PRAISE FOR DEBBIE HERBERT

COLD WATERS

"A compelling story filled with evc
characters, and heart-pounding dran
—Elle James,

"Herbert's haunting language, gothic tone, and vivid portrayal of small-town southern life add layers to this intriguing suspense. I was hooked from the first word!"

—Rita Herron, *USA Today* bestselling author

"Herbert delivers a fast-paced mystery where nothing is quite what it seems. Family secrets and a cold-case murder are at the heart of her compelling novel, where the author masterfully paints the canvas of a sedate southern town with intriguing characters and a crafty plot. Readers won't soon forget the chilling thrill of *Cold Waters*."

—Laura Spinella, bestselling author of the Ghost Gifts novels

"Small towns hide the darkest secrets, and Normal, Alabama, is anything but in this southern gothic thriller that will keep you turning the pages until the very last. A twisted southern gothic family drama that will stay with you long after you've closed the book. A stunning, deftly written journey through the dark corridors of the human heart."

—Sara Lunsford, author of *Tooth and Nail*

"*Cold Waters* is an unforgettable suspense story steeped in decaying old houses, dark family secrets, and rumors in a small southern town."

—Leslie Tentler, author of the Chasing Evil trilogy

NOT
ONE
OF US

OTHER TITLES BY DEBBIE HERBERT

Scorched Grounds

Cold Waters

NOT ONE OF US

DEBBIE HERBERT

THOMAS & MERCER

Published by Thomas & Mercer, Seattle

www.apub.com

Amazon, the Amazon logo, and Thomas & Mercer are trademarks of Amazon.com, Inc., or its affiliates.

ISBN-13: 9781542024921
ISBN-10: 1542024927

Cover design by Shasti O'Leary Soudant

Printed in the United States of America

*As always, to my husband, Tim, who relentlessly
believes in me and supports my dreams.
His encouragement through the years has kept me going
in times when I've been stuck or dispirited. Thank you.
And to my father, J. W. Gainey, who is my biggest
cheerleader and sings my praises to anyone who crosses
his path for more than a few minutes. Many thanks.*

Chapter 1

JORI TRAHERN

May 2006

Moon glowed through pine and cypress, the tree branches forming gnarled, twisted shapes that cast daggers of black in the silvered darkness. The litany of a million insects triggered a Disney-esque *Fantasia* light show in my mind.

My particular form of synesthesia, colored hearing, had its perks. Muted hues of green, blue, and yellow burst onto a black canvas. Mosquito buzzes morphed to pointed-star formations. An occasional long spherical column formed as a frog croaked its guttural song.

But that night, the delight in my mental smorgasbord of sound and color was interrupted by annoyance. And hurt. Deacon Cormier, my boyfriend of eighteen months, had stood me up, and I was determined to discover why.

Friday nights were our standing date night at Broussard's Pavilion, along with many other of our senior classmates from Eric County High School. We both enjoyed the lively zydeco band with its fast tempo featuring an accordion, scrub board, and guitar. All my shyness and reserve melted away when Deacon would pull me onto the wooden deck and we danced. Actually, to say we *danced* is being generous. More like we stomped around with little grace but lots of enthusiasm.

I trudged on across the boggy bayou ground, making no effort to hide the noise of my boots breaking twigs and cones beneath my feet. I slapped at the limbs and vines that diligently, maliciously snaked over the cleared trail no matter how often Deacon's dad hired locals to keep it trimmed back.

These woods had a wild determination that no man could tame. But not being from around here, Louis Cormier didn't understand this land or its personality. South Alabama natives like me knew we were the trespassers and the swamp reigned supreme over us mere mortals—not the other way around.

"Damn it," I cursed as a wisteria vine scratched against the side of my face and neck. I didn't bother keeping my voice low. Why should I? All that was on my mind that evening was talking to Deacon.

At last, lights from the Cormier house appeared, sparkling like a beckoning fairyland promising magic. The large log, rock, and glass structure glowed as though it contained a fallen star within.

Someone was home that evening.

Even after dating Deacon all this time, I was still awed by his house. Our parents' homes might be less than a quarter mile apart, but the white-columned grandness of his house was a stark contrast to our modest old place, so small that Mama and I had to share a bedroom. As a prominent attorney, Mr. Cormier commanded and received a high salary for his services.

I walked up the wooden stairway of the wide front porch. Once I was halfway up the steps, a wave of unease prickled the nape of my neck. Despite the glow of lights flowing through uncurtained windows, the house was too quiet. No sound of a television or voices, or even pots rattling in the kitchen or footsteps from within. Why leave all the lights blazing if they'd gone out?

I could practically hear my grandmother's tsk in my ear. "Such wastefulness," Mimi would declare. At our home, every light was immediately turned off once a room wasn't in use. The less we owed on utilities, the more we could spend on luxuries like store-bought clothes.

I peeked in the living room window, taking in the stack of school-books Deacon had carelessly tossed on an end table. A pillow had dropped to the floor beside the sofa. I glanced to my right, spotting a few dirty glasses and plates strewn on the kitchen island. The slight messiness contrasted with the pristine neatness of the home's interior, signaling that its occupants were confident there would always be some-one else to clear the chaos.

That someone happened to be my grandmother. She wasn't their daily housekeeper, but she came every Friday for the deep-cleaning tasks Clotille Cormier wanted to keep the home sparkling and suited for their many visitors. Their guests seemed impressed with the views of Magnolia Bay, yet whenever they roamed Bayou Enigma, the visitors nervously checked the ground beneath them for gators, snakes, and other unsavory creatures. While they appreciated the primitive beauty of our land, I imagined they were secretly relieved when they returned to Mobile or Montgomery or wherever else they flocked from.

"Wouldn't want their designer shoes to slosh through mud," Mimi would utter about the out-of-town guests. I found her rancor-ous remarks odd, considering that Uncle Buddy, her brother, was so wealthy. The sporting lodge and private fishing expeditions company he'd opened thirty years ago had prospered beyond anyone's wildest expectations. Louis Cormier did well as an attorney, but he was not in Uncle Buddy's league—a fact I had pointed out to Mimi.

I shook off my meandering thoughts and rapped sharply at the door. Deacon should have been at my house over an hour ago. If he had a good explanation for why he'd ghosted me, we could leave then and still have a couple of hours to dance before I had to hustle home to meet my curfew.

"Go without him," Mimi had urged. "Fancy people and their rudeness," she'd harrumphed under her breath. "Everything's all about them. Ain't got no consideration for others."

Unfazed, I'd let her comment roll off me. Deacon wasn't fancy or stuck up, and I liked his parents, too, even if everyone else couldn't stand them. Louis Cormier was universally despised for supposedly paying low wages to his household and yard crew and for his flamboyant lifestyle. Clotille Cormier was seen as glib and "artsy."

Not one of us, the folks in Bayou Enigma whispered through tight-pinched scowls.

There was no answer to my knock. No rush of footsteps from within or a familiar voice calling out, "I'm coming."

My skin tightened with another prickle of unease.

I walked over to the floor-to-ceiling windows of the den. No one roamed inside. It was one of the few weekends they had no planned guests arriving. Mimi had only worked a couple of hours that morning before being dismissed. Naturally, she'd grumbled about the reduced hours, which meant even less money.

Had all three of the Cormiers decided to travel to their Mobile home for some reason? Perhaps Deacon's dad had unexpected urgent business in the city and had asked his son and wife to go with him. That had happened on a few occasions since I'd met them.

But why leave all the lights on?

Maybe they hadn't heard my knock. I strode back to the door and rang the doorbell. Its chime echoed forlornly inside. Pressing my nose to the pane of glass by the entrance, I craned my neck from side to side to see if anyone might be in the hallway or kitchen.

"Hey," I called out, knocking sharply at the door again. "It's Jori. Anybody home?"

No answer.

Gingerly, I tested the lock, and the knob twisted all the way around with a click. I pushed the heavy door open, and it creaked as loudly as thunder. I stuck my head inside. "Anyone here?" I called out again.

I pushed my shoulders through the opening, drew a deep breath, and then took a tentative step inside. They knew me; they liked me. It'd be okay.

The delicious aroma of roasted chicken wafted toward me—they were home, then, or they had been recently. Underlying the scent of dinner was a very faint trace of some kind of disinfectant cleanser. I kept calling out "Hello?" and "Anybody home?" as I stepped cautiously from the foyer to the den.

Two half-full glasses of iced tea sat on the coffee table, one of them rimmed with Mrs. Cormier's ruby lip gloss. Nerves on edge, I entered the kitchen and found the table set for three. Bright cherry-red plates on gold chargers, glasses of melted ice, a bowl of salad greens already wilting. A casserole dish of potatoes sat on the granite counter, and I gingerly touched the baking dish. It was cold. I opened the oven and found a slightly overdone roasted chicken; the oven setting had been lowered to "warm." I turned it completely off, not wanting their dinner to go to ruin. They must have had an emergency call and left the house quickly, expecting to return shortly.

My annoyance morphed to concern. Had something happened to Deacon's dad? Had he and his mom rushed to the hospital in Mobile, where he'd been injured or taken ill? But why wasn't Deacon answering his phone? Had he forgotten to bring it along?

When would they return? I couldn't help it—I pictured my prom dress hanging on the back of my bedroom door. A beautiful peach tea-length dress that had cost me an entire week of the wages I'd earned as a cashier at Winn-Dixie. Were we still on for the prom tomorrow night?

I pulled out my cheap flip phone and called his number. Like before, it went straight to voice mail. His battery must be dead, I decided. I texted him again.

At ur house. Where are u? Turned off oven. Call me.

I strode across the polished walnut floors to the bay windows facing the back of the property and driveway. Mrs. Cormier's Grand Prix was there, as well as Deacon's black Mustang. A chill slid down my spine. They weren't here in the house—or were they?

I punched down the dread churning my gut and slowly walked to the staircase, again calling out and again receiving no answer. The quiet felt ominous, choking and weighing me down. The stairs creaked as I slowly climbed. At the top of the stairs, I checked Deacon's room—undisturbed. His bed was neatly made, and nothing appeared out of place. I headed out, then paused and slowly turned back around. Something wasn't quite right. I scanned the room, stopping when I caught sight of his desk. Deacon's laptop was gone. Had he taken it with him?

I left his room and then passed by the guest rooms before briefly glancing at the open door of the master bedroom. Nothing out of place there either. I relaxed slightly. What had I been expecting? Bloody corpses? I'd been watching too many true-crime shows. I clomped back down the stairs, rechecking my silent cell phone.

They had to have gone in Mr. Cormier's car, then. Maybe after he'd returned home, he'd gotten a call that someone else in their family had fallen ill, and they'd all left in a hurry. Deacon hadn't notified me because his battery was low. He was horrible at remembering to keep it charged.

Yes, that had to be the case. By the time the dance was over, Deacon would call and explain what had happened. No big deal.

And yet . . . it was weird. Creepy. Everything left out on the table like that. Wouldn't Mrs. Cormier have taken five minutes to put up the food before leaving?

I'd do my good deed for the day and put up the chicken and casserole. It took a few tries, but I found the plastic wrap and covered the salad and potatoes and stashed them in the fridge. That done, I scanned the kitchen. Was there anything more I could do?

I strolled back to the den and glanced around. No clues there. I had started to turn when a small flash of something shiny on a coffee table caught my eye. Something I hadn't noticed earlier. I edged over for a closer look.

A small cellophane package lay discarded by a stack of magazines. Gingerly, I picked it up, gasping as I recognized what it was. As I peeled back the cellophane, it made a crinkling sound that caused pink notes shaped like stars to dance in my mind. A single peach rose bloomed amid white carnations. Sprigs of baby's breath poked underneath and around an apricot-colored ribbon. I caressed the rose's smooth petals before lifting it to my nose and inhaling deeply. The scent momentarily soothed me.

Deacon had bought me a wrist corsage for the prom. A silly grin split my face for an instant before worry caught up to my spinning thoughts. What was the corsage doing on the table? They should have stored it in the refrigerator to keep it fresh for prom night. My gaze swept the room more thoroughly, searching for anything out of place or different. All was spotless, including the floors. Except . . . a few tiny clusters of white pilled under the sofa. I couldn't explain what drew me, but I got on my hands and knees by the sofa and peered closer.

A sprig of white baby's breath dotted with bright-red flecks.

How did it get there? What were those flecks? I reached out my hand and touched a dot of red with one fingertip. It felt wet, sticky. I drew my hand back and stared at the drop of blood smeared on my finger. Had he accidentally pricked himself with the corsage pin and dropped the bouquet?

Where the hell was Deacon?

Chapter 2

JORI

Thirteen Years Later

"There he is," Dana said, jabbing her elbow into my side. We were jammed into a booth at Broussard's Pavilion, where the crowd grew more boisterous by the minute. Maybe coming tonight had been a good idea, a welcome change from the stress of returning home last week. The whole place buzzed with cozy conviviality—a shelter from the gathering storm that at the moment was only a whisper of wind rattling the pines and cypress.

I practically shouted into her ear. "There *who* is?" I asked.

She nodded toward a booth on the opposite side of the bar. "Ray Strickland."

Through the slight fog of my two bloody marys, I realized the name was familiar, but I couldn't quite grasp its significance, other than a vague unsettling. It registered that he wasn't a *good* person, although the specific details associated with the name remained fuzzy. My forehead drew together from a vodka-befuddled haze, and my friend elaborated.

"Raymond Strickland," she said again, enunciating each syllable as though speaking to a daft child. Her voice formed green arrows that fizzed harmlessly against a black backdrop. "You know, the guy who murdered your cousin."

Click. There was a blast from the past. Hadn't heard his name mentioned in ages. "They let him out of prison?"

"In February." She shot me an incredulous look. "Your family didn't tell you?"

"We never speak of him or the murder. Ancient history."

Dana's eyes held the tiniest trace of reproach. She quickly sipped her beer, trying to cover it up, but we'd been friends since kindergarten, and she could hide nothing from me. Even though we'd drifted apart a bit since I'd left the bayou years ago, we always got together when I visited to catch up.

"It's not like I knew Jackson," I said defensively. "He was my second cousin, and I was only two when he died."

"Still. Family is family. My folks? They'd have rallied all of us together and devised sneaky schemes to make Ray's free life as miserable as possible."

"Good for y'all." I couldn't quite keep the sour note from my voice. Nobody had to lecture me on family loyalty. If it hadn't been instilled in me since childhood, I'd never have returned to Bayou Enigma two weeks ago.

Dana patted my hand. "That wasn't a criticism. You never knew your cousin. And from what everyone says about Jackson Ensley . . ."

I frowned, not liking her implication. "You saying he deserved to die? I've heard all the tales about what a low-life piece of trash Jackson was. But c'mon, Dana—we're talking about a sixteen-year-old kid."

She held up a hand. "You're right. Sorry. The older I get, the younger sixteen sounds. Who knows? He could have just been going through a troubled adolescent stage and would have turned his life around. Become a respectable, upstanding citizen."

I chose to ignore the doubtful tone as she uttered those words. It was hard to get worked up about such an old crime involving a relative

I never knew. Call me heartless, but I had enough on my plate dealing with present circumstances.

I'd been cruising along just fine with my mostly solitary life in Mobile. Since leaving government employment and striking out on my own as an event coordinator, I'd stayed holed up in my apartment, glued to the computer and dedicated to making a go of my new business. On the few occasions I'd come home to visit my grandmother and younger brother, Zach, I'd tamped down my feelings of uneasiness. Yes, Mimi had grown a tad too forgetful for my liking. But didn't most people become that way as they aged? Trouble was, Mimi was Zach's sole caretaker, and his autism was on the severe end of the spectrum.

Last week's call from Social Services had jolted me from my false complacency. Zach hadn't showed at his regular day program, and the concerned director had driven to Mimi's house. Zach was home alone, unharmed and watching TV. Mimi drifted in a good twenty minutes later, a dazed expression on her face. Turns out she'd walked to the end of the driveway to set out the trash can that morning, talked to a neighbor for several minutes, then apparently become confused and wandered up and down the road until she remembered which house was hers.

So here I was. Back in the bayou. Trying to figure out what the hell I needed to do to understand Mimi's medical condition and get her help and at the same time ensure that Zach was safe.

I shook off my worries as best I could. Tonight was supposed to be a fun evening with an old friend. Last thing I needed was more problems. Still, I couldn't help sneaking a glance at the thin, tatted man drinking his beer alone. His head was bent, his full attention on the glass in his hands. His hair was heavily streaked with gray and pulled severely into a ponytail. He wore a clean but faded T-shirt and jeans. "Surprised he came back to the bayou when they let him out," I observed.

"He didn't. He only came for his mom's funeral a few days ago. I expect he'll be moving along soon. There's nothing to keep him here."

"Good. I wouldn't want Aunt Tressie running into him. Not that there's much chance of that. She only leaves assisted living once a month to get her hair done."

Now that Dana had pointed him out, I noticed other patrons eyeing him with covert sideways glances. Ray appeared oblivious—or was deliberately avoiding everyone by keeping his head down.

"He appears older than he must be," I said, signaling to the waitress for another bloody mary. The noise of patrons mixed with speakers blaring music on the dock and the clink of pool balls in the back room formed a steady drumbeat of colors that swirled and morphed into blackish splatters of ugly blobs. Hence the multiple bloody marys to cope with the cacophony. "My cousin would have been fortyish if Strickland hadn't murdered him."

"Ray was only a couple years older than Jackson. Prison life must really age you," Dana agreed.

"Geez. I would have guessed he was at least in his midfifties." My temples began to throb with the overload of sound, and I rubbed them.

"You hurting?" Dana asked.

Close as we were, Dana didn't understand the half of it, only that I had a sensitivity to sound that could result in headaches.

"I thought you'd be okay since there's no live band tonight."

"Music is fine. It's all the background buzz of people talking."

"You want a pain pill?" Dana rummaged through her purse and produced a bottle. "I always keep some handy. My scoliosis aches kick in when I least expect it."

I raised a brow, remembering her reputation in high school for experimenting with drugs—not that she ever did anything in front of me. She knew my position on the matter. I'd heard talk that she'd gone through rehab a couple of years ago, but since she'd never confided in me, I didn't bring the subject up. My philosophy was that if someone wanted you to know anything personal, they'd tell you themselves.

"No thanks. I took some over-the-counter pills about twenty minutes ago. They'll kick in soon enough."

Dana shrugged and dropped the medicine back into her purse. "If you say so."

I returned my attention to Ray Strickland, imagining the long, thin fingers now wrapped around his beer as the same hands that had held a gun and pulled the trigger to shoot Jackson. I thought of my aunt and her early descent into assisted living. It's like her mind and body slowly checked out of reality with her son's death. Her husband left, and she sat alone in her small house, day after day after day, immersed in her grief. By the time I was old enough to remember weekly visits to her place with Mimi, Aunt Tressie had been a fragile shell, distant and confused, eyes permanently reddened from crying.

Once, I made the mistake of drifting into Jackson's old bedroom, where all his possessions had been left untouched. But instead of being stale and dusty, the room smelled of lemon polish, and every surface gleamed with an unnatural, unlived-in cleanliness. A shrine to her dead son. Aunt Tressie had roused from her vague, passive manner and run screeching through the house to grab me roughly by the shoulders, screaming at me to get out and stay out of Jackson's room. As a child, I'd had a secret terror of the woman after that, always imagining her rousing from a stupor and turning wild with grief, ready to lash out at me. Of course, as I'd grown older, I'd realized she was a tragic woman who meant no harm.

My mouth hardened into a thin line. This man was the one who had done that to her. The waitress brought my cocktail, and I downed a large gulp before setting the glass down hard on the scarred wooden table. "He shouldn't be here," I said darkly. I rose up and slid out of the booth, glaring at Ray.

Dana grabbed the front hem of my T-shirt. "What are you doing? Sit back down," she demanded with a hiss of breath.

But I was pumped with liquid courage and a self-righteous resolve to tell this man how much he'd hurt my family. I easily shrugged from Dana's grasp and made my way around several tables jammed in the middle of the bar.

"Jori!" she called after me several times. People looked up from their drinks or bowls of gumbo, sniffing out trouble. But not Ray. The man appeared impervious to the brewing shitstorm. I slipped into the booth, and his head jerked up with a start.

"What you want?" he asked sourly. His tone was a bruising purple-black, the color of storm clouds accompanied by a howling wind. The shade wasn't particularly vivid since I'd never met him before. The longer I knew someone, the more vivid and distinctive the color and shapes of their voices became.

He scowled, emphasizing the lines around his mouth that betrayed a serious tobacco habit. His eyes narrowed at me with suspicion. "I been drinkin' and mindin' my own bizness. I ain't botherin' nobody."

"Your very presence bothers me," I retorted.

"Who the hell are you?"

"Jori Trahern."

His hard gaze didn't flicker. My name meant nothing to him.

"Jackson Ensley's cousin."

His right eye twitched, and he raised an arm, breaking eye contact. "Waitress!" he called out with a wave, searching through the crowd.

"That's right," I scoffed. "Ignore me, you coward."

"I ain't no coward."

"A murdering coward," I reiterated. "You shot my cousin from the back."

"It wasn't me."

I snorted. I'd have been more impressed if he'd owned up to what he'd done and shown even an iota of remorse. "You're a liar too."

"He was my friend. I didn't kill him!" His voice rose, crescendos of lime squares. The crowd set down their drinks and openly watched us now. He lowered his voice an octave as he placed his hands on the scarred table and balled his fists. "Guess nobody in this miserable bayou will ever believe me."

If he'd thought to intimidate me with his outburst, he was dead wrong. My temper rose at his loud indignation. "The evidence says otherwise," I pointed out. My voice shook in anger, red heat shimmering across baked concrete.

"That shit was planted. Jackson was my friend. I had no beef with him."

His defense flew in the face of what little my family had told me about the crime. It was one of those quiet tragedies no one liked to talk about but that shadowed us despite our best intentions to forget the past. "A drug buddy who owed you money, is what I hear," I argued. "You were a small-town dealer peddling to your friends. Cops caught you with bags of pot and pills when they went to question you. They also found your fingerprints all over rolling papers in Jackson's car. Not to mention your hoodie sweatshirt soaked with Jackson's fresh blood."

Hardness settled on his too-sculpted cheekbones, and he lifted one bony shoulder in a shrug. My eye was drawn to the tattoo of barbed wire encircling his upper-right arm. Judging by the haphazard lines and ashy color, it had been carved in prison by a minimally talented inmate artist. "I was set up," he insisted, his mouth drawn into a childish, surly pout. "Somebody broke into my car and stole that stuff."

"Righhht," I drawled. "You were framed. Isn't that what all criminals say?"

"I didn't do it. Jackson had all kinds of enemies. Plenty of people weren't sorry to hear he'd been killed."

I shifted in my seat. This might be the first truthful thing Ray had uttered. Even all these years later, I heard the whispers. I'd seen the way Uncle Buddy and Mimi looked at each other when I'd heard rumors about my cousin and asked them if it was true Jackson was a bad person. Over the years, whenever Jackson's name came up, a shadow had flickered in their eyes, and they'd immediately shifted the conversation to other topics.

"I was in the wrong place at the wrong time," Ray insisted. "This town's dirty as hell. If you're from the wrong side of the tracks, you ain't got a chance. You're the one who gets blamed for everythin'." He scraped a bitter laugh as he twirled the beer in his glass. "At least I'm alive. Folks have a way of disappearin' 'round here. Gator feed."

My breath drew in sharply, and acute pain knifed my chest. *Deacon.* Just saying his name in my mind created waves of dark violet with tips of white froth at the crest. I leaned in toward Ray. "What are you saying? Are you talking about the Cormiers?"

He glanced around the bar with a furtive, feral air, as though he regretted the slip of tongue.

"Tell me," I pushed, my voice rising. "Do you know something about their disappearance or not?"

"Maybe. Maybe not."

Gator feed. The words pounded through me, drumming despair. Not my Deacon. He couldn't have met such a violent, cruel end. I grabbed Ray's forearm. "If you know something, tell me."

He shook me off and sprawled back into the booth. "Don't. Touch. Me," he growled.

Heat suffused my face. This man knew nothing, hadn't even lived in the bayou for years. His innuendo about the Cormiers was just another theory, one of dozens I'd heard over the years. They'd vanished without a trace that same night I'd entered their abandoned home. It still haunted me, those empty plates on the table, the chicken left roasting in the oven, the fragments of the forgotten corsage under the couch.

Everyone had an opinion: The Cormiers were still alive and had fled the country to avoid legal problems. The Cormiers were murdered by the Mafia because Mr. Cormier had dealings with the underworld. The Cormiers were spotted on a Mexican beach, living the high life with stolen money. The tales grew more outlandish with every year.

At last, I found my voice. "I think your imagination went wild with all the free time you had locked up in prison."

"Free time?" He snorted. "They work the shit out of you in prison. I worked eight hours in the kitchen every day and mopped floors at night."

"Don't expect pity from me. You ruined my aunt's life. After Jackson died she lost her grip on reality, and then her husband abandoned her and left town. Just so you know."

Ray lifted his glass and took a long swallow, his Adam's apple bobbing up and down. "We all got troubles. My life ain't been no picnic either, missy. I served my time. You done harassing me?"

I cocked my head to the side, studying his hard features. What had I hoped to gain by speaking with this man? He couldn't care less that my aunt's life had been forever scarred. Must be the alcohol that had made me so hell bent on making sure Ray knew the impact of that long-ago murder. I'd said what I'd come to say. There was nothing else to discuss, except: "When do you leave?"

He raised a thin brow streaked with gray hairs.

"I'd hate for my aunt to accidentally run into you in town."

"Again, none of yer bizness, but I don't mind tellin' ya I leave in a day or so. Got some private bizness to take care of that should set me up nicely while I get back on my feet." His eyes shifted in a crafty way, and a sly grin slid over his wan face. No doubt this business was something highly illegal.

"Now that Momma's dead and buried, ain't no need for me to ever come back to this hellhole," he continued.

"Good." My face suffused with warmth. "Not that your mother died," I hastened to assure him, even though I had no need to explain myself to this loser. But politeness had been drilled into me all my life, and I couldn't be a total jerk. "Good that you're leaving, that is."

Message delivered, I started to rise to my feet when a group of four men with pool cues marched deliberatively over to our table. Our raised voices had attracted the attention of the bar bullies. I'd seen them around over the years, always stumbling about half-drunk and taking offense at folks for the least provocation. Luckily, they mostly stuck to the back poolroom and were easily avoided. But tonight, the beasts had been roused. Their eyes were narrowed to mean slits, and one of them slapped his cue menacingly into an open palm.

"Ray Strickland," their ringleader groused. His thin mouth tightened into a grim line. "Can't believe you have the nerve to show your face here."

Ray cradled his hands around his beer glass, the calloused knuckles white, emphasizing a row of tatted crosses lining each knuckle joint. "I ain't botherin' nobody."

Dana hovered by my side. "Let's *go*," she whispered in my ear, her hand on my arm.

"He botherin' you?" one of the guys asked me. With a start, I realized I recognized this one. Eddie Yaeger. He'd been several years ahead of me in school and was always being called to the principal's office for fighting or some other mischief.

"Nope. Thanks, Eddie. Y'all go on back to your game." I pushed onto slightly unsteady feet. I despised Strickland for what he'd done to my family, but to be fair, I'd been the one to approach him. Man didn't know me from Jack. I had no stomach for fistfights, either, especially when it was unfair. Surely Ray had learned a few slick moves protecting himself in prison, but tonight's four-to-one odds meant an ass whoopin' I'd rather not witness.

"Why you showing your face here, Ray?" the ringleader asked, not willing to retreat just yet. "This is a respectable joint. No convicts allowed."

"I ain't a convict no more." Ray's tone was truculent, and the muscles in his arms tensed as though preparing for a fight.

The men edged closer to the table in a semicircle, blocking his exit. Chairs scuffled all around us, the other patrons sensing trouble and hastening to put distance between themselves and the brawl's epicenter. Dana's grip tightened on my arm as she pulled me away. "Come on."

I couldn't abandon Ray to this fate. I should never have approached him. This was all on me.

"He was just leaving," I offered, pointing to Ray's nearly empty glass. "Isn't that right, Ray?" I asked, beseeching him to gracefully exit the danger.

He dug in, his jaw hardening even more. "Ain't going nowhere 'til I'm good and ready."

Stubborn jerk. I backed away from the inevitable scene.

Eddie turned to the ringleader. "Ray ain't worth our time, Tommy. Let's go."

But the man nearest to him wrapped his hand over Ray's bicep. "Go now," he threatened.

"Or what?"

"Or I'll kick your ass."

"I don't want no trouble. Get yer hands off me. Ain't warning ya again."

Instead of backing off, the man tugged on Ray's arm.

Ray picked up his glass and threw what was left of his drink into the guy's face. The golden, sticky brew trickled down into his eyes and made tracks in the scrubby stubble of his jaw.

An awful silence descended throughout the room. Everyone recognized the split second of stillness for what it was: a signal of coming disaster.

One moment Ray was seated at the booth; the next he was on his feet, easily flicking off the man's hold on his arm. The attacker shoved at Ray's chest, and Ray shoved back, sending the guy flying into the nearest table. Bowls of gumbo and pints of beer crashed to the concrete floor as the table was upended. A woman screamed somewhere nearby. Hot liquid scorched my right calf, bits of rice and crawfish dotting my jeans.

The other three men were galvanized into action. Eddie swung his pool cue at Ray's head, but Ray snatched it before it made contact and snapped it in half. He clutched the pieces of the broken stick in either hand like a weapon. Tommy lunged toward Ray, only to be walloped on the side of his head. The contact made a nasty crack, the noise creating a whip of black that exploded in my mind's eye.

A trickle of blood streamed down Tommy's left temple. "Son of a bitch," he cried, raising a hand to swipe at the blood.

The third man wisely did nothing but shoot Ray a scowl.

But Tommy exploded to his feet and lunged again at Ray, this time making contact. The men fell to the ground, breaking a chair leg from the nearest table on the way down. Tommy was on top as they hit concrete, but Ray quickly maneuvered out from under him and straddled Tommy, his right arm raised overhead, hand fisted to land a punch.

The bouncer, a lumbering six-foot-five giant weighing at least three hundred pounds, ran over with surprising speed. "Break it up," he ordered, grabbing Ray's raised fist and pulling him off Tommy. Both men quickly rose, glaring at each other. Tommy was breathing hard but shallowly, as though it hurt his ribs to draw a full breath. "All of you—out right now," the bouncer ordered.

The first attacker crossed his arms over his ample belly. "You're going to be sorry," he warned Ray. "Better stay away from us." For all the world, he sounded like an elementary school bully displaying false courage in the bouncer's presence.

Ray snorted. He dug his wallet out from his back pocket and slapped a ten-dollar bill on the table. "I was just leavin'," he said drily. His dark eyes slid over the men. "You pansy-ass boys oughta pick yer fights better."

Tommy balled his fists at his sides. "Oh yeah? You just better watch your back and get the hell out of our town."

Ray shuffled toward the door, shaking his head. "I'm real scared."

"You should be," Tommy called to Ray's back. "You come near me, and I'll kill you, motherfucker."

Ray didn't bother turning around as he raised his right arm and flipped off the crowd.

"The rest of you get out of here too," the bouncer ordered, turning to the attackers. "Mister Broussard don't tolerate no fighting in here. I've warned y'all before. Something like this happens again, you're all banned."

The four of them huffed and blustered as they strode to the door, muttering about revenge.

"Cops already been called," the bouncer warned. "Better not start no scuffle in the parking lot either 'less you want to spend the night in lockup."

The door slammed behind the last of them, and I hurried back to the booth I shared with Dana and stared out the window. Ray had strapped on his helmet and mounted a beat-up motorcycle. The engine roared to life and emitted a cloud of noxious black smoke as he sped out of the parking lot, spewing gravel in his wake.

Tommy and his friends piled into a battered pickup truck that had a shotgun mounted in the rear window. The driver hit the accelerator, and they made an equally loud exit from the lot, their tires spitting up dust and gravel.

"Think they're following Ray?" Dana asked.

"They're just stupid enough," I said with disgust. "Let's hope their chase is only for show, a way of saving face after getting their asses kicked and thrown out of here."

"Maybe," she agreed, though her eyes looked doubtful.

I settled into my seat and sighed, the slight alcoholic haze already stripped away by Ray's oblique mention of the Cormiers. All I'd done was upset myself. Regret roiled in my gut. And if I'd never gone to talk to Ray, would he have escaped notice from Tommy and his gang of rednecks?

Still, he'd piqued my curiosity with his remark about people disappearing around the bayou. If there was a connection between my cousin and Deacon's murder, I couldn't just let that go. If there was a way to find out what had happened to Deacon and his parents, I'd do anything to know. Damn the danger.

"Need another bloody mary?" Dana asked. "After all, I'm driving tonight. Remember?"

I pulled my gaze from the window. "Yeah, I need one, but I'm going to pass." It wouldn't do for me to arrive home all liquored up. The whole point of my return to Bayou Enigma was to help take care of Mimi and Zach. I'd be useless to both if I drank any more.

"I understand." Dana's eyes radiated sympathy. "How is your grandmother?"

"Fine until she's not." So far, I'd only glimpsed a few lapses of memory—Mimi wandering into the den and leaving a pot of okra to burn on the stove, repeating herself in a conversation, with no recall of telling the same story minutes before. I'd insisted she see a doctor, and she'd been diagnosed with dementia. Specifically, he'd determined she was at stage four Alzheimer's with moderate cognitive decline. The doctor had warned that her condition would grow progressively worse, although no one could predict how fast the fall from normalcy might be.

"And Zach?" Dana pressed.

"Same as ever." I'd already told her about my family's precarious situation.

"I'm glad you're home with them. It's a good thing your job is so flexible."

Thank heavens for that, at least. I took a deep breath, calming the ever-present worry about what was necessary for Mimi and Zach in the long term. Before Mom had died, I'd promised her that I'd always make sure they were okay. Over the next few weeks, I'd have to decide exactly what fulfilling that promise might entail. Not for the first time, resentment flared in my gut that Zach's and my father had cut loose and run shortly after Zach was diagnosed at age two. No help would come from that quarter. A few pellets of rain plopped against the window, a prelude to the gulf storm expected to arrive later that night. The day grew darker by the second, matching my apprehension. What if those idiots caught up to one another on some lonely road in the boondocks and one of those men got hurt? What if, right at this very moment, Mimi was cooking dinner and had left food on the stove and started a house fire?

I had to get home immediately. It felt like the storm—and trouble— were about to break.

Chapter 3

DEPUTY OFFICER TEGAN BLACKWELL

Yellow crime scene tape wrapped around the small shotgun-style house. The place possessed a tired vibe, with its faded paint peeling off cheap pressboard and drooping shutters missing several slats. A frail-looking older woman with a head full of hair curlers visible underneath a scarf spoke with two police officers, rubbing her hands together. As she talked, her neck kept craning back toward the house as though pulled by an involuntary force. On the drive in, we'd spotted several curious neighbors already striding down the dusty road, drawn to the commotion and the sniff of impending drama.

We pulled into the gravel driveway and stopped a few feet from the threesome. I spilled out of the passenger-side door of the sheriff's cruiser with my partner, Joe Oliver, Erie County's head investigator. I still couldn't believe my luck that Oliver had chosen me to mentor.

Neither could my fellow officers and coworkers, especially the older ones who knew me from high school. Back then, I'd weighed fifty pounds more and had a reputation, both of which led me to the unfortunate nickname "Big Easy." In the years since, I'd done my best to shrug off the moniker, eventually marrying and losing the extra pounds.

For the most part, my contemporaries let bygones be bygones, especially since I'd entered law enforcement.

Although I'd been employed at the sheriff's office nearly two years as a deputy, I'd finished my field training and probationary status only six months ago. The others still jokingly referred to me as a rookie—and although they said it in jest, I sensed they believed I'd not yet been truly tested.

As I'd been trained, I scanned the area, taking in all the details. Houses in this older neighborhood were spaced far apart, and despite the obvious worn-down and lower socioeconomic level of the place, the house in question was tidy and well maintained. The owner had gone to some lengths to pretty up its faded plainness with colorful hanging flowerpots on the porch. Pink pansies lined the gravel path to the front steps, and the sparse grass was freshly mown. An old motorcycle and an ancient Plymouth Duster were parked in the dirt driveway. The air smelled fresh and clean from last night's rain.

The few houses we'd passed were mostly occupied by older couples who enjoyed the spring warmth from the comfort of rockers on the porch. There were also a couple of residences where the lawns were littered with tricycles and kids' toys. The sort of area for old folks on a fixed income and young couples or single moms on a tight budget. I could relate to the whole single-mom-tight-budget scenario. By the thinnest of margins, my bimonthly paycheck separated me from this downtrodden neighborhood.

A sudden gush of gratitude rose in me for my own humble home. It wasn't often I thanked the stars for the old twelve-hundred-square-foot brick house that sheltered me and my two children, but we had a roof over our heads and plenty of food on the table, thanks to this job. When my ex-husband, Josh, deserted us five years ago for a model-skinny paralegal, I'd worked a string of minimum wage jobs that had left me tense and exhausted. Between my meager earnings and court-ordered child support, we'd barely scraped by. Just months later, Josh sent a few signals that he was tiring of Darlene and willing to return home, but exhausted or not, I'd nixed that straightaway.

Surprisingly, that burst of defiance gave me the confidence to search for a better job. My brother Liam, a cop in Montgomery, learned of an opening in the local sheriff's office and urged me to apply. I never expected the opportunity to pan out or that I'd actually make it through the required training should they hire me.

The past two years of law enforcement training hadn't been easy, but to everyone's surprise, including my own, I'd made it, easily sailing through the police academy curriculum and shooting qualification test. I even enjoyed the job sometimes, though I wouldn't admit it to my fellow officers. The one time I had, they'd laughed and rolled their eyes, promising that my tune would change after I'd been there long enough to witness the crimes that they had.

I had a feeling that was about to change today.

I swallowed a lump of dread when we approached the house and I recognized one of the cops. Gilbert Dempsey was one of my ex-husband's closest friends, one that I'd never cared for. Not then and certainly not now. He and Josh had worked together a couple of years after high school in the local fish processing plant. It had surprised us all when Gilbert, a heavy drinker and equally heavy gambler, was hired by the Enigma PD. But Gilbert's new career never slowed down his dicey extracurricular activities or turned him into a polite gentleman. He always slid me covert, sly glances when he thought no one was watching, even when I was married to Josh.

Oliver immediately took charge of the situation, greeting the uniformed cops and addressing the woman as we approached. "I take it you're the neighbor who called?" he asked.

She nodded, still rubbing her arms. "Yes, Reba Tankersley."

Dempsey volunteered more information. "We arrived less than five minutes ago and secured the scene." He motioned for Oliver and me to follow him as he took a step backward. He nodded at his partner, Leroy Granger. "You stay here and keep everyone away."

"What's happening? Is Raymond in there?" Reba asked, her voice thin and reedy.

Four more of the neighbors wandered up the driveway. A baby squalled where it sat propped against her mother's hip. "You all right, Reba?" an older man in the crowd asked, pushing forward.

We left Granger to deal with the gathering crowd.

Dempsey led us around the side of the house. Once we were out of range for the others to hear, he spoke. "Forensics has been called and are en route."

This was bad. Very bad. A tingle of apprehension ran down my spine. I was about to get my first murder case—or possibly it was a clear case of suicide. Either way, what lay inside that house was going to be my first on-the-job brush with an unnatural death.

I strode to the rear of the small house. The back door was cracked open a couple of inches.

"The door was open when we arrived," Dempsey informed us. "No sign of forced entry, though."

Plenty of folks in the backwoods didn't bother locking their doors at night. My folks never had while we were growing up, and my three siblings and I had survived into adulthood.

I scanned the small yard, which backed up to a densely wooded area. Nothing seemed amiss, but someone could have hidden here earlier, lying in wait to murder the residents inside.

"We looked through the window here," Dempsey said, pointing at a window to the left. It was the old-fashioned kind with roll-out panes that were cranked out from inside. "That's when we discovered the body," he continued. "Granger and I immediately entered through the back door and checked to see if the victim might still be alive." He paused a heartbeat. "He wasn't."

Oliver nodded. "Who is the victim?"

"According to the neighbor, the house belongs to a Ms. Letitia Strickland, who died earlier in the week. Her son, Raymond, was down here for the funeral."

Raymond Strickland. The name instantly clicked, followed immediately by another name, another image: *Jackson Ensley.* My gut roiled. Once again, I tasted the sour tang of Jackson's tongue thrust down my throat, his hips grinding painfully into me, my back scraping against cold leather in the back seat of his car. The rising terror as his hand covered my mouth, stifling my screams.

I shut down the memory, snuffing it out as quickly and completely as a candle doused by water. Too bad I hadn't heard earlier that Strickland was in town and that our call this morning would lead to his mother's home. Surprising, since the crime was still talked about, almost as much as the mysterious disappearance of the Cormier family years later.

"Ahh . . . Raymond Strickland," I drawled, trying my best to appear nonchalant, wishing I'd had time to prepare for this reminder of the past.

"The one and only," Dempsey confirmed.

Oliver frowned. "Who's this victim? Enlighten me."

Joe Oliver had been working for the sheriff's department only four months. After Sheriff Lancaster died unexpectedly, Oliver was brought in from Mobile County to supervise the office until elections were held that fall to vote in a new sheriff. The county commission and mayor's decision to do so rankled several of the investigators hoping to fill the vacancy left by Lancaster's death. Temporarily running the office would have given them a leg up on the competition to impress voters.

"Ray was convicted of murder when I was a senior in high school," I volunteered. "Shot his best friend in the back of the head, supposedly in a drug deal gone bad," I explained before turning to Dempsey. "When did he get out of prison?"

"Been a good little while, but he'd never showed his face here until his mother died."

Oliver cut our reminiscence short. "We'll take a quick look around until forensics arrives."

He slipped a pair of rubber gloves from his pockets, and I did the same. As I pulled the latex over my hands, I couldn't resist peeking through the window. A double bed took up much of the room. And on the bed . . . I blinked once, then twice.

The victim, a tall man wearing boxers, lay facedown on the mattress. His head was a mangled mess. Blood and gray matter splattered the walls and white sheets. Long, thin strands of dark hair, streaked with silver and mixed with blood, hung down his neck and shoulders.

My mouth went dry, and I instinctively pulled away from the window. It didn't seem real. The morning was too pretty, too calm, and the damn birds were chirping up a storm. As if to mock me, a finch chattered close by as it winged its way toward the woods. Everything was too normal—except for the man inside.

I gave myself a moment to get it together before following Oliver up the back porch steps. This was my first time seeing a body, and I wanted to respond in a calm, professional manner. If I didn't, I'd never hear the end of it at the station.

The day of reckoning had finally arrived. I wasn't going to blow it. I'd worked too hard trying to gain everyone's respect to lose it now. I needed this job. My kids depended on my paycheck.

Oliver pushed through the door, and I followed him inside. The back entrance opened into a kitchen so tiny its width could be spanned by holding out my arms in both directions. All was clean and tidy. A mountain of plastic food containers sat atop a folded kitchen towel, clean and neatly stacked. Whether Ray was an ex-convict or not, his mother must have been a decent sort of person for the community to have dropped off casseroles for her son in this time of family tragedy.

Now the emptied containers had been washed, ready for their owners to return and pick up.

To our right was a dining room with a table and four chairs. Straight ahead lay a comfy den with shabby furniture, a worn area rug, and an old, bulky TV that sat atop a plain but functional wooden stand with shelves beneath.

No sign of a disturbance. Not even an errant scrap of paper lay on the cheap linoleum floor.

Oliver started down the hall, glancing over his shoulder at me, a question in his eyes.

I gave him an I'm-just-fine nod, and we proceeded down the hall, passing a cramped bathroom. The victim would be in the next room to the left. Across the hall was another bedroom, the bed neatly made with a threadbare chenille bedspread and a painting of Jesus wearing a crown of thorns, the blood trickling from his forehead and into his piercing brown eyes before trailing down his cheeks and disappearing into his beard.

"Morbid spirituality," I grumbled under my breath. My gaze remained transfixed on the painting's droplets of blood as though preparing for the grisly scene awaiting me only fifteen feet away.

"You ready for this?" Joe paused at the open bedroom door, and I nodded, squaring my shoulders and then following him into the room.

My mouth tingled with the metallic odor of blood and decay. I registered the details up close—the pattern of blood and brain splayed on the white bedsheets and the beige wall behind the bed. Bullet holes grazed the torn flesh of his scalp. A half glass of water undisturbed on the nightstand, a worn Bible open beside it. Scuffed leather motorcycle boots neatly tucked under the bed's edge. A pair of jeans and a T-shirt folded onto a rocking chair in the corner.

"Jesus," Oliver muttered, scurrying to the body.

No one could have survived this devastation, and the cops had already checked, but Oliver's large hand touched the side of the man's neck, feeling for a pulse. In the heartbeat of silence that followed, I continued scanning the room, searching for a discarded gun or anything the killer might have dropped. On the dresser was an empty whiskey bottle and a crumpled pack of cigarettes. A pair of dirty socks lay on the linoleum floor. A cardboard table in the far corner sported a baggie of what appeared to be marijuana and several prescription pill bottles. I picked my way over and bent close, reading the labels for opiates prescribed to Letitia Strickland. I glanced again at the baggie, distaste shuddering through me as I remembered that night and the one time I'd indulged in smoking weed, at Jackson's urging. Look where that had got me.

Joe straightened and removed his hand. "Don't touch anything," he said, turning to address me.

I barely restrained myself from rolling my eyes. "Gee, thanks, I wouldn't have known that. I don't see any wound other than the obvious gunshot to the head," I noted, proud of my level tone. "No sign of a struggle. Wonder if he was shot in his sleep?" That would be the most merciful way to go. To never see it coming. I'd rather go that way, to not have to face the horror of a killer pointing a gun at my face. I wouldn't want to be sentient in my last moments, impotent and frightened as I stared into the hate-filled eyes that would be my last sight on earth.

Oliver's take was different, immediately homing in on the killer and his mindset. "Cowardly, cold, and calculating."

"Just the way he shot his victim in the back of the head all those years ago," I mused aloud.

"Poetic justice."

"A revenge killing, maybe?"

"Maybe," he agreed grimly.

More voices rose from outside, drifting in from the open window. I strolled over and looked into the yard. "Forensics has arrived."

Two men and a woman cut through the gathering spectators. They carried evidence kits and cameras, their hands already gloved, their hair covered in nets to prevent shedding and adding to the proliferation of DNA the old house was bound to contain.

"Take a good, long, last-second look around. It's about to get chaotic," Oliver advised.

Involuntarily, my attention drifted to the nightstand and the open Bible. I walked to it and leaned over, curious as to what might have been the last thing the victim ever read. A dirty crocheted cross lay across the thin, yellowed pages. A few verses were underlined. My eyes drifted over the markings, settling on the verse underlined twice in a bold black pen:

Vengeance is mine, and recompense, for the time when their foot shall slip; for the day of their calamity is at hand, and their doom comes swiftly. Deuteronomy 32:35.

Vengeance. Calamity. Doom. The printed words rumbled through my mind, and the fine hairs at the nape of my neck bristled.

The kitchen's storm door opened and banged shut. Footsteps approached down the hallway. An older man dressed head to toe in a white suit stood in the doorway and cast a quick, impassive glance at the scene, then gave a low whistle. "Bad one, eh?"

"Worst I've seen in years," Oliver agreed, then gestured at me. "This is Deputy Blackwell. She'll be assisting me in the investigation."

Despite the horror of the body only a few feet away from us, I couldn't help the burst of pride and excitement Oliver's words sent through me. I wouldn't let him down.

The rest of the forensics team entered the room and immediately set to work. Camera flashes strobed the room, highlighting the gore in vivid detail.

Dempsey nudged my elbow as I swept past him to go speak with Reba Tankersley. He leaned into me, keeping his voice low and confidential. "Hey there . . . Big Easy."

I'd had a long, long time to learn how to mask my reaction at the old nickname. I didn't blink or tense a single muscle. "At least I had the good taste not to screw you," I answered with a practiced, slightly contemptuous upturn of my lips.

Anger flushed his already-ruddy face, and he barked a laugh that didn't match the fire in his eyes. "Touché," he grumbled.

Oliver entered the hallway, and we both turned.

"There's justice for ya," Dempsey said. "The man Ray killed years ago was a rough son of a bitch by all accounts, but he was only sixteen. A kid. Someone around here figured an eye for an eye. That Ray should suffer the same fate as his victim."

"Vigilante justice will get you the death penalty same as a random murder," I noted drily. "Nothing we can ever condone. Murder is murder."

"Course," Dempsey agreed, but his back stiffened, and he drew away. "Just sayin' Ray might have had this coming to him, that's all. He was a low-life scum who lived life on the edge."

I didn't respond. If Dempsey had even the slightest peek inside my mind, he'd be shocked. Because as far as I was concerned, Raymond Strickland was a fucking hero.

For a microsecond, displeasure crossed Oliver's face, but he quickly suppressed it, and I doubted Dempsey even noticed. My estimation of Joe Oliver grew. Whether or not Strickland was considered a scumbag victim by others in law enforcement, Oliver sincerely believed in justice and the sanctity of life. Perhaps the fact that I recognized and approved of his old-fashioned values is why he'd chosen to lift me from property crimes and minor thefts to work alongside him.

"Why don't you escort Mrs. Tankersley to her home and interview her further?" Oliver asked me, completely ignoring Dempsey. "I'll talk to the neighbors gathered outside and then join you over there."

"Gotcha," I agreed, hastily putting space between me and Dempsey. I took a final look at the home's interior as I entered the den. The furniture was shabby, but brightly colored afghans were draped over tattered cushions. White lace doilies were placed under lamps, and an old-fashioned braided rug centered the area. A small collection of cobalt-blue bottles lined the front window shelf, and two healthy peace lilies anchored either side of the window. Beside a rocking chair was a basket holding skeins of red and yellow yarn, and knitted rows were loaded on the needles, as though waiting for their creator to pick up the project again and finish. A framed counted cross-stitch hung nearby, the serenity prayer painstakingly crafted.

All was tidy, and the atmosphere cozy and warm—unless you were aware of the grisly scene tucked away in the back bedroom. I imagined Mrs. Letitia Strickland as the kind of older woman who made her guests feel at home with a cup of coffee and freshly baked cookies. Her son Raymond must have been a huge disappointment and a constant source of heartache.

I thought of my own kids, Linsey and Luke. Fifteen-year-old twins, now sophomores at Erie County High. A vulnerable age, right on the cusp of danger. If I had the money and aptitude, I'd homeschool them, keeping both kiddos tucked safely inside our home under constant supervision. No learner's permit. And dating? Out of the question until they'd graduated college, at least. My lips curled in a wry smile. Good thing I didn't have unlimited funds and time—they'd chafe under my overprotective nature.

I stepped onto the back porch and scanned the crowd for Mrs. Tankersley. She held forth between two other women, dabbing her eyes with the hem of a floral apron and shaking her head. "I just knew something was wrong," she wailed. "I had a premonition and came straight over this morning."

Her words gave me pause. I didn't believe in premonitions and omens. Either the woman was being dramatic for an audience, or something in the normal routine of this sleepy street had subtly shifted, alerting her that all was not right. I'd dig it out of her.

"Mrs. Tankersley?" I said, striding up to the little group. "Deputy Blackwell. I'd like to speak with you."

She puffed up with importance and lifted her chin. "I expect you do. Seeing as I'm the one who called you out here and all."

One of the women standing beside Reba, her head also plastered with sponge hair curlers—who didn't use hot appliances these days?—patted Mrs. Tankersley's shoulder. "You call me later, Reba," she gushed. "I want to hear everything."

I bet she did.

I cocked my head to the right and lifted a thumb, gesturing for us to move away. Reba fell in alongside me. "Let's walk to your place," I suggested. "You'll be more comfortable and perhaps recall some small detail that can help us."

"I'll do whatever I can. Never cared much for Ray, God rest his soul, but Letitia was a fine woman. A good neighbor." Her eyes dried, and she shot me a sidelong glance as we crossed the dirt road. "Ray must not have died of natural causes?" she asked, prodding for information. "I mean, if he had, y'all wouldn't have sent for those men from Mobile."

No harm in telling her the truth about that, at least. "Appears he was murdered," I conceded.

Reba licked her lips. "Gunshot?"

It was time for me to be the one asking questions. "Did you hear anything last night?"

"Only his motorcycle. Like I told the police earlier, it must have been close to eleven o'clock. I'd finished watching the ten o'clock news, taken a bath, and tidied up in the kitchen, same as always."

"Anyone with you?" I pressed.

"Lawd, no." She gave a breathless laugh. "My Ralph died near five years ago. Heart attack." Her tone turned wistful. "I been alone ever since."

I understood that tone. Sometimes, when I woke in the middle of the night or the twins had gotten on my last nerve, I missed Josh—until I remembered the final year of our marriage. All the lies, all the betrayals and anger and pain. Then I'd assure myself that I was much better off alone.

We reached her house, and she invited me inside, urging me to take a seat. "Would you like some coffee?" she asked.

"Just water, if you don't mind."

While Reba bustled about the kitchen, I studied her living room. Her decor was surprisingly modern, with leather furniture and an expensive large-screen TV banked against the opposite wall. Interesting that her choice in personal grooming was not. Besides the pink sponge hair rollers, I noted a jar of old-fashioned cold cream on the coffee table. She returned with a glass of water, and we sat opposite one another on each end of the couch.

"You stated that you heard Mr. Strickland's motorcycle about eleven last night. Do you think it could have been another motorcycle? Another driver?"

Reba shook her head, removed her scarf, and began snatching the rollers from her hair with trembling hands. "I must look a fright. Didn't realize I'd end up being seen like this by the whole neighborhood." The rollers fell into the lap of her floral muumuu.

"This must be difficult for you," I said. "But I need you to focus on the events of last night. For Mrs. Strickland's sake."

Her eyes filled with tears as she ran a hand through the tight curls. "Of course. Letitia would want her son's killer caught." She drew a shaky breath. "It was Ray's motorcycle. I looked out the window and checked. I get nervous here living alone at night. Ya know?"

"I understand. Was he alone on the bike? Was another vehicle following him?"

"Not that I noticed. I only peeked out the window once and then went to bed." She bit her lip. "Not to speak ill of the dead, but . . ."

"Go on," I urged.

"I guessed he'd been drinking. The bike weaved a bit on the road, and when he turned in the driveway, he lurched it to a stop."

"Did you observe him go into the house?"

Her face flushed slightly. "I did. Just wanted to make sure he got in safe. The front porch light was on, as always. Ray tripped on the first step but didn't fall. Took him a minute, but he fished keys out of his pocket and stumbled in the door."

This was more than the quick peek out the window she'd originally claimed. "Were there any lights on inside the house before he arrived?" I asked, wondering if someone had been waiting, hidden, for Ray's return.

"No, the house was dark. Hadn't seen or heard anyone pass by, either, except for Tillman Ragsdale and his wife driving by after a night out."

"And after that?" I prodded. "Did Mr. Strickland turn on any lights?"

"I don't know. Once he went in, I went to bed."

"You didn't hear anything else the rest of the night?"

"Nothing. I sleep like a well-fed baby," she admitted. "But when I woke up this morning, I got to thinking. What if Ray had fallen and hurt himself last night in the house? He's usually up early and sits out on the porch to smoke. Letitia never let him smoke in the house, and I was glad to see he still honored her wish."

"But this morning, he wasn't outside, and that alarmed you."

"That, and like I said before, I had a premonition. Just like I had when Letitia had a heart attack, and again when—"

I cut her off as I pulled out a business card with my contact information. "Thank you for your time, Mrs. Tankersley. If you recall anything new, please give us a call."

"Of course." She glanced at the card as she palmed it in her shaking hand. "Don't mind admitting I'm nervous knowing a killer was so close by. What if he comes back? What if he knows I've been talking to you?"

"You didn't see anyone. There's no reason you should be in jeopardy. If it makes you feel better, we'll have a police patrol make periodic drives by your house the next few nights."

She nodded and swiped at the sudden swelling of tears. "I know Ray's been in lots of trouble. Done some bad things. But I remember when he was just a tiny boy. Always so polite. Full of mischief too—the harmless kind," she hastened to add.

It heartened me that someone had a kind word for Raymond Strickland. That another soul besides his dead mother would care that he'd left this world. I exited Reba's house in time to meet Oliver crossing the street. I filled him in on our conversation, and he nodded thoughtfully.

"That matches up to what another neighbor relayed. He saw Mr. Strickland drinking last night at Broussard's Pavilion. Claims Strickland got in a fight there last evening with several men who threatened to kill him."

My first murder case might turn out to be easy to solve. With any luck, we'd have an arrest by nightfall. If so, I'd be sure to call Reba and let her know. "Who were these men?" I asked, curious if a name might be familiar.

Oliver pulled the notes up on his phone. "Tommy Sims, Eddie Yaeger, Jayrod Booker, and Alden Knight. From what I gather, Sims was the ringleader. We'll check him out first."

A ball of dread formed in my gut. As if running into Dempsey this morning hadn't been bad enough. Now I'd have to face more men I knew from high school, one of whom I had a past with. An intimate past. I shook off my misgivings. This wouldn't be the first time. And if they were jerks like Dempsey—which they likely were, if they'd been involved in a bar fight—then that was their problem, not mine. I knew when I went into law enforcement that situations like this were bound to happen.

We climbed in the cruiser, and while Oliver drove, I obtained Tommy's address: 1649 Mulder Drive. I was familiar with the area, located only a couple blocks past Main Street. We proceeded into the older, historic part of town, neighborhoods that featured charming cottage homes with white picket fences and well-manicured lawns and gardens. But three streets over and down, the older homes were ill kempt and falling into various degrees of disrepair and neglect. Peeling paint, broken shutters, and rusted vehicles in the yard were the norm. The more wrecked the house, the greater mass of accumulated junk littered the front porch and driveway.

Tommy Sims's place was about the worst of the worst. From the windows hung with ugly sheets as curtains to the unfortunate lime-green shade of the shutters and trim, its general air was one of neglect.

The doorbell didn't work—no surprise—and it took several minutes of loud rapping on the front door before a dispirited woman grudgingly opened it. She looked as if she'd just tumbled out of bed with her short hair sticking up at awkward angles. Her sleepy eyes instantly widened in alarm at the sight of us.

"We're with the Erie County Sheriff's Department," Oliver informed her. "Is Mr. Sims available?"

Without bothering to answer, the woman stepped away, yelling for Tommy. A deep baritone sounded from inside, the words indecipherable.

But the woman's shrill voice was not. "Cops are here," she proclaimed. "What the hell have you done now?"

More unintelligible mumbling.

"Tell 'em yourself," she yelled. A door slammed inside.

Oliver and I exchanged a wry glance. Marital harmony this was not.

Tommy appeared at the door, eyes wary and pulling a faded T-shirt over his beer belly. A red welt streaked across the left side of his face. That must have been some bar fight. "Yeah?" he asked by way of greeting.

The years had not been kind to him. In high school, he'd been a tall, lean baseball pitcher with longish brown hair and a chiseled jaw. I'd been thrilled when he'd paid attention to me one day at school and had foolishly agreed to meet him at the bleachers after his game that night. Turned out he'd been interested in only one thing. I'd discovered this at school the next day when he and his buddies had walked right past me in the hallway as though I were a nobody. Even worse, it became apparent in the days and weeks that followed that he'd run his mouth about what went down between us. I credited Tommy for the "Big Easy" nickname, which had stuck to me like superglue the rest of the year.

I hadn't expected Tommy Sims to look the same as he was when a teenager—and I'd seen him a time or two from a distance at the grocery store—but I hadn't been prepared for a close look at the weathered, wrinkled face and sagging jawline. His once dark-brown locks were threaded with gray, and his hairline had receded several inches at the front.

I tried to be generous. After all, I had my own wrinkles and stretch marks and a fierce reliance on dye to keep my hair its once-natural light-brown color. But my figure these days was trim and athletic, a far cry from my chubby adolescence.

"Lieutenant Oliver and Deputy Blackwell with the Sheriff's Department. We'd like to ask you a few questions," said Oliver.

Tommy barely glanced my way as he responded to my partner. "Son of a . . . if this is about last night, Strickland provoked us." His hand lightly touched the welt on his face. "Man gave as good as he got." Tommy's eyes narrowed. "He file a complaint or somethin'?"

"What was the fight about?" I asked, bypassing his question.

Tommy leveled his gaze at me and shifted uneasily on his bare feet. "We thought he might be bothering Jori Trahern, so we stepped in."

The name didn't ring a bell. "Why did you think there was a problem? Did you observe any violence or distress between them?"

"Nooo," he drawled slowly. "It was more because of who she is."

I quirked a brow. "Which is?"

"A cousin of Jackson Ensley's. Guy was murdered by Ray back in high school. Shot in the back of the head. Cold blooded."

A shiver eased down my spine like a melting ice cube making tracks. This marked the second time today I'd heard Jackson's name. I'd have to brace myself for more of the same in this investigation.

Tommy's eyes narrowed on me. "Do I know you? You look kinda familiar."

A flush crept up the nape of my neck. So he didn't recognize me. I didn't know whether to be relieved or affronted. I ignored the question and asked one of my own. "Had you ever observed Mr. Strickland and Ms. Trahern together prior to last evening?"

"Nah. First time I'd seen Ray in ages." Tommy crossed his arms over his chest, a half sneer painting his face. He'd sported that expression in high school whether on the ball field or hanging out with friends.

Images from over three decades ago flashed through my mind—Jackson and Tommy milling together with others at a party and the two of them sitting in the school cafeteria with a dozen others. But I couldn't recall seeing them alone together. They always seemed to have a more "friend of a friend" type relationship. The two couldn't have been more opposite—the clean-cut jock and the guy who acted too cool for school and slightly dangerous. Jackson had a reputation as a heavy drug user. As far as I could tell, the only thing the guys had in common was their callous treatment of me. Not that either knew or cared.

But if they weren't close, why did Tommy seem so bent out of shape about seeing Ray and Jori together? Did Tommy have a thing for Jori Trahern? She was a lot younger than him, but that didn't necessarily rule out the possibility.

"What caused the fight?" I asked abruptly.

"Man had no business being at the Pavilion." Tommy's chest puffed out, and his tone rang with righteous indignation. "It weren't right that he was just sittin' there chattin' it up with one of Jackson's kin. Ray needed to be put in his place."

Was this merely a male territorial move? Tommy showing off to his friends by bullying Ray?

"Hey, I *do* know you." Tommy raised a hand and pointed his finger at me. His lips pressed together and breathed out a puff of sound. *Buh.*

I braced myself. *Here it comes.* The old moniker. But Tommy stopped himself midword. I was surprised he possessed this modicum of self-control.

"Yeah, I recognize you now," he continued, a smirk settling over his mouth. "You look lots different. Better." His eyes did a slow scan up and down my body. I kept my poker face on, revealing nothing.

Oliver's sidelong glance burned into me, and I felt him assessing this development in the interview. Before I could respond to Tommy's insult-wrapped-in-a-compliment, Oliver took over the questioning, pressing for more details on the altercation. Tommy insisted there wasn't much of a physical fight, but I suspected he was downplaying the situation. We'd check with Broussard's staff who were on duty last night and take statements from witnesses and the other three men involved.

"Did you threaten to kill Mr. Strickland?" Oliver asked at last.

Tommy shook his head in disgust. "It was just words said in the heat of the moment. Don't tell me that hardened convict claims he's scared for his life now." Tommy crossed his arms over his potbelly, and his mouth turned down in a scowl. "So are you arresting me, or what?" he demanded.

Oliver tucked his notepad in his vest pocket. "Depends."

"On what?"

Oliver leveled him with a stern gaze. "On whether or not you were the one who murdered Raymond Strickland last night."

Tommy paled, as though Oliver's words had landed like a punch to his gut. "Murder? Ray's dead?" he asked, blinking rapidly.

The woman who'd opened the door to us appeared immediately by Tommy's side. She'd evidently been listening in on us. She sidled up to Tommy, and he wrapped an arm around her waist. "What's this about?" she asked. Her voice was loud with a false bravado.

"It's okay, Sandy," Tommy reassured her. "Just a misunderstanding."

Her chin lifted. "My husband was with me all last night."

"What time did you return home from the bar?" I asked Tommy.

He rubbed his face and turned to Sandy. "I'm not sure. About eleven?"

"Yeah, maybe even a little earlier." She answered with her gaze fixed on me, dislike and mistrust brimming in her faded blue eyes.

"You willing to come to the station for a GSR test?" Oliver asked.

Tommy blinked. "A what?"

"Gunshot residue test."

I retained my poker face. Oliver was trying to assess Tommy's frame of mind. The GSR test would be useless at this point. It was only relevant four to six hours after a shooting, and that was only if the suspect hadn't washed his hands and had also been inactive. While I'd talked to Strickland's neighbors, Oliver had spoken briefly with the coroner and pressed him for a quick assessment. According to the coroner, Raymond Strickland had probably been dead over eight hours by the time his body was discovered.

"Yeah, I'll—"

"No way," Sandy interrupted. "He ain't doin' nothing without a lawyer present."

"If your husband is innocent . . ." I let my voice trail off.

"I told you, he was with me last night. I just don't trust y'all not to try and pin him with the crime."

Oliver ignored her outburst. "We'll be in touch, Mr. Sims."

It sounded more like a threat than a casual comment.

A cowed Tommy nodded. "Yes, Officers." The door began to close as Oliver and I stepped off the porch.

"Who was that woman?" I heard Sandy ask before it shut behind us.

"Nobody."

A nobody. That's what he thought of me. I pressed my lips together. After all these years, his opinion didn't matter. I regarded Tommy Sims as a low-life scumbag, so all things considered, I thought less of him than he did of me.

Oliver didn't address me until we were safely ensconced in the cruiser. "Mind telling me what all that was about? How well do you know Sims?"

"Not well at all. Especially not these days. He's just someone I knew from high school."

"Somebody from high school, eh?" he asked, gently probing.

"We went out once." I practically choked on the euphemism. What we'd done hadn't even been on an official date.

"Hmm," Oliver noted, backing out of the driveway. His tone was neutral, inviting discussion.

I shut it down with a dismissive shrug. "It's a small town. Lots of connections and paths crossed over the years. So. Who are we interviewing next? Eddie Yaeger, Alden Knight, or Jayrod Booker?"

"You know them too?" he asked wryly.

"I've seen them around. They all like to hang out playing pool at the Pavilion and trying to act like tough hotshots." I held the radio mike in my hand. "Which house directions do you want next?"

"Actually, I'm more intrigued by Strickland's association with Jori Trahern. She might be the last person he ever spoke with. Let's visit her first."

Chapter 4

JORI

Drinking the evening before had been a bad idea. Zach and Mimi had both been restless last night, wandering around the house for no good reason in the wee hours before dawn, which meant that I couldn't rest either. All it would take was one slip on the rug for Mimi to fall and get injured, or for Zach to decide to fix something to eat and turn on a stove burner, and disaster might ensue. The possibilities had kept me up and coaxing them both back to bed whenever I heard wooden floors creak in the hallway.

As I poured Zach a glass of iced tea in the kitchen, I tried to rub away the dull throbbing in my temples.

Zach bit into the sandwich I'd prepared and frowned. "Pick . . ." The final consonant of the word was a garbled glug.

"Pick *what*?" I asked.

His brows drew together in concentration. "Pick . . . ," and he again uttered some strangled syllable.

I stared blankly at his face, which was puckered with agitation.

"Mimi knows," he said. Those two words were his favorite expression, and he joined them together as a single word: *Mimiknows*.

I turned to Mimi, who was putting away the dried breakfast dishes. "What does Zach want?"

"Pickles," she said. "He won't even eat peanut butter sandwiches without them."

Mystery solved. I opened the fridge and moved around contents. No pickle jar. "It's not here."

Mimi turned away from the dish rack, her brows drawn together, echoing Zach's expression. I'd never noticed the resemblance in my brother and grandmother before, but it struck me suddenly with full force. Mom had also used to wear that same pinched look, especially in the latter stages of cancer, when she'd been heavily dosed on painkillers and in that twilight world where she was neither here with us nor there on the other side of life. For a moment, the memory squeezed the breath out of my lungs.

"It's got to be there," Mimi asserted, striding over. Her house slippers flapped against the linoleum, blending with the tiger-orange cubes my colored hearing produced.

"Pickles," Zach insisted, his voice rising. Zach's tone was similar to Mimi's, the same cubed shape, but the color was marigold with blended specks of orange and yellow. My own colored sounds were a bronzed sandstone of shaved ice, not near as flashy and pretty as theirs but still genetically related.

I opened the pantry cabinet and spotted a half-empty jar on the top shelf. "Here we are," I said triumphantly.

"It shouldn't have been in the pantry," Mimi said. "Zach must have moved it."

Or she had done so and just couldn't remember.

"Did you take your medicine this morning?" I asked her.

"Can't rightly remember," she hedged.

I checked Mimi's pill dispenser on the counter. The donepezil pill sat forlorn and neglected in its Saturday slot.

I poured her a glass of water and then handed it to her with the pill.

She frowned. "I don't like taking them. They make me tired."

Her tone was that of a recalcitrant child, and I silently tamped down my irritation. "The doctor said this might help you."

"*Might*," she emphasized bitterly.

"It's worth a try. If you won't do it for yourself, do it for Zach."

The defiance in her dark-blue eyes faded, and she held out a hand. Was I doing the right thing insisting she take the medication? The doctor had warned it only worked in half the patients, and even then, the effects were limited to six months or a year. There was no cure. The most it could possibly do was slow the progression of the disease.

Just as there had been no cure for Zach's autism or Mom's brain cancer, it seemed the Traherns were a cursed lot. At least our branch was. Was my own neurological quirk with synesthesia a product of some faulty brain chemistry I'd inherited from the maternal side of the family?

My hands fluttered involuntarily to my empty stomach.

A knock sounded at the side door. Before I could answer, it squeaked open and Uncle Buddy strode in, bringing with him a breath of fresh air into the tense kitchen.

"Morning, y'all," he said easily, his deep voice filling the room. His eyes settled on Mimi scowling at the pill in her hand. "You taking your vitamins this morning, Oatha?"

In a swift move, she popped the pill in her mouth and swigged it down with a gulp of water. Scowling at the both of us, she set the glass on the counter. "Y'all happy now?" Without waiting for an answer, she shuffled to the den.

Uncle Buddy raised a brow. "Always was a grump in the morning, even as a kid. Tressie was the same. The two of them used to snap at each other every day until noontime."

Hard to picture Mimi as a child. Especially since she never talked about her childhood. "Was she always this stubborn?" I asked.

"You bet." He slanted me a curious look and cocked his head toward the door. "Got a moment?"

"Sure. Back in a minute," I called to Mimi and Zach. Once outside, I turned to him. "What's up?"

He withdrew a wallet from his back pocket and pulled out a check. "A little something to tide y'all over," he said, handing me the check.

I accepted it, whistling softly at the amount. "I'm sure this is way more than—"

"Got a call from the bank late yesterday," he interrupted. "Oatha was overdrawn."

I groaned. Seemed I'd have to add managing Mimi's financial affairs to my growing list of duties. "I won't let it happen again," I promised.

"Not your fault. I'd have just directly deposited this in her account but figured you needed to know what was going on."

No telling how many times Uncle Buddy had to "help out" his sister over the years. I suspected he assisted with Tressie's bills too.

"Thanks. How about you and Aunt Sue coming over one night soon for dinner?"

"Sure thing. I'd reckon Sue would appreciate a break from cooking."

If she did have a complaint, I couldn't picture his wife ever voicing it. To me, she'd always appeared a mousy kind of person, shuffling about quietly in the background while Uncle Buddy took center stage with his huge personality. Both of their daughters favored Aunt Sue in looks and personality. Quiet people. I'd never been especially close with my cousins. They were a generation older than me, and both had moved out of state decades ago.

He fixed an intense stare on me. "Anything else I can do to help, give me a call."

With that, he waved and climbed into his truck. I reentered the house and stepped into the living room, where Mimi and Zach sat together on the couch, chuckling at demolition footage on HGTV.

"Boom," Zach squealed as a construction crew hammered a wall, slashing holes into slabs of sheetrock.

My heart warmed as I watched. How many times had I observed them laughing together like this? They seemed to bring out the best in each other. I swallowed past a lump in my throat.

Before I could join them, the front doorbell clanged, emitting bursts of green triangles, and we all startled. Nobody ever rang the bell. Friends and family just knocked once on the side door before entering. Like a call after midnight, this signaled something that could not be good.

"I'll get it." I wiped my sticky palms on the front of my jeans and headed to the door, stoically pulling it open to face whatever bad news awaited. Two strangers, a man and a woman, stood on the porch. I glanced over the khaki uniforms and the official-looking patches on the shirts. Cops or detectives. My mind raced with questions. Had someone died? Were we in some kind of trouble? Maybe someone had called Social Services again. My heart skittered wildly as I imagined these cops poking into our business and deciding we provided an unsafe environment for Zach. What would become of him then?

The woman spoke first, her voice a blue-gray herringbone pattern. "Are you Jori Trahern?"

I swallowed with difficulty. "Yes." My answer came out squeaky and timid.

"I'm Deputy Blackwell, and this is Lieutenant Oliver with the Sheriff's Department. We'd like to ask you a few questions."

"About what?"

"Your conversation last night with Raymond Strickland."

I let out a deep breath. Zach was safe. Along with the relief, my manners returned. "Please, come on in," I invited, opening the door wider and motioning them to enter. Raymond Strickland. What the hell was this all about? Was he angry that I'd spoken to him last night and drawn the ire of the redneck pool players? Perhaps he'd filed a complaint or restraining order against me. Fine. I had no desire to ever see the man again anyway.

Mimi stepped into the den and frowned as the officers seated themselves on the couch. "What's all this here about?" she demanded, crossing her arms at the waist. Mimi had never much been the gracious kind, always suspicious of strangers, especially cops. But either old age or the Alzheimer's disease had made those rough edges sharper.

I gave her a reassuring smile. "It's about a bar fight I witnessed last night while I was out with Dana. Why don't you go ahead and finish eating lunch with Zach?"

"I don't want these people in my house," she sniffed. With one last glare of distrust, Mimi turned and left us alone. I shrugged an apology to the officers, who acted as though they hadn't witnessed my grandmother's rudeness. They were probably used to rude receptions in the course of their duties.

"Has the guy filed a complaint against me?" I asked, getting right down to business. "I didn't talk to him but a few minutes. And anyway, he told me he was leaving town soon."

"There's been no complaint," Lieutenant Oliver assured me in a deep baritone, forming steel-wool coils. "We just want to know the nature of your conversation with him."

Whew. I wasn't in trouble. "But . . . why do you care what we talked about?"

"Raymond Strickland was murdered last night," Deputy Blackwell said. Her brown eyes bored into me, curious and searching.

"Holy crap," I breathed, shock dousing my body like ice water. "Those men at the bar . . . I thought they were just full of hot air. What happened?"

"It's under investigation," she said smoothly. "Now, if you could tell us what the two of you talked about?"

My face heated in embarrassment. "To tell the truth, I'd had one too many cocktails. I was with a friend, and she pointed out Raymond

Strickland, reminding me that he was the one who'd murdered my cousin years ago. So I decided to confront him."

"And your friend's name?" the woman asked, taking notes on her cell phone.

"Dana Adair."

"Go on," she said, looking up from her phone.

I was conscious of Mimi in the next room and the fact that she could clearly hear every word of this. "Well, I—I told him who I was and that I wanted him to know how he'd pretty much destroyed my aunt's life."

Lieutenant Oliver cocked his head toward the kitchen. "Is that the aunt in question?"

"No, no. That's my grandmother, Oatha Jean Delpeche. Her sister—my aunt Tressie Ensley—was the mother of Jackson Ensley, the man Raymond Strickland murdered."

I could feel Mimi's displeasure all the way from the next room. We never, ever talked about this old crime, and my grandmother sure as hell hated family business being paraded in front of strangers.

"How did he respond to that?" Blackwell asked.

I snorted a bitter laugh. "Just what you'd expect. He denied having killed Jackson. Typical con man, right? Said he was framed. Like I'd believe anything he had to say." I stopped abruptly, wanting to bite my tongue. The guy, after all, was now dead. Murdered.

The two officers stared at me, willing me to continue.

I held out my hands, palms up. "That's about it. We didn't talk long before Eddie and them came over and started harassing him. I do feel bad about that. Maybe if I'd never confronted Strickland, he'd still be alive."

Zach unexpectedly entered the room and took Deputy Blackwell's hand. He tugged at it and she half rose, fixing me with a questioning look.

"Bye-bye," Zach stated, trying to guide her to the front door.

"Not yet, Zach," I said, hurrying to his side and trying to lead him back to the kitchen. "Wait a few minutes. Go eat your lunch, okay?"

He shook his head. "Bye-bye," he said again, louder.

"Mimi?" I called out, beseeching her to come get him. Zach didn't much cotton to strangers in his house either.

"Maybe it'd be better if we continued this on the porch," the woman said, gently releasing her arm from Zach's hold. The officers both rose from the couch, and I followed them out.

"Sorry about that," I apologized. "My brother has autism and likes to stick to familiar routines and people. Strangers make him uncomfortable."

"No problem at all," she assured me. "Returning to last night, did Mr. Strickland indicate that he was worried about anything, or did he mention any enemies? Is there anything else you can tell us about his state of mind? You might be the last person to ever speak with him."

The melting-ice-chip shiver returned to trickle down my spine. "He was angry. Disgusted with the world and everyone in it. Mentioned that he was only passing through and that his mom had recently died. Like I said before, he claimed to be innocent and that he was set up for murder. He also said something to the effect that people around this bayou have a way of disappearing."

"Did he mention specific names?" Lieutenant Oliver asked, his tone sharp and intense.

"No, he kept it all vague. I assumed he was talking about the Cormiers, of course."

"We're familiar with the case. Anything else?" Blackwell asked.

I started to shake my head no, then stopped. "Oh! I almost forgot. He sort of implied that he had a secret deal in the works. A lucrative one that he needed to complete before leaving town."

"Secret deal?" Blackwell's eyes lit with interest, and she and her partner leaned in toward me.

"I'm trying to remember his exact words." I racked my brain, picturing his sly grin at the bar as he mentioned it. "*Private business* was how he phrased it. I assumed he was talking about a drug deal or something else illegal."

"Why did you assume it was illegal?" Oliver asked. "He could have been talking about finalizing his mother's inheritance."

My chin lifted. "Because he acted awful secretive, dropping his voice and glancing around the room as he spoke. He shot my cousin in the back in cold blood, his supposed friend. Call me cynical—I assumed the worst about him."

The female deputy withdrew a card from her uniform pocket and handed it to me. "If you think of anything else, give us a call."

The April breeze nipped into the thin fabric of my T-shirt as I watched the officers pile into their vehicle and back out of our driveway. I rubbed at the goose bumps on my arms, unsettled at the idea that I might be the last person Ray spoke to before he was murdered.

Welcome home, I thought sourly as I reentered the house. It suddenly felt too crowded, too stuffy, too warm. Mimi stomped into the den, Zach close behind. "They gone?"

"Yes, ma'am." I had the feeling she was about to let loose on me.

Zach loped over to the window, staring after the cop car. "All gone," he pronounced after their vehicle was out of sight. Although he spoke in his usual flat affect, I could tell he was pleased. He sauntered down the hallway to his room. Once he'd shut the door behind him, Mimi rounded on me.

"What the hell were you doing talking to Raymond Strickland, of all people?"

"It seemed like a good idea at the time. I'd been drinking too much," I admitted with a wry smile.

"You could ply me with all the whiskey in that bar, and I'd still never speak to that lowlife. He ruined my sister's life. Don't you have any family loyalty?"

Her words stung. "Of course I do. That's why my besotted brain thought it was brilliant to confront the guy and let him know how his murder hurt Aunt Tressie."

Mimi's anger thawed; I could see it in the relaxing of tension in her shoulders. "Humph. Let that be a lesson to you. You hang with trash, it will bring you nothing but trouble. No good ever comes of it."

"Yes, ma'am."

"We'll speak no more about it."

"But—"

"But nothing. Raymond Strickland got what he deserved in the end."

I couldn't argue with her logic. Nor could I fault her anger. Some might call my grandmother cold and unforgiving, but they didn't see the soft side to her that I did. She'd nursed my mother through a terminal illness and then raised her challenged grandchild without a single complaint. I doubted I'd ever possess half her fortitude and compassion. Lately, I'd done nothing but throw myself a big ole pity party while moaning and groaning to Dana at every opportunity.

I resolved to do better by Mimi and Zach. They were family, and family stuck together. No matter what.

Chapter 5

JORI

I crept through the house, careful to avoid the wooden planks in the hallway and den that I knew creaked the loudest. I hadn't sneaked out of the house since I was seventeen, yet I remembered every inch of these old floorboards and how to escape with no one the wiser. If I lived to be a hundred, I'd never forget my old, intricate tiptoeing choreography as I slipped out to be with Deacon. The weather was never too cold or too rainy or too humid for those late-night rendezvous.

Carefully, I lifted the latch and opened the door. The yard and trees were etched in silver shadows from the full moon. I probably didn't even need the flashlight clutched in my right hand. Tonight held none of the wild, frantic excitement of my youth, when I'd exalted in temporary, stolen freedom and raced through the woods to meet Deacon in our secret place. Back then, I could never get enough of him.

But now there was only a gnawing hunger to revisit and remember. I deserved this respite.

Despite my sincere intention, formed only this morning, to be more compassionate with Mimi and Zach, my patience was shot by evening. At long last, they slept soundly. As I'd lain in my old childhood bed, I'd been awash with a painful nostalgia that insisted I return to the old smoking shed on the Cormier property. Rather, what used to be the Cormier land.

Over the years, their showcase home had switched hands several times. Each time the house was resold and inhabited by new owners, its grandeur had sunk, until at last Uncle Buddy bought it and expanded his thriving tourism business to include vacation forays for fishermen. He'd bought it at a steal and restored the interior to cater to his clientele. But the upkeep, especially of the outside grounds, never lived up to the standard Clotille Cormier had set. Her old rose garden was reduced to weeds and patches of invasive saw palmetto. Only a few dead shrubs remained, pitiful brown stumps that did not flower, their branches barbed with thorns. The house itself was no longer the modern, gleaming structure of its heyday. Instead, it was decorated in a hunting lodge style, replete with mounted deer heads and bass, and lots of leather and dark paneling. A taxidermy wonderland that its former mistress would have despised.

Twigs and leaves snapped beneath my feet as I marched the abandoned dirt path. Vines and low-lying tree branches clawed at my clothing, scratching into my flesh. Years ago, the path had been wider, but now it was almost entirely closed in as nature did its work, expanding and creeping over man's attempts to carve order. A pungent smell of damp earth combined with the briny air. It pressed upon me as thick as the smothering vegetation scraping against my body. Thorns, spindly branches, and the sharp edge of palmetto blades sliced my skin like a rebuke and a warning to retreat.

Even now, thirteen years later, I shuddered at the memory of that innocent, naive version of myself tromping about these woods by the Cormier house property, blissfully unaware of hidden danger. Had I missed the kidnapper—or killer—by mere seconds? Fifteen minutes? An hour? Or had he still been around, lurking out in the shadows—watching me—ready to slit my throat if I caught a glimpse of him?

I realized I should be grateful for having been spared whatever mysterious fate had been dealt the Cormiers that long-ago night. But even though I'd been spared the tragedy that had played out in their beautiful home, I lived with this omniscient *unknowing*, a vague uneasiness that anyone close to me, at any moment, could be snatched from my life—devoured in a black hole of silence, ripped from the fabric of my life's familiar landscapes.

And I felt so much older, too—my emotions in sync with the bayou night's atmosphere, weighed down by past pain and buried secrets. But I was determined. Resolved to remember the good, all that had been pure and innocent and hopeful. It was there that the memories still lived, despite the mysterious aftermath of my missing lover. And tonight, I wanted to relive each past meeting, each kiss and touch and murmured word of love that had passed between Deacon and me.

I'd been so absorbed in my thoughts that I almost collided with the ancient smoke shed. A mossy wall gleamed just a couple of feet ahead, illuminated by my flashlight's elliptical beam. I reached out my hand, my fingers touching the wet condensation on the moldy concrete blocks. Arcing the flashlight to the right, I followed the outline of the structure to the front. A rotted wooden door angled against the opening. After checking for snakes, I pushed it to the side and aimed my light at the interior.

It was empty. All that remained was the old bricked-up pit in the corner used a century ago for smoking hogs and venison. Empty pine shelves lined one wall of the small building. The floor was in surprisingly good shape. Mrs. Cormier once had a grand whim to convert the building into a pottery studio, but after the expense of replacing the dirt floor with oak planks and ordering a kiln and supplies, she'd quickly lost interest in the project and left it abandoned.

I entered farther into the room. Whatever had happened to the kiln and pottery supplies, not a trace of them remained. I checked behind the pit, and sure enough, folded inconspicuously behind it was a rough wool blanket. Heat flooded my body, and my heart pinched. I kicked at it with my boot—who knew what kind of spiders, snakes, or critters might have bedded in there? When nothing scurried out of the material, I knelt down and picked it up. Could it possibly hold some faint scent of Deacon, left over from the many nights we'd lain together on top of this very blanket? Feeling foolish, I nonetheless held the coarse fabric to my nose and sniffed. It stank of wet rot and mold. Still, I refolded it carefully and returned it to its rightful home.

I sank to the floor and wrapped my arms around my knees, my head sinking onto my thighs. The cold crept up all the way from my ass to my spine. I thought of the first night I'd met him out here. The way, earlier, he'd lightly pecked my cheek when he dropped me off at the door to my home, the gleam in our eyes, knowing that in less than an hour we'd meet here, extending the kisses and exploring each other's bodies until we sneaked home again before daylight.

It was a wonder we'd never been caught.

Although, in the end, there was always a reckoning.

I don't know how long I sat there, remembering long, slow kisses and the heat and wonder of skin against skin. All the fervent vows and promises we'd made. All the plans and dreams. I'd never doubted Deacon's love. In the years since, with all the rumors flying about the Cormiers still being alive and living incognito, I knew it wasn't true. We were young and rash, but Deacon would never, ever have cut me out of his life so cruelly. He would have sent word to me somehow, sent for me to leave the bayou and join him wherever he was hidden.

At last, I slowly rose, my back and hips cramped from sitting so long in the cold. I considered extending my foray down this adolescent memory lane to the one spot in the woods I never revisited. Yet, no matter the years that passed, I was certain I could find that exact location even if I were blindfolded.

I straightened and walked across the floorboards, my footsteps echoing like gunshots in the ghostly silence. No, I decided. Not tonight. I didn't think I was up to it yet. Perhaps I never would be.

Outside, I was shocked to find coral and violet rays bursting from the eastern horizon. Time to hurry home. My lips curled in sad irony. How many times had I said the same thing to myself as I'd left this shed and waved goodbye to Deacon? And the last time I'd said goodbye had been nothing special—there'd been no premonition or anything in his manner to indicate it would be the last time I saw him alive.

I tucked the small flashlight into my back pocket, not needing it anymore. As I turned to find the tangled path, a moving pattern of olive and gray caught the corner of my eye. I whirled around, and it was gone. I waited, and seconds later, I heard the faint sound of twigs crunching underfoot. Whoever or whatever roamed the woods was coming my way.

People have a way of disappearing around here.

Raymond Strickland's words howled in my head with their unique color of eggplant purple edged in black. My throat clogged with sudden fear, and I froze where I stood—a frightened bunny exposed to lethal prey. My legs were rooted to the ground with a nightmare paralysis.

A figure emerged from the copse of pines. The man was decked head to toe in camo, a twelve-gauge shotgun propped against his shoulder. Judging by his gaping mouth, I guessed he was as surprised to run into me as I was to see him.

I let out a shaky laugh. "I forgot. Turkey season started this week, didn't it?"

"Yesterday." His voice was a boxy medium brown, the color of rich dirt. "Came in with some buddies from Wetumpka. There's three of us out here this morning. Be careful, Miss."

"Right. Thanks for the warning." With the start of turkey season and only six weeks out from the Blessing event, I should expect to see more hunters and tourists.

Bayou Enigma's annual Blessing of the Fleet was our town's biggest event of the year. And ever since Uncle Buddy was elected to the county commission four years ago, he'd made sure to throw business my way, including this event. My freelance event planning job had turned out to be profitable beyond my expectations, but the Blessing ceremony was a big deal for my bottom line too.

"I'll be careful." I threw up a hand, eager to return home before Mimi and Zach stirred and not particularly wanting to chitchat with this armed stranger. "Happy hunting."

He tugged the bill of his camo cap, and in two seconds, he'd completely disappeared into the woods, silent and inconspicuous, with the skill of a practiced hunter. I blinked, slightly disconcerted at the speed with which he'd blended into the green foliage. Shaking off my bemusement, I headed down the path, a great deal noisier than the hunter, just in case his friends were around. At the bend in the trail, I glanced over my shoulder at the smoking shed, its outline visible in the emerging morning light.

Even with all the whispered promises and long conversations with Deacon held inside the old building, there had also been things left unsaid. Words that would never be spoken aloud.

Dead secrets that haunted.

Chapter 6

JORI

"He was adopted, you know."

Mimi had slipped that little bombshell in today, totally out of the blue. I was dropping her off at the home of Rose Sankey, one of her oldest and dearest friends. Rose was the same age as Mimi. She'd never fully recovered from hip surgery last year, but her mind was sharp as a tack. Mimi helped Rose with the housekeeping while they gossiped and then settled in for a mammoth game of gin. Rose kept a steady eye on Mimi, providing my grandmother a safe outing for the day. The arrangement worked out perfectly for both of them.

"Hmm . . . what was that?" I asked, my mind focused on safely pulling through the four-way stop downtown.

"Jackson. He was adopted."

I gaped at her. "I can't believe this is the first time I've heard of it."

"Well, you just asked me about him."

"You mean a couple of days ago?" My brow furrowed as I turned onto Ocala Drive.

"No," she said, her voice rising. "Just now."

I'd done no such thing. Instead, I'd been mentally listing all my to-do tasks for the week. While Zach was at his adult day program, I could focus better on my business. But correcting Mimi would only make her more edgy.

"Why haven't you told me about Jackson before now?" I asked. "What's the big deal?"

"It was a huge deal for Tressie. She and Ardy tried for years to have a baby, and it was clearly not working."

"I meant, why the secrecy?"

Mimi rubbed a hand over her brow. The skin of her hands was so transparent and paper thin now. More than any other aspect of her appearance, they showed her age, betraying a fragile vulnerability. "Well, you wanted to know about him," she said querulously. "What he was like."

I waited, silently willing her to continue in her own bumbling, confused way.

"He was a bad boy," she said at last, her voice so soft I had to lean in to catch the words. "Bad blood, I always said."

It was hardly fair to blame Jackson's behavior on his biology, but arguing the point with her served no purpose. "How was he bad?" I prodded when it appeared she had nothing further to say.

"He was a liar. And whenever he got caught in a lie, he knew just how to manipulate Tressie. Ardy, I think, began to see through Jackson by the time he was a teenager."

"What did he lie about?"

"Drugs, stealing, a bad temper." Mimi clamped her mouth shut. "Enough about him."

She maintained a stony silence until I pulled into Rose's driveway. With one hand on the car door latch, she turned to me, eyes serious and clear. "Don't go digging up the past, Jori. Nothing good will come of it—mark my words."

"Why? That was all long ago. It can't hurt anyone now."

To my surprise, her eyes filmed with tears.

"It's okay," I assured her, patting her arm. "I won't ask you any more questions about Jackson."

Mimi let out a sigh and then nodded before leaving the car. I watched as she walked up the sidewalk and knocked on the door. Rose opened it and waved at me, a signal that I could go on my way.

This wouldn't be the first time I'd lied to my grandmother. But what was the point in needlessly upsetting her?

Less than ten minutes later, without any conscious decision on my part, I found myself sitting in Aunt Tressie's room at Magnolia Oaks Nursing & Assisted Living Home, a private one, thanks to Uncle Buddy's generosity. The home was magnificent and grand. Although small, Tressie's room had polished mahogany floors, crown molding at the ceiling, and a brick fireplace that gave off a cozy vibe, which was further enhanced by my aunt's flowers, afghans, stacks of books, and a few framed photos scattered on her tasteful furniture. She even had her own private bathroom and kitchen galley.

Speaking with my aunt Tressie was hit or miss. Some days, she was lucid and eager to talk about old times, and other days, she was wrapped in a mental fog that was nearly impregnable. Today fell in between on the spectrum. She sat in a recliner, shuffling through a parcel of photos and yellowed papers. This seemed to be her favorite activity. She greeted me with a smile of recognition, and then a frail hand fluttered to her hair. "Oh, dear. Is it my day to get my hair done? I'm not ready."

Her voice was golden amber, shaped into cubes of frozen honey. The color was in the same happy orange family as the rest of my blood relations, but mellower in tone.

"No. I just stopped in to visit for a bit." I sat on the sofa beside her and pointed at her lap. "What are you looking at?"

She held up a black-and-white photo of a young couple standing on the shore, holding a pudgy baby. "This was Jackson at seven months old. His first trip to the beach."

"Hmm. Sounds fun."

Tressie held up another photo. "And here he is at age three, playing with Tinker Toys. Such a sweet baby."

I'd seen all the photos dozens of times, but I nodded appreciatively. "What about all those old letters?" I asked.

"I used to have a pen pal from Germany named Ann Marie. Her father was in the army, and she was in the American school. Do people have pen pals anymore?"

"Nah." I smiled gently. "There's this new thing called the internet, and we all keep in touch on social media."

She blinked at me, and I suppressed my amusement. Mimi and Tressie were sisters, but so different. Mimi was remarkably modern and was always piddling around on her laptop and smartphone.

"Actually, I came to ask you about Jackson," I began nervously. "Mimi happened to let it slip today that he was adopted. How come I never heard about this before? Why did everyone keep it a secret?"

Aunt Tressie shifted her weight in the chair, clearly uncomfortable. "I don't think I'm supposed to talk about it."

"But why?"

"It was all arranged very quietly." Her eyes looked dreamy. "And quickly too. We didn't have to go through an agency and wait for months or years." She flashed a triumphant grin. "We decided we wanted to adopt, and in no time, we had our Jackson."

"If you didn't go through an agency, then how—"

"Mrs. Ensley? Time for . . ." A male nurse entered the room, then stopped short at the sight of me. "Sorry. Didn't know you had company. We can reschedule your social worker appointment, if you'd like."

Disappointment and frustration whipped through me. I wanted more time alone with Aunt Tressie to dig out information.

"What appointment?" Aunt Tressie asked, brow furrowed.

"Your monthly interview with Mrs. Prescott." He faced me to explain. "She interviews all the residents monthly to see if they need anything or have any concerns with their care. I can reschedule for later in the day, though," he offered.

I rose, forcing a smile. "No, no. I don't want to interfere with her routine."

"If you're sure . . . ," he said.

He offered his hand to Tressie, and she frowned. "Where am I going now?"

"To see Mrs. Prescott."

"But all my papers." She gestured at everything in her lap.

"Don't worry. I'll put them away for you," I said, beginning to gather her stuff.

"If you're sure . . . they go in the cedar chest by the TV."

"Right. Go on along, and I'll come back another day for a nice, long chat."

I waved at her as she left and then went to the old-fashioned hope chest where she stored her sentimental memorabilia. The lid creaked open, and the faint scent of cedar and dried rose petals greeted me. I laid the papers on the top fold-out drawer and then paused. Maybe there were answers in this chest. Guiltily, I looked over my shoulder and saw that the room's door was shut, leaving me with total privacy. When would I ever get this chance again?

I riffled through the papers and photographs in the top drawer, but I'd seen them all dozens of times. I dug deeper, dragging out handfuls of photo albums, papers, and envelopes. I wasn't even exactly sure what I was searching for. I quickly shuffled through letters, then Jackson's elementary and junior high school report cards, smiling at the occasional old photos of Mimi and my mother. Back before Mom had children. Before the cancer. She looked so carefree and happy, unencumbered instead of beaten down by life—which is mainly how I remembered her these days.

I tore into an eight-by-ten manila envelope and saw it was filled with official-looking mimeographed documents. I scanned the contents, and my pulse quickened as I found a birth certificate.

Jackson Earl Fairhope
Born: March 13, 1975, 5 pounds 3 ounces, father unknown. Mother:
Grace Lee Fairhope, Hospital: Mobile General, Mobile, Alabama.

Quickly, I photographed the birth certificate and continued rum-
maging, hoping to find the private adoption papers. There were none.
If there had ever been any, Aunt Tressie hadn't kept them.

Grace Lee Fairhope. Mobile was less than an hour away. Was there
any chance the birth mother still lived nearby? What the hell, it was
worth a shot. I entered her name and location on my phone and immediately found links to several newspaper articles. I clicked on the first
one, which pulled up a stark black-and-white photo of a woman staring
into the camera with dead eyes. Thin, scraggly hair framed a sunken
face. Her lips were chapped and split, her cheeks pocked with scabs.
Mobile Woman Charged with Prostitution & Drug Possession.

The article mentioned Fairhope's previous arrests for the same
crimes, dating back over three decades. No wonder Jackson had been
born on the thin side if his mom had been using while pregnant. Had
his biology contributed to his delinquency later in life? Guilt pinged
in my chest at the thought. It was unfair. People were more than their
biology. They had free will and made their own choices.

This latest arrest had occurred only four months ago in Mobile. If I
left now, I'd have plenty of time to make the trip before Zach returned
home from his day program. Again, my body seemed to move of its
own accord, just as it had when I'd driven on autopilot to the nursing
home. Now I found myself on Highway 10 East, my GPS set and ticking down the ETA to the address I'd googled of this unknown woman.

What the hell did I expect to gain? All I had was a suspicion that
my murdered cousin's death was linked to Deacon's disappearance—
which had sprung forth from Raymond Strickland's words, hardly a
reliable source. Yet on I drove. The day was pewter, and clouds swirled
mercilessly, always at the whim of the gulf's capricious winds. Light

rain drizzled, and the roads were slick, a black track leading out of the primitive bayou and into a large commercialized city.

My GPS efficiently guided me off the highway and onto a county road that led to a residential area. I wasn't familiar with the area and braced myself to drive into a housing project peopled with loitering drug dealers. I promised myself that if it looked too dangerous, I'd get the hell out of Dodge and instead call Grace Fairhope. I tried to formulate my approach if by some miracle she was still at the listed address, but my brain refused to function past the moment-to-moment tension of moving forward.

I'd have to wing it when I arrived.

Surprisingly, I was only a couple of miles from my final destination, and the neighborhood wasn't half-bad—a lower-middle-class area that was, frankly, better than what I expected. The homes were small and close together. I felt as though I'd traveled back in time to the 1950s, before the vogue of today's McMansions or the long, sprawling ranch houses popular in the 1960s. Each house was different—no cookie-cutter construction here—and the streets were laid out in no-nonsense square grids. Stately magnolias and live oaks shaded the properties, some of them so large the roots had broken up driveways and sidewalks, and their branches towered over the rooflines. If a strong hurricane gale uprooted them and they toppled, these tiny homes would be crushed.

My palms sweated against the steering wheel as I pulled up to 945 Cypress Lane. After parking the car against the curb, I dried my hands on my jeans and studied the house. It was all redbrick and white trim with overgrown azaleas along the front and sides. Light glowed from inside, and a tan, slightly rusted Toyota Camry was parked in the driveway.

Someone was home. I didn't know whether to be thankful or nervous. Probably a combination of both. Best not to think too hard. I grabbed my purse and exited my car, heart thumping as my sneakers squeaked with each step along the cracked cement of the Fairhope driveway. Something about the cheeriness of the bright bottle collection shimmering by the window gave me comfort. Anyone who could appreciate their delicate beauty must have goodness inside them.

Or so I reasoned.

Before I knocked on the door, the drone of a TV set, familiar and reassuring, further quieted my qualms. The door squeaked open a few inches, and a woman regarded me, eyes narrowed. It could be her. She certainly seemed old enough, judging from the lines etching her eyes and lips and the gray roots by her temples.

"Grace Fairhope?" I asked.

"Yeah," she admitted in a husky smoker's voice colored with fuchsia and navy coils. Her eyes raked me up and down. "You from the court or something?"

My casual attire should have tipped her off that this was not the case, but she opened the door wider and beckoned me inside.

"I was getting ready for my AA meeting," she informed me as I followed her into the den. She sat down gingerly on the couch and pointed to a high-back chair opposite. Her pale arms were streaked with scars slicing through the translucent skin. The thin white track lines looked as though they were healing. Nothing was raw, red, and fresh.

Grace caught my stare and flushed. "I been clean four months, two weeks, and six days," she said, facing me down with defiant pride.

I smiled in what I hoped was an encouraging manner. "That's great. Congratulations."

She wore faded jeans and an old Led Zeppelin T-shirt. The skin on her face, neck, and arms was no longer scabbed, albeit her pallor was tinged with a gray sheen, as though she'd been dragged through fire and emerged with a faint trace of ash. A reborn woman.

From beyond the side door, a teakettle whistled shrilly.

"Excuse me," she murmured, disappearing into the kitchen. I took the opportunity to study the surroundings. A TV was in the corner of the room playing *Jeopardy*. The carpet was old gray shag, but clean.

Dark paneled wood lined the walls. My attention was captured by a bank of framed photographs atop the stone fireplace mantel. I walked over and scanned them, but there were no baby pictures or any others resembling photos I'd seen of Jackson. Mostly, they were photos of an elderly couple.

"Those were my parents."

I whirled around, face burning at being caught snooping.

"They both died last year, within three months of each other. They say that happens, you know. When two people have been married a long time, they can't live without the other. My parents were like that. Dad died of lung cancer, and Mom died in her sleep weeks later. Heart attack, the doctors said. I say she grieved herself to death."

"I'm so sorry."

A sad smile tugged the side of her mouth, transforming her look. I caught the shadow of the handsome girl she might have been long ago, before the drugs. Her son had inherited her high cheekbones and a similar disarming smile.

Grace returned to the sofa, and I sat across from her again. "I inherited this house," she informed me. "You may not think it's much, but after living on the streets a few years, this place is like the Taj Mahal to me."

"It's a perfectly nice house," I hastened to assure her.

A ginger kitty sprang up from nowhere and leaped into Grace's lap. She stroked its fur as gently and reverently as though it were a baby.

"With God's help, I'm going to make it this time. Muffin here is depending on me." With a final rub behind its ear, she looked up at me. "I'm going to AA every night. I've got a steady job at the Suzy Q Diner, and I'm paying restitution for court costs. I had it garnished from my check so's to make sure it gets paid first thing."

"Sounds like a solid plan. I imagine it's hard to start over and work through everything."

"You a psychologist or something? Or a social worker?" Again, the flash of suspicion crossed her face.

"No, nothing like that." I squirmed in my seat, unable to keep up the charade. There was nothing for it but to get down to the matter at hand. "I'm here about the baby you gave up for adoption. Jackson Earl Fairhope."

Grace's back went rigid, and her arms lay still in her lap, Muffin temporarily forgotten. Her face registered a mixture of hope, dread, and shock. "Wh-what?" Then her eyes darkened with stark fear. "Is something wrong? He doin' okay?"

I skirted the question. "It must have been hard, giving him up for adoption."

She didn't speak for several moments, her throat spasming as she visibly tried to regain composure. A single tear slid down her cheek, inky with black mascara. "No," she choked. "You're wrong about that. It was easy. Too easy. I could blow smoke up your ass and tell you I did it for the baby's sake, to give him a better life with a nice family. But that would be a lie."

Her throat clogged with emotion before she drew a deep breath and spoke again. "I was offered ten thousand dollars, a fortune, more money than I'd ever seen at one time in my entire life. And you know what was important to me? Not raising my baby, that's for damn sure. All I could see was a life full of blissed-out highs. One after another after another. And so on, and so on. Ecstasy."

The tears came faster now, and she gave a hollow laugh.

"Who was it?"

She blinked at me, and I had the feeling she'd been a million miles away, experiencing a quantum jump to the past when the monster of her addiction had swallowed up any love and hope for a better life with her child. "Who was what?" she asked numbly.

"Who offered you the ten thousand dollars?"

"I-I can't rightly remember. It was some young man, an attorney arranging a private adoption. Can't recall the name."

"Did you sign any papers?"

"I reckon so." Grace tapped an index finger against a rotted front tooth as she considered the question. "Yes, yes, I did, come to think of it."

"Do you still have those documents?" I asked hopefully.

She snorted. "Even if I had wanted to keep that miserable reminder of what I'd done, I was hardly in a position to be filing away important papers. I was on the streets with no thought but how to score my next high and where to eat and sleep for the night."

"Is there anything you can tell me about the arrangement you agreed to?"

"No. That period of my life is nothing but a blur. Thank God. Why are you so interested? Am I in some kind of trouble after all these years?"

"Not at all. I'm, uh, a friend of the family who adopted your child." I rose quickly—there was nothing more to be gained interrogating the woman. "Thank you for your time. I don't want to keep you from your meeting."

I tried to sweep past, but she grabbed the sleeve of my jacket and held on with a surprising firmness. "And Jackson? He's all right?" A smile lit her eyes. "Does he want to meet me after all these years?"

"No, I didn't come to arrange a meeting."

Hope washed out of her body in a whoosh, and her shoulders slumped.

My words were true enough. But I had to leave Grace with something, some small measure of comfort. I wouldn't be the one responsible for destroying her recovery. Let her live in her respectable little house, attend her AA meetings, and keep the illusion that her son was living a good life.

I extracted myself from her grip. "Thanks for your time, Grace. Your son was raised by a family who loved him well. I'm sure you made the right choice."

Chapter 7

TEGAN

"Hey, rookie. Surprised you're late for work today. How's your big case going?" Deputy Mullins greeted me with a sardonic grin as I entered the station. Deputies Sinclair and Haywood looked up from the paperwork on their desks.

"Got it solved yet?" Haywood asked, not bothering to hide his amusement.

Sinclair had to chime in with his two cents. "Heard you were looking a little green around the gills the other day."

"Screw y'all," I answered cheerily, heading to the coffeepot and pouring a cup. This morning had been a disaster with the twins. Llnsey had overslept, and in the rush to eat breakfast and catch the bus, Luke had knocked over an entire carton of orange juice. The kids had tried to help mop up the mess and missed the bus . . . which meant I'd had to drive them to school and get caught up in the mommy lane drop-off for twenty minutes.

"You need any help with the case?" Mullins asked, openly smirking.

"I'll let you know if I do." I opened a pack of Splenda and stirred my brew. I spared a brief, longing glance at the croissants someone had brought in. These days, I didn't allow myself real sugar or high-carb pastries. Sometimes I wondered if being slim was worth it. I sipped the coffee as I sat at my desk. About the only good thing I could say was that it was hot and strong. After a restless night thinking about the murder, it was exactly what I needed. Mug in hand, I sat at my desk and logged in.

"Wouldn't surprise me if Tommy Sims killed Strickland," Mullins said. "Man's nothing but a hothead. We've arrested him half a dozen times over the years for assault and battery."

I certainly had no lost love for Sims, but I couldn't picture him shooting a man in the back of the head as he lay asleep in bed. That was much too premeditated. If Sims ever crossed a line, it would be while in a fistfight that escalated his anger to a white-hot rage. And his weapon would be his hands, not a gun.

My computer screen lit up, and I opened my email, scanning to see if anything needed an immediate response. Nothing pressing there, nor was there anything on my calendar. Excellent. I wanted to review the notes on the interviews with Tommy and his pals and make a plan of attack. I scribbled a few notes and guzzled more coffee.

"I almost forgot," Haywood said in a way-too-casual voice. "Oliver asked to see you immediately when you got in."

I practically spat out the coffee in my mouth. "Thanks a lot, guys. You could have told me that ten minutes ago." I grabbed a notebook, pen, and coffee cup and hurried to the door, sloshing hot liquid down the front of my uniform pants. Terrific. The snickers followed me down the hallway.

I knocked on Oliver's door and entered. He was writing on a whiteboard and didn't bother turning around. "Sorry I'm late . . . rough morning," I began. "The kids—"

He raised an arm and brushed away my explanation. "Not important." Oliver moved to the side of the board, and I read the timeline he'd been working on. He pointed at the first line with a black dry-erase pen and read his scribbles aloud. "One. On April 13, 1991, sixteen-year-old

Jackson Ensley was shot in the back of the head after attending a late-night party. His friend Raymond Strickland was arrested the next day and charged with murder. According to the prosecution, the motive in the killing was a dispute over a drug transaction.

"Two. Strickland is released from prison on parole February 8, 2019. He returns home to attend his mother's funeral and is killed on April 19 in the same method in which Ensley was murdered.

"Three. The coroner estimated the time of death to be anytime between ten and eleven thirty p.m. Victim was last seen at approximately ten fifteen on Friday night, when, according to his neighbor, Reba Tankersley, Strickland arrived at his house.

"Now moving on to possible suspects—"

"Hold on," I interrupted. After walking up to the whiteboard, I picked up a spare dry-erase pen on the easel and drew an arrow between the first and second points he'd outlined. "Let's make an addition between *one* and *two*." I drew an asterisk, labeled it "1.5," and wrote, *May 19, 2006, all three members of the Cormier household are reported missing.*

Oliver frowned. "The Cormier case has no bearing on the Strickland murder."

"Probably," I agreed. "But we should keep it in mind, since Strickland made a reference to people disappearing in the bayou. It's one of the last things he said to one of the last people who saw him alive that night. You probably don't know since you're not from around here, but Louis Cormier was widely suspected by townsfolk of being involved in shady business like money laundering for drug traffickers. And since Strickland was a known drug dealer, maybe their paths crossed over the years or they associated with the same underworld criminals."

"Don't let the Cormier case sidetrack you," he warned. "We need to focus on the most obvious suspects first."

"Of course." Warmth blossomed on my neck. Had I overstepped work boundaries by adding to my boss's outline? After all, this was my first murder case, and Oliver had solved many while working in Mobile. I sat back down and dutifully made arrangements to interview the bouncer at the Pavilion and check on the details of Letitia Strickland's will while Oliver would continue digging around to explore a possible drug connection to the crime. I had to admit that the drug angle made sense. Strickland had been a known dealer in his youth and had hinted to Jori Trahern that he was working on closing up some kind of deal before he left town.

Oliver ran a hand through his white, unruly hair and sighed. "Would've helped if Strickland's cell phone hadn't gone missing. We could've traced his calls for possible leads."

"The killer's got it. Has to." I scanned through the most recent investigation notes, hoping that the phone records would reveal something of interest. We'd received the records quickly, thanks to Oliver's connections. He had a mountain of sources everywhere after working in the field for so long. But the record only confirmed the phone's last location. "The GPS showed it was last active on his street at 10:18 p.m., April 19."

"Yep. Our killer disabled it. The phone's probably at the bottom of some swamp out here."

We sat in gloomy silence for a moment.

"Any fingerprints or other forensic evidence?" I asked.

"Haven't heard anything yet from the team. I'll let you know as soon as I do. Let's get cracking."

"Yes, sir." I took my leave, eager to resume my investigation. In the hallway, I paused, listening to the familiar muffled sound of computer keyboards and ringing phones behind closed office doors and muted voices from the lobby. What would it hurt to take a look at the old Cormier case files?

Impulsively, I turned right instead of left and walked the opposite way from the office I shared with the other deputies. One quick glance over my shoulder assured me no one else was around. I opened the door leading to the stairwell and headed to the basement, where old files were archived.

Ginger Ledbetter sat at her battered desk, flipping through a magazine. She hurriedly slipped it under a mountain of paperwork as I approached. "Morning, Tegan. What brings you down here?"

Ginger had worked at the sheriff's office longer than anyone else and was deliberately informal when it came to addressing employees. As far as Ginger was concerned, she was the ultimate ruler down here in the basement, the potentate of old records.

"Morning." I found myself shifting on my feet uncomfortably. "I'd like to check out a file."

"Which one?" she asked, steepling her fingers together and peering at me through her bifocals.

"The Cormier case."

Her eyes widened, and then she snorted in amusement. "Haven't you got enough on your plate with the Strickland murder? Why you wanna look at the Cormier file?"

Technically, it was none of her business. Why couldn't the woman just hand it over without the attitude? I didn't have to answer her question, but I wasn't stupid. If I pulled the superior position card, Ginger would hassle me at every opportunity I needed to research old files. I pasted on a smile.

"Never know where there might be connections in different cases," I said breezily. "Is it on microfiche?"

"Yep."

My heart sank. I didn't have time to sit around in the basement reading on the microfiche machine.

"But I also have it digitally scanned," Ginger added, a smug smile spreading across her plump face. "You think you're the first deputy to ever request this file? It'd be a real feather in your cap if you could solve that old case. Every deputy working here for the last thirteen years has read up on the case, so why not you?"

She turned away from me and typed on her keyboard. After a minute, she swirled back to face me. "There. I sent it to your email. It's a huge file. Might take a few minutes to load."

"Thank you." My smile was genuine this time.

"You might not thank me when you get it," she warned. "That file's monstrous. Over the years, seems like every citizen in the county has called in with a theory or thinks they've spotted one of them. Course, none of it ever panned out. It's all duly noted in the records."

I hadn't expected this to be easy, but my eagerness to rake through the material plummeted like a rock sinking in water. "Is the file searchable by keyword?" I asked hopefully.

"Nope." She laughed. "Good luck, kiddo. Don't expect you'll have any more luck with this case than the dozens who've looked at the file before you."

Her words pinged around inside my brain, mocking my enthusiasm as I trudged back up the stairs. As I reached the landing, I drew a deep breath and squared my shoulders. What I might lack in experience, I'd make up for with hard work. If there was any connection between Ray Strickland and the Cormiers, I would find it.

Chapter 8

JORI

A frisson of unease shivered down my spine as I entered my bedroom, an unsettling deep in my gut that was out of place with the ordinary routine of my day. After speaking with Grace Fairhope yesterday, I'd returned home to an uneventful evening, and this morning had been no different. After Zach was at his day program, I'd spent a couple of hours running errands around town with Mimi and then taken a long walk in the woods. Mimi was in the kitchen now, and Zach was home. Pots and pans rattled as she began to prepare a gumbo that would simmer until suppertime.

I cocked my head to the side, trying to understand why the fine hairs on the nape of my neck had risen. At first glance, all was in place. The modest room, with its scuffed but clean wooden floors, slightly battered furniture, and an oil lamp on the dresser, had a shabby-chic vibe that was cozy and warm. A small rolltop desk, where I used to do all my schoolwork, was shoved into one corner. Growing up, I'd pretty much regarded my room as shabby and not at all chic, but as an adult, I saw it had a retro charm that some people now paid a hefty price to emulate.

My quilted bedspread was smooth and unruffled. The book I'd been reading was where I'd left it on my nightstand. My gaze swung to the dresser, but the lace doily, jewelry box, and perfume bottles were in the same spots, if slightly askew. Still, I couldn't shake the sensation that someone had been in my room. There was a faint but definite musk in the air that hadn't been there when I'd dressed this morning.

I looked around the room, noticing that my closet door stood open and all the hanging clothes had been pushed to one side. *That* had not been my doing. I always kept the closet shut and my clothes tidy. I walked over and saw that the boxes of photos, journals, and old board games I kept on the top shelf had been knocked to the floor.

Who'd been rifling through my stuff? Zach had no interest in my old junk. He never came in my room and didn't tolerate anyone entering his bedroom, either, unless invited. Mimi had never been one to come in my room. Ever since junior high, I'd been responsible for cleaning my space and doing my laundry.

I bent down and picked up scattered Monopoly money and stacks of spilled photographs, intent on tidying the mess. But I paused at the sight of my old notebooks and journals, which lay open as though someone had been reading them.

Why? Who would care about the journals of a teenage girl? It was hardly gripping reading material. Thank God I'd torn out and burned the section chronicling my last semester of school before leaving the bayou to strike out on my own. Tonight, I'd burn what was left of these journals. The idea of someone violating my privacy made my skin crawl.

I picked up a couple of notebooks and flipped through them. Random pages had been torn out. I began separating the journals from the rest of the other junk on the floor, but I stopped short when my hands brushed against something sticky. I held up my hands and gasped at the brownish liquid coating my fingers. What the hell? I scrambled backward and then kicked at the pile with my foot.

A tiny snake, no longer than four inches, was slit down the middle, its organs sagging out of its body. It was skewered onto a cardboard chessboard with a bent safety pin. A single dried flower petal and a note were pinned to its dissected, ruined body. Trembling, I bent back down to read the block letters written in all caps: *LET DEAD DOGS LIE.*

Bile rose in my throat, and I jumped backward again, staring at the words in disbelief. Who would do such a thing? Why would they do it?

Let dead dogs lie. The only possible explanation was that someone had not liked my speaking with Jackson's mother yesterday, but I hadn't told anyone about the visit. Not even Mimi, who would have disapproved of my digging around the past.

And what was up with the flower? I had a sneaking suspicion that the petal had been torn from the pressed corsage Deacon would have pinned to my prom dress if he hadn't disappeared. I hurried to my jewelry box, where I kept the treasured memento.

The rose had been crushed into desiccated shreds.

Tears stung my eyes, and I raked through the ruins. Had anything else been destroyed or gone missing? It wasn't as though I had anything valuable in this childhood jewelry box. It was only the size of a book, wrapped in lavender satin with a ballerina on top. The brass key on the side wound up, and she spun en pointe in her pink tutu. The box was so old and worn that the music played warped and out of tune. It had been from my mom the Christmas when I was nine. Inside, my small childhood treasures were still there—a pin from Bayou Enigma First Methodist Church for perfect attendance one year; a few tumbled stones from a visit to Rock City, Tennessee, when I was twelve; an empty sample tube of Avon frosted-pink lipstick I used to sneak-wear in junior high after my mom had forbidden me to use makeup; and a cheap bracelet from elementary school with rusted charms.

The dried corsage had been the last treasure I ever stored in the box. It had seemed a fitting resting place for the posy that symbolized the death of my first love and of my childhood.

Anger seeped into my emotions of fear and shock. How dare someone come into my bedroom, go through my private things, and destroy my property? Was it someone I knew? Someone I trusted?

It had to be. Who else would even know I had old journals and keepsakes? Unless the intruder had browsed and stumbled upon my private mementos while delivering his threat.

I marched out of my room and into the kitchen. Mimi was humming as she tossed okra and onions into a sizzling cast-iron pan. She glanced up from her work. "Want to chop up the garlic for me?" she asked. Her gaze narrowed, and she held the knife poised in the air. "Something wrong?"

"Have you been in my room today?" I asked in a hard, flat voice.

Humph. Her chin lifted, and she began to chop a garlic clove. "No, I have not, missy. What's with that tone?"

"Has anyone else been in the house today?"

"Only Rose. Why?"

"Someone came in my room and tore up my stuff."

The knife hovered over the cutting board. "Zach never goes in your room."

"It wasn't him."

Mimi dropped the knife on the counter and hastily wiped her hands on her apron. She walked toward me, her face a ghastly gray color. "What stuff?"

"Nothing of value, just sentimental things. My journals and other private items."

Her face turned a shade grayer. I was a little surprised she hadn't brushed off my complaint, claiming that I must be imagining the entire thing.

She followed me to my room, and I pointed at the mess on the bottom of the closet. "They went through here and tore pages out of my journal. They also opened my jewelry box and destroyed some dried flowers. But the worst—"

Mimi bent over for a closer look. Before I could warn her about the bloody carcass, she let out a shriek. "Oh, my God. A dead snake."

"Not only that. It's sliced down the middle and has a note jabbed in its body."

Her eyes widened, and a hand went to her throat. Her voice came out in a guttural croak. "What does it say?"

"Let dead dogs lie."

Mimi sat on the edge of the bed, drawing in a labored breath.

Guilt immediately sluiced through my gut. She was as upset about the invasion as me. Maybe I shouldn't have even told her about it.

"Rose wouldn't have done such a thing."

"I agree." I walked to the window and lifted the sash. As always, it wasn't locked. That would change. Outside, the miniature boxwoods and surrounding mulch looked undisturbed. If the intruder had entered this way, he'd covered his tracks well. I clicked the latches shut with a resounding snap.

"He must have sneaked in while I was here," said Mimi.

"Were you in the house the whole time?"

She nodded her head, then stopped abruptly. "Except for when Rose helped me hang out the wash."

"We need to start locking all the doors and windows." I shuddered to think what might have happened if Mimi had stumbled upon him in my room. Would he have hurt her?

"To think it would come to this," she muttered, shaking her head.

The remark seemed odd. "What's that supposed to mean?"

Mimi placed her hands on her knees and slowly stood, looking all of her many years and then some. "Never thought we'd have to lock our doors like city folk."

"Crime's as rampant in the country as anywhere. Nobody's safe." But Mimi appeared even more upset than me, and I wanted to reassure her. "Maybe this was a onetime fluke, someone who just gets his kicks from scaring folks, but we should be careful."

I didn't believe my own words. I'd have felt more optimistic, less violated, if the intruder had stolen items of value. Maybe then I could convince myself it was merely a random crime of opportunity, motivated by greed. But the particularly deliberative nature of his acts, the singling out of my sentimental possessions, and the cruel, disgusting message for me pinned to a dead animal . . . well, it shook me.

But I forced a smile and patted Mimi's arm. "I'm calling the police to file a report. Try not to worry too much."

Her eyes darted to the closet. "I want that—that . . . *thing* out of my house."

"I'll take care of it after I talk to the police," I assured her. "Go back to your gumbo."

She shuffled from the room.

"Lock the doors first," I called out, grabbing my phone. Revulsion snaked over my body, but I squared my shoulders and walked to the closet. There it was, bloody and sinister. I snapped a photo. One picture was worth a thousand words when it came to describing this over the phone.

I'd left the officer's card in my nightstand, so I opened the top drawer and pulled out the plain black-and-white card Deputy Blackwell had given me. My mouth went dry as cotton as I dialed the number and listened to it ring. Doubts swirled through me. Would she laugh it off as a childish prank someone had pulled? Was this important enough to bother her with? After all, she was involved in a murder investigation. I pulled the phone from my car, ready to disconnect the call, when she answered on the second ring.

"Deputy Blackwell speaking." Her tone was crisp and firm, but not unfriendly.

I cleared my throat. "This is Jori Trahern. You may not remember me, but—"

"Of course, Ms. Trahern. You were the one who spoke with Raymond Strickland hours before he was murdered. Have you recalled anything else about the conversation you think might help us with the investigation?"

"It's not about him." I swallowed hard.

A heartbeat of surprise followed. I could picture her brows rising with interest. "Oh?"

"I'd like to report a break-in at my house."

"I see. Was anybody hurt?"

"No," I admitted. "But it was creepy. We're a little freaked out."

"Understandable. I can have an officer at your house immediately to investigate."

"I want you. It's, um, complicated." I hurried to my bedroom door, listened to Mimi puttering in the kitchen, and then shut it.

"How so?" she asked. The woman didn't waste words.

"They didn't steal anything valuable. It was more of a threat. He— or she—ransacked and vandalized my personal stuff, and then they left a note."

"What did the note say?"

"Here, I'm texting you a photo. That'll be easier than trying to explain." I selected the disgusting photo from my gallery and clicked send.

"Got it," she confirmed moments later, then added, "Is that a . . . a snake?"

"Yep. Sliced down the middle."

"What does the note say? The paper's bent, and I can't quite make it out."

"Let dead dogs lie."

"I can be at your house in ten minutes."

"Here's the thing. I'd like to speak with you in private. My grand-mother's already agitated enough about this, and if she overhears every-thing I want to tell you, she'll only get more upset."

"You'd rather come to our office?"

"Yes—only, I hate to leave her and Zach alone. What if the intruder sees me leave and then decides to return?"

"I'll arrange for a police cruiser to drive by your house while we talk and then sporadically after that for the next few days. If you're being watched, the presence of the cruiser should act as a deterrent."

"Thank you," I said with a rush of breath.

"As soon as you see the cops going by your place, come on down. After I get your statement, I'll send someone over to get photos and prints."

"The sooner that snake is out of here, the better we'll all feel."

I hung up the call and headed to the door. Zach was seated at the kitchen table, tasting a small bowl of mint chocolate chip ice cream Mimi had placed before him.

"How's it taste, Zach?" Mimi asked. "Is it good?"

"Good," he confirmed, shoveling down spoonfuls. He held out the empty bowl. "More."

"Coming right up."

As always, there was something very comforting about Zach. No matter my level of anxiety, Zach's focus on the here and now was a beacon of calm.

The sheriff's office was in the same location it had been all the years I'd grown up in Bayou Enigma, one block east of the courthouse down-town, a redbrick, two-story, no-nonsense type of building with a modest sign out front and a parking lot filled with patrol cars. I'd never had reason to visit until now.

Inside, the place was brightly lit from unforgiving fluorescent fixtures. The walls were a dull green, and the floors were a worn, speckled linoleum. I walked into the lobby and noted the metal folding chairs where nearly a dozen people slouched, sporting various expressions of boredom or anxiety. Across from the chairs was a glassed-in booth where a receptionist sat.

"Got an appointment?" she asked in a bored tone when I walked over.

"Deputy Blackwell is expecting me."

"Name?"

"Jori Trahern."

Without responding, she pressed a phone button and murmured a few words before speaking to me again. "Deputy Blackwell will escort you back in a moment. Have a seat."

I took my place among the weary, the despondent, and the agitated. Evidently, there was no happy reason to be in this place. The only person immune to the atmosphere was a young boy who ran back and forth from the water cooler to his mama's lap, shrieking with laughter.

The door off to the side opened, and we all turned expectantly. Deputy Blackwell scanned the crowd, then nodded at me. "This way, Ms. Trahern."

I stood, catching the scowl of a young man decked in camo and exuding a surly attitude. His lower lip protruded farther. "I been here two hours. This ain't right."

Pretending not to hear, I quickly strode to Deputy Blackwell and followed her down a long hallway. The farther we walked, the louder the muffled noises emerged. She caught my puzzled look. "We share a wall with the county lockup. It can get really rowdy at times. This way."

She beckoned me into a small office devoid of everything but a metal table and chairs. Not even a window to dispel the stark institutional vibe.

"What's this? An old prison cell?" I joked.

"Sorry. It happens to be the only room where we can have a modicum of privacy at the moment."

I gingerly took a seat, the cold, hard metal unwelcoming to my bones. "Is this where you interrogate criminals?" I asked, serious this time.

"Sometimes," she admitted, smiling kindly. "Certainly not the case now, though."

Sitting only a foot apart from one another in the cramped space felt surprisingly, uncomfortably intimate. A slight citrus smell wafted in the air, refreshing and incongruous. She wore no jewelry, only a touch of mascara and a subtle lip color. In spite of the shapeless uniform and the hair pulled back into a messy ponytail, I was surprised to discover she was quite beautiful, even though she seemed at pains to downplay it. Couldn't blame her, though, in this type of job.

"How did you get interested in law enforcement?" I blurted. "I mean, I know it's not unusual for women these days, but you must get sick of dealing with all the creeps."

My question didn't faze her. She must have been asked hundreds of times before. "Same reason any person, male or female, chooses this for a career. We want to catch the bad guys and help the good guys." I flushed at the asperity in her tone, but she shot me a conspiratorial grin. "Plus, it pays the bills. I have two kids and a mortgage."

Kids. She appeared only ten years older than me. Not for the first time, I wondered if my life had been in a state of perpetual hold since high school. These days, a woman didn't need children for validation, but I had to admit my life often felt pointless, as though I was merely going through the motions. College, then work. It wasn't that I still grieved for Deacon, even if I thought of him often in odd, lonely hours of the night, but none of my relationships had ever lasted more than a year. I felt as though I floated from one day to the next, planning events that other people went to and enjoyed and returning to my solo apartment in the evenings. Hell, I didn't even own a cat.

Blackwell placed a manila file on the battered table and opened it up. The photo I'd sent her was printed out, blown up to eight-by-ten size. "We'll send an officer to your house to dust for prints and take photos. We'll remove the carcass and secure it in our evidence room in case we discover any suspects."

"Thank you." I was relieved I didn't have to deal with getting rid of the thing.

Blackwell folded her hands on the desk and regarded me soberly. "What was written in those journals?"

"The usual teen stuff. Nothing earth shattering."

"No potential blackmail material?"

"None." Relief washed over me again that I'd long since destroyed the pages that were the most painful. Keeping my secret buried deep inside felt right. What had happened was nobody's business. Just my own private grief.

Blackwell tapped at the photo. "Why do you think you were sent this message?"

"I'm not sure."

She stared at me, waiting for me to start talking. I'd requested a private meeting, after all.

"Where's your partner?" I asked. "Why isn't he here?"

"Lieutenant Oliver is my boss, not my partner. We're only working together on the Strickland case. He's out interviewing this morning, but he should be back shortly if you need to speak to us both together."

"No. That's okay. I'd rather speak to you alone." I found her less intimidating than the older man.

"Tell me, Ms. Trahern, do you think this threat is related to the Strickland murder?"

I blinked in surprise. "No."

A brow rose. "A mighty big coincidence, then. And I, for one, don't happen to believe in coincidences. Is there something you haven't told us about your conversation with the victim? Do you know anything that would help solve this case? If you do, speak up now."

Her voice had taken on a hard edge, and her eyes sharpened on me. Had I thought her less intimidating than Oliver? Now I wasn't so sure. "I don't know anything about it," I protested. "I was in the wrong place at the wrong time. Dana warned me it was stupid to go talk to Ray. I wish I never had."

"You must have some idea why an intruder targeted you and your private belongings. The threat he left was very specific."

"I think this is about my cousin," I said with reluctance. "Not Raymond Strickland."

Blackwell stiffened, then leaned back in her chair. "Jackson Ensley?"

"Right." Something about the faint tinge of dislike as she spoke his name made me wonder if she might have known Jackson. He would have been about her age, had he lived. "Hey, did you know my cousin?"

Was it my imagination, or was there a slight hesitation before she answered? "We were in the same grade at Enigma High."

"What was he like?"

"He had a reputation." White lines etched the contour of her pursed lips. Like everyone else in town who knew him, Blackwell was clearly not a fan.

"Yeah, I've always heard he was a bit wild."

"*Wild* is one way to put it," she said crisply. "Explain why you think there's a connection between this threat and Ensley."

"Because this happened the day after I went to Mobile to speak with his biological mother."

"I didn't realize he was adopted. Why did you go see her?"

"Because it's weird. Mimi and the rest of my family are so close-mouthed about him. I didn't even know he was adopted until Mimi

88

let it slip yesterday." I drummed my fingers against the battered table, trying to explain my compulsion to dig into his past. "I've heard the rumors about him. That he used and dealt drugs, that he'd had a few minor scrapes with the law and was generally not a . . . not a *nice* person. Nobody ever has anything good to say about the guy. And with his former best friend also being found dead with a bullet to the back of his head, hours after talking to me, well, I just . . ." I cleared my throat. "I got curious."

"And you think this visit with his mother got someone upset."

"What else could it be?"

Blackwell folded her arms and tapped an index finger against her mouth. "Did she tell you anything that bears a relation to these two murders?"

"I don't know if it has any bearing, but Grace claimed she was paid ten thousand dollars for her baby."

Blackwell let out a low whistle. "That's a lot of money, especially way back in 1975. Who paid her?"

"Says she doesn't remember the details of the private adoption, and I believe her. Grace was a drug addict who took the money way back when and ran with it. For all it's worth, she's recently got her life back together and is remorseful."

Blackwell slowly nodded. "I'll check into that with my contact at Family Social Services. Private or not, the adoption had to have been registered. It's illegal, of course, to pay for a child. But the adoptive parents can provide money for maternity expenses."

I frowned. "That wasn't the impression I got from her. I asked if she had any adoption records, but she didn't."

"Illegal or not, it's a stretch to say that the matter might be related to either murder."

"It's the only dredging up of the past that I've been up to," I pointed out. My stomach flipped as I pushed on with my next theory. "Other than mentioning to Dana and a few family members what I told you when Ray's body was discovered." At her blank face, I pushed on. "That Ray brought up folks had a way of disappearing in the bayou. Like the Cormiers."

"I haven't forgotten," she assured me. "I'm reviewing the old Cormier files. Seems you were also the last person to see Deacon Cormier alive." She paused a moment, eyeballing me curiously. "You were the last to see Raymond Strickland and Deacon Cormier alive."

Blood pounded in my ears, and my heartbeat pulsed madly. I hadn't made that uncanny connection. Silence stretched between us, drumming a loud pulse of swirling vermilion and gunmetal tension in the cramped room. "Wh-what are you implying?" I managed to croak.

"Just making an observation."

"If you're reviewing the case, then you know Deacon and I were dating. Those notebooks I told you that the intruder went through and tore up? Those were my old high school journals. They were filled with, you know, silly stuff a teenage girl would write."

"Angsty poems about true love and endless details about your dates?" she guessed.

"Exactly. Why would the intruder be interested in them? Unless . . . unless it was a message to stop bringing up the subject of Deacon and his parents."

"Your theory tying the Cormiers to Strickland's murder is still a stretch."

"I know, but just in case there is one, I feel bound to tell you everything."

"And have you?"

"Yes." I faced her dead on, my voice steady. Certain things from the past would stay buried there, too private and painful to be shared.

"I'm going to ask again. What was written in your old diary pages that are missing?"

"It's been so long since I wrote them, I can't give specifics. But it was in the time frame I was seeing Deacon." My face twisted in embarrassed chagrin. "So I feel confident in saying those pages were all about him. After all, he was the subject matter of at least ninety percent of my scribbles."

"No secret from the past you aren't telling me about?"

"Absolutely no secrets."

"There could be a more current, more logical explanation. Are you currently seeing someone?"

"No."

"Have you had a past romantic relationship that ended badly?"

The notion was laughable. All my relationships since Deacon had ended amicably, dying a slow, neglectful death for which I was entirely to blame. There'd been no explosive breakups, no jealous stalking or recriminations from either party. Only my failure to completely commit.

"There's nothing of the sort," I assured Blackwell. "I don't have some psycho ex-boyfriend out to intimidate me. And if I did, I'd report him."

"Some women don't," she countered. "I have to ask these questions."

"I understand. Is there anything else you need from me?"

"Only your assurance that you'll contact me if anything else unusual occurs."

"Of course If anything happened to Mimi or Zach, I'd never forgive myself."

Blackwell rose from her chair, and I took my cue the interview was over.

"Thanks for meeting me," I said, scraping back my chair and also rising. The metal legs ground in a high-pitched squeal against the hard floor. "And thanks for reviewing the Cormier case," I added. "Didn't think anyone cared about them after all these years."

She merely nodded, and I followed her out of the room and back down the hallway toward the lobby. As I approached the exit door, Blackwell turned to me and took out papers from the manila envelope.

"Fill out this official report and leave it with the receptionist. If we have any leads or any more questions, I'll give you a call."

I scanned the two-page document she'd given me. Should be easy enough to complete. I nodded and had started to turn away when Blackwell spoke again.

"By the way, if no one was willing to discuss Jackson Ensley's adoption with you, and you don't have any papers, how did you discover his birth mother's name?"

"I visited my aunt Tressie, Jackson's mother, at her assisted living home and saw his birth certificate."

"She's one of the family members you discussed the Cormier case with?"

"Not exactly." Heat traveled down my neck. "She asked me to put some papers and pictures back inside a trunk she keeps in her room. The certificate was in there."

"Leave the investigative work to us," she admonished. "Just in case there is any present danger."

I shot her a wry smile before exiting. "Seems you are the second person today to issue me a warning."

The lobby seemed even more crowded than before. I took a seat and quickly filled out the incident report before dutifully handing it over to the woman behind the glass wall. Had my meeting with Deputy Blackwell accomplished anything? The only thing I'd learned was that she had listened to me and was looking into the past.

Once outside, I breathed easier. I'd done everything in my power. Surely this would all blow over now. There was nothing else for me to pursue. If someone was watching me, they'd be bored to tears at my mundane life and eventually leave us alone. From here on out, it was back to working at my freelance job and keeping an eye on Mimi and Zach. Tonight, after they'd gone to sleep, I'd take what was left of my journals and burn them—like I should have done long ago. Destroy the written ramblings and stop dwelling on the past.

You were the last to see Raymond Strickland and Deacon Cormier alive. Blackwell's words crawled like a nest of spiders let loose in my brain. It had to be a coincidence, nothing more.

Yet when the wind whipped up the sides of my unzipped black coat, I fancied that I must appear like a giant crow flapping its wings, an unwilling harbinger of death.

Chapter 9

TEGAN

"What are you looking at?"

Oliver's voice thundered by my ear. I'd been so engrossed in reading the old Cormier investigative transcripts that I'd been oblivious to his presence. He leaned over my right shoulder, peering at the computer screen.

I flushed as though I were ten years old and had been caught misbehaving by the school principal. "Just exploring links between the various cases."

He straightened, displeasure evident on his face. "Come into my office, and let's talk."

"Be right there." Quickly, I closed the document and gathered my notebook and pen as he left our room.

"You're in trouble now, rookie," Haywood stage-whispered loudly enough for everyone to hear.

"If he kicks you off the Strickland case, I want first dibs on it," Mullins added, wagging a finger in my direction. I was sure his remark was only half in jest.

Oliver was already seated when I entered his office and didn't immediately look up from the papers on his desk. I dropped into a chair across from him and waited for him to acknowledge me.

Finally, he folded his large hands on the desk and faced me. "Why were you reading up on that cold case? We've already discussed this. Our attention should be focused on the present, not events that occurred nearly two decades ago."

"Yes, sir." I vowed not to read it anymore in the office. What I did at home in my own time was my own business. And I would pore over every detail—present and past.

He nodded, satisfied. "We just received an initial report. I forwarded a copy to your email. The substance found in Strickland's bedroom was marijuana. No prints were found that couldn't be traced to Strickland or his mother. The nine millimeter extracted from the body was from a Glock. Unfortunately, one of the most common makes and models."

It was an unsettlingly perfect crime. "Is there reason to believe this was an execution?"

He hesitated. "Safe to say it was probably no amateur. Whoever it was, they were clever and calculating. It wasn't done in the heat of passion."

"So you're ruling out Tommy Sims and the other men from the Pavilion."

"Seems highly unlikely to me that any of them has the brains or cool deliberation for this crime. Sims did agree to an independent polygraph test last evening, and the results indicated he's telling the truth when he claims to be innocent of the murder."

Much as I disliked Tommy, I had to agree with Oliver's assessment. "If it wasn't a crime of passion, then are we talking about a hired gun? Maybe someone employed by a drug ring?"

"We have to consider that possibility, especially given that there were drugs in Strickland's room and that he was a known drug dealer in his youth."

"Never would have thought our small town would have a problem of this magnitude. I always believed drugs came in from the Port of

Mobile and on to a few outsiders who distributed to a small clientele here in the backwoods."

"No town, no matter the size, is immune to the opioid and meth crisis. And our state's the worst. Alabama has the highest filled-prescription rate for opiates."

I shouldn't have been surprised. Finding out my beloved state was last or next to last in any positive category—years of education, median salary—was nothing new. We only made the top of the national list in places we did not want it—things like *most obese* or *most incarcerated*. Now this.

"Damn. It's logical to conclude that if we have the highest prescription rate, then there are a hell of a lot of addicts wanting the drug. Even if it's off the streets." I couldn't help thinking of Linsey and Luke. They were at a vulnerable age with peer pressure and the need to fit in, to experiment because everyone else did. I knew this as well as anybody. Drugs had been easy to come by when I attended Enigma High, my friend Lisa being the perfect case in point. How much easier was it now to get them? How much more prolific was drug use these days?

"Exactly. Where there's a demand, there's always someone willing to become the supplier at a hefty profit."

Discouraged frustration raked my gut. "So, what's our next move?"

"We shut them down." He gave me a warm smile, the first real one I'd gotten from him this morning. "Don't be so upset. That's why we're in law enforcement, right? To fight back against the kinds of people who prey on others."

"That, and the cushy lifestyle it provides."

He barked out a surprised laugh. "Yeah, right. The first order of business for us is to infiltrate their operation."

"How?"

"We petition the mayor to foot the bill for a narcotics agent."

Surprise washed over me. That seemed like a huge expense to fork over on mere speculation. "Does our little PD even have one?"

"Not that I'm aware of. But if they don't, we can have the mayor try and work out a deal to pay someone to come in from Mobile."

Oliver's gaze drifted to the small window banking the side wall of his office. Suspicion pricked down my spine.

"And if that doesn't work out?" I asked, feeling certain it wouldn't. "Can we possibly get an agent from ALEA?"

The Alabama Law Enforcement Agency was an executive branch of state government that coordinated public safety matters. ALEA was an important resource for small towns like us.

"We can try. In the meantime, we'll meet with our local police." He glanced at the utilitarian wall clock to his right. "We're due over at their station in half an hour."

Inwardly, I groaned. Terrific. Another opportunity to be insulted by Dempsey. Immediately I brushed away my petty insecurity as I left Oliver's office and returned to my own. Despite his warning, I spent the next twenty minutes sneak-reading the old Cormier file. If there was any connection between the past and present murders, I'd find it.

If we found and shut down a drug distributor in our bayou, we'd be a safer town. A safer place for my kids to grow up in. This job was more than a paycheck to me. It was my way of trying to shield the innocent and the vulnerable from danger. I didn't want anyone to go through what I had as a teenage girl.

Chapter 10

TEGAN

April 1991

He knew my name! He called me *cute*!

I didn't think Jackson had ever noticed me all these years I'd been crushing on him. Tonight was my lucky night. As much as I'd dragged my feet about coming to this party, Lisa had been right. If she hadn't convinced me to come with her, I'd be doing my usual Saturday night thing—sitting in my bedroom, reading a book while half watching some lame sitcom.

Jackson freaking Ensley knew my name and was actually talking to me—*me*—fat nobody Tegan Atkins. Maybe even flirting with me? My head was dizzy with excitement before I even swallowed the whiskey he offered. Disgusting stuff, but I didn't tell him that. If I hadn't wanted the hard liquor, I for sure hadn't wanted to smoke pot. But he held it out to me and smiled oh so charmingly.

Aw, come on, Tegan, don't be a drag.

So I smoked the joint. It took several attempts to inhale without coughing up my lungs, but I discovered that I liked it much better than the whiskey. When he threw his arm over my shoulder and began carting me off to who-knew-where, I offered no resistance, wobbling on my feet and giggling.

First party, first-time high.

The music, laughter, and loud conversations dimmed behind us as we walked away from the barn. Jackson removed his arm from my shoulder and opened the door of his red Mustang, motioning me toward the back seat. My excitement pulled up short, and I planted my feet, balking.

"What's wrong?" he asked, flashing that crooked smile that made my stomach turn flips.

"I, uh . . . I'm not sure about this."

"Why not? It'll be warm in my car."

I stared at the black leather seats and gulped.

"C'mon, baby," he said, his voice husky as he nuzzled his nose against my throat and neck. And when I turned to face him, his lips fanned my hair, my cheeks. So gentle, so sweet. I closed my eyes and sighed as his mouth pressed against my right temple and then my forehead. My first kiss—if you didn't count the peck on the mouth Bucky Rodgers gave me in third grade at recess.

This kiss was nothing like that one.

How many times had I dreamed of this moment? Of kissing Jackson. *Don't be such a baby. Get in the car.*

I caved to that inner whisper. Jackson wouldn't like me if I was a prude. He dated girls like Natalie Clecker. Pretty, popular, and, I assumed, putting out. What harm could a few minutes of making out do? I'd never get a chance like this again.

He pulled away from me, again beckoning me into his car. I slipped inside and ungracefully plopped onto the cool leather seat, shivering as much from nerves as cold. I pulled my skirt down over my thighs pockmarked with cellulite. He climbed in beside me and shut the door, sealing us off from the rest of the world. We were in our own little bubble. He kissed me again, right on the lips, a little more insistent this time.

I responded, lost in the heady newness of whiskey, pot, and my first real kiss. Too quickly, his hands began roving toward my back. Inwardly, I cringed, thinking he had to notice the roll of fat beneath my bra. Thank God we were in the dark, where he couldn't see it as well as feel it. Some of my giddiness seeped away at the thought. I should have refused to get in the car. Better he think I was a prude than a disgustingly fat slob.

With expert fingers, Jackson unbuckled my bra with a flip of his hand. The guy had obviously done it hundreds of times before. I was in over my head. Nothing special. I pulled away from him.

"I—I'm sorry," I mumbled. "I think we should go back to the party."

He laughed. A disbelieving, unkind laugh. "You're kidding me, right?"

I tried to fasten my bra but couldn't get it snapped together. I drew my coat closer around me. If I kept it on, no one at the party would know my bra was undone.

He'd hurt my feelings with that laugh, and it reinforced my decision to get the hell out of the Mustang. Although handsome and with an abundance of surface charm, Jackson was not a nice guy.

"I want to go back to the barn," I said with as much dignity as I could scramble together.

He changed tactics; his voice lowered to a husky note as he cajoled me. "Aw, come on, baby. It'll be fun. Haven't you ever done it before?" He reached up and palmed one of my breasts.

I jerked away from his touch and grabbed the door handle on the passenger side of the vehicle.

"What are you doing?" he growled, all trace of huskiness gone.

"Leaving."

"The fuck you are." He grabbed my arm and yanked me away from the door.

"Let me go. I changed my mind." I tried to sound firm, tried to keep the quiver of fear out of my voice. This was not how I imagined our getting together in my dreams. In my fantasies, Jackson was kind and romantic. I tried to pull from his grip, but his fingers squeezed my biceps so tightly that I was afraid the bone beneath would snap in two. Tears sprang to my eyes, and I gasped from the pain. "Stop it!"

He chuckled. "Stop it," he mimicked in a high-pitched falsetto.

I fought him in earnest then, kicking and squirming. His weight slammed against me, pinning me to the seat. A loud, metallic rip rent the air as he unzipped his jeans. I screamed, and he clamped a hand over my mouth.

I was trapped. I looked out the car window, focusing on a cypress whose limbs swayed in the breeze like beckoning witchy fingers. This was not happening. My mind left me, drifted far, far away. This was a nightmare. I was at home in my cozy pink bedroom with my fluffy comforter wrapped snug around me and the smells of Saturday night's roast beef dinner drifting upstairs from the kitchen down below.

It would be over soon. I'd find Lisa and hightail it home. I couldn't tell my parents. If they knew I'd sneaked off to a party and drank and did drugs, they'd be angry. Anger I could handle, but not their disappointment. I didn't want anyone to know how stupid I'd been. I could hear my classmates snicker about fat Tegan hollering rape. *Who would even want her lard ass?* they'd say.

No. I'd tuck this memory of Jackson down so deep that it would never hurt me again. Everything that happened tonight would be relegated to a black chasm of oblivion.

Chapter 11

In hindsight, perhaps sending that message hadn't been a good idea. It had been way too specific.

Stubborn woman went straight to the sheriff's office. I hadn't counted on that. Not that the investigators would find anything to incriminate me. But still, the vandalism and its timing provided a link to my past misdeeds—a past I couldn't allow to surface.

That initial crime necessitated a string of felonies that grew increasingly worse. How much longer did I have to keep paying? I thought after Ray Strickland was convicted, I was home free. But Strickland had put a kink in everything, threatening to expose me. He couldn't prove anything, and yet I couldn't risk calling his bluff. I'd anonymously deposited cash into his prison canteen account over the years. Small change, mostly—it wasn't like he could spend much money on the cigarettes and candy bars sold at the inmate store. But he had bigger plans for the future. He'd plotted revenge, and once he was paroled, he kept tightening the screws, demanding more money, until I had no choice but to pull the trigger.

I turned my attention back to the matter at hand, trying to be optimistic. Maybe the message would work after all. Jori may have reported the threat, but that didn't mean it hadn't shaken her. Wouldn't hurt to cover my bases.

So far, everything was contained.

Strickland's murder investigation would be hot for a few weeks, and then, as they found nothing to discover the killer's identity, the trail would grow cold. Other crimes would be committed, and manpower would be split in different directions.

Besides, it wasn't as though anyone cared about Strickland's death. He was a parolee convicted of murder. A person to be regarded with, if not fear, then mistrust. The convenient death of his mother left the man with no more ties to the community. No one cared that he'd died. There'd be no political pressure or moral outrage placed on law enforcement to find his killer.

All I had to do was sit tight and wait it out. I was no rookie to that game. Circumstances had been far more nerve-racking for me with the Cormier disappearances.

Meanwhile, I'd wait and watch.

I might like Jori. But that wouldn't stop me from doing what had to be done. She'd been warned.

Chapter 12

JORI

It was difficult to concentrate on my job when all I could think about was the threat against me. I shifted uncomfortably in my seat at the small table, longing to make my escape. Mayor Hank Rembert finally adjourned the special county commission meeting. I'd answered every last question volleyed at me by the half dozen folks who composed the entertainment subcommittee—no easy feat, considering my thoughts kept circling back to the dead snake left in my closet. But I knew I had to focus as best I could, both for my work's reputation and for the town who depended on this successful event for the local economy. Enigma's population doubled from its usual twenty-five hundred during the festival weekend, when the archbishop from Mobile arrived to bless the boats and sailors. Before and after his blessing, there were land and boat parades, arts and crafts vendors, bands, dances, boat and kayaking tours, a race, and a gumbo cook-off. And since this was the South, a beauty pageant to crown a queen and her court.

I'd been selected queen one year in high school. I smiled at the recollection of a happier time before Deacon's disappearance. Dana and two other runners-up had been part of my court. The duties were fun, consisting only of dressing up in our sashes and tiaras for various town events.

One thing our small town had going for it—we loved to celebrate old traditions. Our intimate connection to this remote land and the surrounding sea bound us together in a way many modern cities and their inhabitants probably didn't experience.

Even though the local fish processing plant was now our largest employer, nearly half of the town's population was still made up of small, family-owned shrimpers. They embraced the challenge of netting the daily catch while the sun shone on them from above and the mysterious depths of the sea below tantalized them with its bounty and beauty. The occasional storm was to be expected alongside the peace and majesty of the sparkling vista.

I'd tried to stay calm and focused at the barrage of committee members' reminders—had I booked all the speakers and entertainers? Sent application forms to past vendors and boaters? Arranged for rental of all the needed equipment? Gently, I reminded them that this was my fourth year coordinating the event and that I had everything under control.

Uncle Buddy, a commissioner and board member, had stealthily winked at me across the table. He knew me too well to be fooled by my strained smile.

At last, Mayor Rembert clapped his chubby hands together. "Seems like everything is running right on schedule. Thanks, Jori. Our last meeting is scheduled for Thursday of next week. Let's pray for fair weather."

"Amen," several members mumbled.

Last year's Blessing had been a bit of a nightmare. It had rained the entire weekend. I'd managed to secure extra tents for vendors and moved the band from playing outdoors in the park to Broussard's Pavilion, and to my surprised relief, the rain had little impact on the festivities. The crowd was huge and enthusiastic. Afterward, visitors and locals had assured me that nothing could dampen their enjoyment of the event.

I'd never loved my hometown more.

Thank heavens the meeting was over. I wanted nothing more than to return home and make sure Mimi and Zach were safe. As people shuffled out of the room, Rembert swaggered over and patted me on the shoulder. "Excellent job as always, Jori," he boomed. He never seemed to talk in a normal tone of voice. It had the loud ring of a politician's forced hardiness and cheer. "Heard you were staying in town awhile. Everything going all right with Oatha Jean and Zach?"

"We're fine," I lied, feeling like nothing could be further from the truth. "Thank you, sir."

"Good, good." His attention had already slid to someone else even as he responded. "Hey, Jeeter," he said, extending a hand to a commissioner who'd arrived after the meeting had already started. "How you been doing these days?"

Uncle Buddy slid into the vacant chair beside me and grinned. His tall frame and broad shoulders dwarfed the small chair. Sixty-six years old, and he had the physique and energy of a man half his age. Only the weathered lines on his face betrayed the depths of his experience.

"You handled that well. As usual," he said.

"Thanks for the vote of confidence." Secretly, I was relieved I'd pulled off a professional display of competency given my shattered nerves.

"Don't let all their questions get to you. They have to speak up and act like they're paying attention and earning their pay."

"Our tax dollars at work," I quipped, leaning back in my seat and running a hand through my hair. "It's fine. They kept me on my toes and stopped me from worrying so much about . . . other things."

His grin faded, and his brows drew together in concern. "What troubles you? Is Oatha doing worse? Or is it Zach?"

"Nothing like that. They're both fine," I assured him. "Guess you didn't hear the news. We had a break-in yesterday at the house."

"Break-in?" His eyes widened and jaw slackened.

"It's okay. We didn't encounter him. Nobody got hurt, and nothing valuable was stolen. It's just . . . it's scary to know someone sneaked in."

"I don't understand. If no one saw him and nothing was stolen, how do you know someone broke in?"

"They went through a bunch of my personal stuff and left a threatening message."

"Damn. What kind of threat? Did you report it to the police?"

I started to wish I hadn't brought up the subject. I'd been sure either Mimi or someone else had already mentioned it to Uncle Buddy. Word spread fast around the bayou.

"Of course. Do you know Deputy Blackwell? She was helpful."

"Tegan? Yep. She's good people. Went to school with her daddy." He frowned and rubbed his stubbled jaw. "I don't like the idea of y'all living so remote from everybody."

"It'll probably never happen again. Just some sick prank." I wished I could convince myself of that.

"What kinda threat did they leave?"

"Just something vague. Uncle Buddy, what was Jackson like?"

"Jackson?" He snorted with surprise. "Why are you bringing him up?"

I preferred not to tell him that I'd been snooping. No doubt he'd disapprove. "Simple curiosity. The Strickland murder got me thinking of him—that's all."

He drummed his fingers on the table. "Your cousin was a challenging child for your aunt to raise. Always experimenting with drugs and defiant as all get-out."

"No one seems to have a good word about him. Was he that bad?"

"Pretty bad," he admitted grudgingly. "He'd been caught stealing a time or two, got in fights, that kind of thing. Hung out with the wrong crowd. I even heard tell he was dealing in drugs. Kid was heading down a bad path. I felt sorry for Tressie and Ardy."

Poor Jackson. No one had a good thing to say about him except for his mom. "Did Aunt Tressie ever talk to you about the adoption?"

"Not really. If you're asking if she was sorry she adopted Jackson of all people, then no, she never said anything like that. Never would. Tressie was blind to how seriously troubled Jackson had become."

Uncle Buddy had nothing to add to what I already knew. I gathered my notes together and slipped them in a folder. "So tell me, are all your rooms already booked for the Blessing?"

The concern in his eyes instantly cleared, and a smile lit his craggy features. "Sold out weeks ago. Did I tell you we're thinking of building more cabins out back? Business is great. Hunters are coming down from places as far away as Ohio and Pennsylvania."

"Always expanding. That's terrific."

"Speaking of expanding the business, I have a proposition for you. How'd you like to come work for me full time after the Blessing of the Fleet is over?"

The offer caught me by surprise. "Really? Full time?"

"Absolutely. Along with the job, you'd get health insurance as well as sick and annual leave."

The mention of benefits made me suspicious. I regarded him with narrowed eyes, my pride on the defensive. "Are you offering me this just because you're trying to help us out? We're doing okay financially."

That was slightly stretching the truth. We got by, but barely. I'd have to decide soon about letting go of my apartment. I couldn't keep it up while also helping out Mimi and Zach. If I needed to move here permanently, there was no sense paying rent in Mobile.

Still, as much as the thought of stable employment with benefits enticed me, I hesitated. "Don't you need to check with your partner?" I asked, hedging.

"Already talked it over with Cash. He's in one hundred percent agreement with me. This isn't doing you a favor—you'd be helping us out."

"Do you do that many events? I can't imagine it would take me forty hours a week to schedule them."

"You wouldn't just be doing special events. My company needs marketing to draw more hunters and other kinds of visitors. I was thinking that during the off-season, we could offer things like bird-watcher tours and wildlife adventure classes. That kind of stuff. Plus, you could help out with admin work if you had more time. Cash and I are a mess when it comes to keeping up with all the paperwork."

I was so tempted. Only the thought of giving up my independence reared its ugly head. This felt so permanent. But wasn't it? I was only kidding myself that I could move back to Mobile and leave Mimi and Zach to fend for themselves. Especially not now after our home had been invaded. I'd once broached the idea of them coming to live with me in Mobile, and Mimi had laughed in my face. "I've lived here all my life. Ain't got no plans to be leaving now."

Uncle Buddy nudged my arm with his elbow. "Besides, you'll be working with family. No stress or mean bosses."

"If you're sure . . ."

"Positive." He rapped his knuckles on the table and stood. "I know you're tied up working for the city right now, but whenever you're ready, come on by, and I'll draw up the papers."

I also stood up. Any other time I'd have been thrilled with the offer, but after recent events, my joy was tempered. "Thank you, Uncle Buddy. I'll work hard and do my best."

"I know that." He cocked his head to the side and gave me a slow grin. "What kind of businesswoman are you? You haven't even mentioned salary. What seems fair to you?"

Mentally, I tallied my freelance income for the past year and quoted Uncle Buddy a number slightly under that amount.

"We can do better than that."

"No, really. You don't have to—"

"Enough said. Come on—I'll walk you to your car."

We walked down the marbled hallway and passed by office doors where county employees sat typing away on computer keyboards.

"I appreciate what a help you've been to Oatha and Zach," Uncle Buddy said. "You're awful young to take on so much responsibility."

"Not a problem. They're family." I shot him a sideways glance. "And thanks for helping them out with the bills. Once I start working for you, I can take over."

"How are Oatha and Zach doing?" he asked, his face grave.

"Zach's as set in his ways as ever. If I deviate from his routine or don't understand what he's trying to communicate, he tells me, 'Mimi knows.' I worry how he'll react if she goes into a nursing home one day."

He nodded solemnly.

"I don't know how much you realize it, since you don't see her every day, but the moments of confusion have turned into minutes where she forgets who she is and what she's doing. And typical Mimi. She refuses to admit how dire the situation is."

A wry smile lit his face. "Sounds like Oatha. She always was stubborn growing up. Mama used to despair of her. Said it would take a special man to put up with Oatha Jean's bossy ways."

It was my turn to chuckle. "From what I hear tell, Big Daddy was a match for Mimi."

"Those two could fight dawn to dusk, but they were inseparable until Jimmy's heart attack. Wish he were still around to take care of her."

"She's got me now."

"My sister's a lucky woman for that. Are you at the point y'all need a home health care worker? I can pay for what her Medicare doesn't pick up."

"I'll let you know when the time comes. Right now, we're fine. The house isn't much, but it's paid for. Between my salary and Zach's SSI, we should get by from here on out. More or less."

We exited the back door, which emptied into the parking lot. Sunshine slammed into me, the air thick and sticky with droplets of water that attached to my skin in a fine film. Uncle Buddy waved good-bye, heading the opposite direction. I'd made it halfway to my car when I realized I'd left my file in the conference room. I backtracked and returned to the building. Voices spilled from an open doorway in the hall. One was familiar. Their urgent tones swirled like a symphony in my mind.

At the first open door on my right, Dana and a long-haired man in grungy clothes stood close together by the file cabinets, eyes locked. I stopped cold in my tracks at the tension crackling between them. Dana's job as the mayor's administrative assistant didn't normally include speaking with people on courthouse business.

"I've already told you everything," Dana said with a hiss. "Why don't you get a warrant and search his records?"

The man shook his head, although I couldn't see his expression since his back was to me. "I need something besides your suspicions. I need proof."

"Isn't that like . . . your job?"

"I'm trying. If you really want me to trust you, then—"

From a connecting side door, Hank Rembert strolled into the room where the two were talking. Both of them abruptly halted the conversation.

"So the driver's license renewal is downstairs?" the stranger asked Dana, his manner as smooth as an oil slick.

"Right. After you exit the elevator, turn to your left and follow the signs. Actually, I was leaving anyway. I'll go with you."

Before they could turn and catch me eavesdropping, I hurried down the hall, heart skittering. What in the world had they been talking about? Search whose records? Was there a political scandal brewing in the bayou?

Chapter 13

TEGAN

Only six days into my first murder case and I was more confused now than the day we discovered Strickland's bloody corpse. What we'd initially suspected as a barroom fight that had carried over when the victim returned home didn't hold water. Ray's confrontation with Sims and his bully-boy friends hadn't produced a valid suspect. Oliver theorized, and I agreed, that someone had been lying in wait for Strickland to get home from the bar that evening. While Oliver felt confident this was a drug-related crime, my meetings with Jori raised other possibilities in my mind. It couldn't hurt for me to examine those possibilities away from Oliver's scrutiny and disapproval.

I wearily climbed my porch steps, wanting nothing more than a quiet evening at home reading over the Cormier file, but loud voices from the kitchen assailed me as soon as I opened the door.

"Pepperoni and sausage," Luke said. "Thick crust."

"No. I want onions and mushrooms," Linsey insisted. "Thin crust."

"If you want vegetables, why don't you just eat a salad?" he argued.

I shut the door and sighed. You'd think twins would have similar tastes, but not these two. And special closeness? Forget about it. Ever since they'd turned thirteen, the two went at it regularly. Two years now of bickering. I crossed my fingers, hoping this was a phase about to end.

Linsey turned to me and pleaded her case. "Mom, we had pepperoni and sausage last time. It's *my* turn to get what *I* want."

A good mom would have fixed a nutritionally balanced meal for her family, something I hadn't done for the past week. I'd been working almost nonstop, eager to prove myself on my first murder investigation. So, once again, I opted for the easy way out. "Call in one of each and have them delivered. And no more fighting, please."

Luke called in the compromised order. Appeased, Linsey plopped onto the sofa in front of the TV, shooting me a hesitant look full of hope and dread all at once.

"Mom, have you thought some more about the dance next week?" she asked. "You've met Max. He's been over here several times, and I know you like him."

Not that again. I rubbed my eyes, feeling too weary to make a decision. It was almost as if Linsey sensed this and homed in, ready to strike while my defense was down. I hated to keep outright denying her permission to go on a group date to a school function. After all, her sixteenth birthday was in less than two months anyway. I'd long promised her that she could begin dating at that age.

Frankly, it scared the shit out of me.

My protective mama-bear nature warred with my sense of fairness. Max had always been friendly and respectful when over at our house. I'd even met his parents at a few football games, and they seemed perfectly normal as well. Neither of the parents, nor Max himself, had any kind of local criminal record. I'd secretly checked, not that my daughter knew that little factoid. It was one of the few perks of my job that I could make inquiries on my children's friends. I felt no compunction to apologize for it.

"Okay, okay," I finally relented. Linsey's face lit with excitement. "But you have to meet my conditions."

Her face fell. "Like what?"

"Your brother goes in the car with you and Max to and from the dance."

Luke groaned from his position on the couch.

"And you have to be home by ten o'clock," I added.

"Eleven o'clock," she immediately countered. "All my girlfriends' curfews aren't until midnight."

"Ten thirty. Take it or leave it."

She scowled a moment and then nodded, her frown turning to a grin. "Deal."

Had I just been bamboozled? I shook my head ruefully. I couldn't shelter my kids forever. It was a school event, and Luke would be around as their unwelcome chaperone. Just because I'd experienced that horrific experience at age sixteen, it didn't mean that Linsey would meet the same fate.

I needed to believe that. Or lose my mind with worry every time one of the twins left the house. It had been so much easier when they were little and content to stay home and play with their mother. I missed those days, hectic as they'd been, keeping up with their double trouble of mischief.

Pizza was delivered within twenty minutes, and after they'd scarfed down their slices, they adjourned to their rooms. I slouched in the recliner with my laptop and pulled up the old Cormier file. It was massive, but I was determined to review the facts. The scanned officer notes in the PDF were often hard to decipher, so it was slow going. The first big surprise was that the police had always worked under the assumption that the family was murdered and not just missing.

They'd found an old camcorder tossed in a bookshelf drawer. Bloody fingerprints on the machine were identified as Deacon Cormier's. According to the transcript, the video started with the image of Deacon Cormier standing in the den wearing a tuxedo, looking uncomfortable and holding a corsage. There was a short, garbled conversation between him and the camera operator, whose voice was identified as that of his mother, Clotille. A loud noise blasted in the distance. A startled scream followed as the camera suddenly dropped to the floor with a crashing explosion. The video showed only the floor and the base of the fireplace as the audio continued running. Unfortunately, its aim prevented filming of the actual murders. A door creaked open, and Clotille spoke again, her voice high-pitched and terrified. A male voice answered before another gunshot rang out, this time loud and close. Deacon screamed, "Mom!"

A male voice again muttered something unintelligible in the background. Presumably the killer.

A deafening burst of noise erupted, and a second later the picture jolted and went black.

An ominous silence of six seconds ensued, followed by the heavy thud of footsteps and then a door squeaking open. Experts agreed that the most likely scenario was that the killer had walked to the bodies to check and make sure they were dead before leaving the scene of the crime.

Another long silence ensued, only broken by the eerie whir of the recorder. After twenty-two minutes and twenty-eight seconds, the camcorder was lifted and thrown into a drawer. Shortly after, other voices were recorded, their words even more muffled and garbled. Then the picture and the whirring came to an abrupt halt, as eerie and chilling as the stroke of a ghostly, cold finger along the spine.

Information on the video had never been released to the public. It had been held back in hopes of identifying the killer or killers. The tape had been sent to a forensics lab, but they were unable to clearly identify the garbled voice or vocal pattern of the unidentified person in the room, much less match it with any of the persons questioned in the Cormier case.

Also found and not released to the public was a single sprig of flowers with droplets of Deacon's blood on it.

Had Deacon hidden the camcorder after being injured but before bleeding out? Had the killer been distracted while his victim had the presence of mind to hide evidence that might lead to the man's identity?

I stopped reading and glanced out the window, stunned by the revelations. I'd only heard gossip about the case prior to now and was surprised to learn that law enforcement officials didn't buy into the locals' theory that the Cormiers had staged their own disappearance to either escape legal trouble or avoid some type of Mafia backlash.

One of the original investigators even suggested that the recording itself could have been a hoax deliberately planted by Louis Cormier to make police believe there'd been foul play. Most of the cops didn't buy into that theory.

But because of Deacon's bloody fingerprints and the blood on the flower, more than one law enforcement officer theorized that Louis and Clotille might have murdered their son. In a panic, they'd disposed of his body somewhere and then fled the country.

I wiped a hand over my face and got up, pacing the living room. How was it possible that no trace of violence had been detected? If Louis hadn't been shot inside the home, I wasn't surprised that no clues had been found on the scene. But two people shot inside? If the killer and/or any accomplice had cleaned up the evidence, they'd done a thorough job. However, it *was* possible to cover his tracks if all the blood had been wiped away with an active oxygen bleach. The luminol test would not have been able to pick up traces of blood, especially if the cleaning had occurred fairly soon after the crime. Oxy-type products were popular and widely available prior to the 2006 disappearance.

I wished I could call Oliver and talk over the information with him, but he'd already told me to focus my attention elsewhere.

Having at last absorbed those bombshells, I sat down and resumed reading. On a photocopy of Louis Cormier's business calendar I discovered a new surprise. A small notation on one of the dated squares had me sit up straight, my brain tingling at the unexpected bit of information.

May 4, 2006. Fountain Correctional Facility. Atmore. 2:30 p.m. Raymond Strickland ALDOC# 894502.

The date was about two weeks before Louis Cormier and his family disappeared.

Finally. A tangible connection between the two cases. The men had known each other. Had Cormier followed through with the appointment? What reason did he have for wanting to meet with Strickland? Was it all coincidence?

There was no further information on why Cormier was meeting Strickland or whether the scheduled meeting had ever occurred. I'd be extremely lucky if there was any record of their conversation, since attorney-inmate discussions were supposed to be confidential.

So far in my reading, the police report made no further mention of the appointment. Instead, the investigation had focused on meetings and phone calls between Cormier and his other clients with known criminal backgrounds.

My first order of business tomorrow morning would be to request Strickland's inmate records and the prison visitation and phone logs for the first three weeks of May 2006. I shut down my computer and swiped a hand across my face, again questioning my decision. Was I doing the right thing pursuing this and risking Oliver's anger? After all, he had years of experience. My colleagues would be only too glad to jump in and work the Strickland murder should Oliver remove me from the case.

Hours had passed; the twins were already in bed. I rose from the sofa and peered out the living room window. The obsidian darkness of night was punctuated by rectangular cozy glows from a few of my neighbors' windows. But were those really cuddly gleams of warmth that shone? Even this modest bayou town housed its own dark secrets.

Contained within the four walls of individual homes were addicts and thieves and killers and violent persons who hid their dangerous shadow sides during the day.

I'd expose whoever I could, whenever I could. I'd made that vow the day I entered law enforcement, and I wouldn't forsake that promise now.

Chapter 14

JORI

"No! Not going."

"Zach, you have to go to your day program. Now let's get dressed."

"No!" He backed away from me, flinging his shoes across the floor.

I sighed and put my hands on my hips. I hadn't seen him agitated like this since I visited at Thanksgiving last year. The midweek holiday from his day program had left him cranky.

"What's wrong? Are you sick?" I asked, trying to figure out the sudden resistance to his normal weekday routine.

"Sick," he repeated.

"Where do you hurt?"

He thumped his forehead with the palm of his right hand—hard enough to leave a red mark.

"Headache?"

"Headache," he agreed.

I stared at him, seeking clues as to what had set him off. His echoing my words didn't mean he was actually sick. For people on the severe end of the autism spectrum, echolalia was a common phenomenon wherein they either repeated the last word they heard or spoke words and phrases repetitively, whether or not it was situationally appropriate.

I bit my lip, trying to decide the right thing to do for Zach. If he really didn't feel well, what was wrong? Did he need to see a doctor? Or did he just not want to leave the house?

Some days my brother didn't like going out and preferred to watch TV and play with his LEGOs. Not that he played with them in the conventional sense of building structures. Zach liked to rattle them in a plastic bin or stream them from one hand to another. For hours.

It was so hard to know how best to proceed. Didn't Zach have the right, like anybody else, to make his own decisions about his day-to-day activities?

"Be right back," I said, leaving his bedroom to ask Mimi's opinion.

She was in the den, pacing and muttering what sounded like gibberish words under her breath.

"Zach's upset this morning," I told her. "Any idea why?"

She looked up at me, startled. "Who?"

"Zach. He's upset."

Her eyes regarded me vacantly. "Zach who?"

The back of my throat burned with dismay, and I swallowed back a swift rush of emotion. I hadn't ever seen her at the point where she didn't recognize me. Apparently, Mimi didn't remember Zach either.

I approached slowly and gently took her arm, felt its frail weight under my hand, the skin wrinkled and loose. "Let's go in the kitchen. I'll make you a cup of coffee, and you can take your medicine."

Surprisingly, she allowed me to guide her to the table and seat her in a chair. I opened the cabinet where we stored medicine and rifled through the wicker basket. Her prescription bottle was gone. My heart dropped as I pulled out the odds and ends on the bottom cabinet shelf to see if it had fallen out of the basket. It wasn't there. Had she thrown it away? I hurried to the trash can and opened the lid, then dug through the pile of leftover grits and eggshells. Not the most fun way to start a morning. I found the amber bottle sludged in a mess of bacon grease.

I straightened and gave Mimi a stern glare, but the far-off look in her eyes was still there. I didn't have the heart to scold. Maybe she hadn't done it on purpose, and it had been an accident. I rinsed the bottle in the sink and started the coffee maker before returning to the meds. I removed Zach's blister pack, then stared in consternation. Last night's dose was still enclosed. How had that happened? I thought back, remembering that Mimi had offered to do it last night when we'd all been in the den. Sometime between leaving the den and entering the kitchen, she'd forgotten what she'd gone in there for.

Guilt panged my gut. I should have been paying closer attention. From now on, I'd keep the meds in my room and be the one to distribute them. No wonder Zach was so agitated and out of sorts this morning. It was a wonder he'd even slept last night. I'd have to call Zach's doctor, confess the snafu, and get his guidance on how to get his medicine properly regulated today.

No day program for Zach. That wouldn't be fair to the staff or the other clients. I'd let him stay home and play with LEGOs to his heart's content until his meds normalized.

Once I'd made the doctor call and straightened out the med situation, I had Mimi and Zach sitting in the den, relatively content with a movie and popcorn. It was their favorite pastime, and I figured it might be calming for them—and give me a breather. The sounds of a western action adventure floated to the kitchen, where I cleaned up the last of the breakfast dishes.

That done, I sank into one of the kitchen chairs and buried my face in my hands. I was overwhelmed, feeling unequal to the task of caring for the two people I loved most in the world. Could this day get any worse?

The doorbell rang sharply, and I jerked my head up in surprise. Now what? I rushed to the door to find Deputy Blackwell standing on my doorstep, her expression solemn.

Yep. Apparently, this day could get worse.

"Got a few minutes?" she asked. Her gaze slid to Mimi and Zach on the couch. "We can sit on the porch if you'd like."

"Fine." I shut the front door behind me, and we sat across from one another on the porch rocking chairs. Had she found the culprit who'd broken into our home? I waited expectantly.

"I'm reviewing the old Cormier case and have a few questions for you."

I blinked. Hadn't expected the conversation to take that route.

"According to the notes, you spent a great deal of time at the Cormier house. I know you were questioned as a teenager, but with the space of time and distance, I'm wondering if anything has changed from what you originally told investigators. Could you have overheard any snippet of conversation that might shed some light on their disappearances? Perhaps the mother was having an affair with a jealous lover?"

"No," I protested, quick anger flushing my face. "I don't believe it."

"Why not?"

"She was crazy about her husband. Never heard her say a bad word against him."

"He was gone a good bit, traveling back and forth to Mobile and meeting with clients from all over the southeast."

I crossed my legs. "Are you accusing me of lying back then? Because I didn't. I wouldn't. I was crazy about Deacon and really liked his parents. If I had any insights or suspicions, now or then, I'd immediately tell the cops."

She held up a hand, as though to ward off my defense. "I believe you. I'm on your side."

The stress rushed out of my body, and I relaxed in my seat.

"It's a small town. I'm sure over the years you've heard the rumors that Mrs. Cormier was having an affair," Tegan said.

"Yeah. With our librarian, Adam Logan. Apparently he took an interest in her paintings and displayed them at the library."

Blackwell appeared surprised that I provided a name.

I shrugged. "Like you said, it's a small town." I considered her words. Maybe Clotille had been lonely. I'd been so involved with Deacon and so young that maybe I hadn't picked up on the signs. "I suppose she could have been," I reluctantly conceded. "But I never saw Adam at their house or even heard his name mentioned by Deacon or his mother. I'm sure he was questioned, wasn't he?"

"Yes. He denied it, and there was no scrap of proof that they were romantically involved." She tried another tactic. "Did you ever overhear arguments between Louis and Clotille?"

I started to shake my head no, then abruptly stopped.

"What is it?" Blackwell asked quickly. "Did you remember something?"

"Only a little back-and-forth about how much Clotille had spent on her art studio. Nothing major."

"How did Deacon get along with his parents? He ever confide anything to you about being mistreated?"

"He got along as well with his parents as any teenager. I mean, there were a couple of times he got in trouble at school and they'd ground him over the weekend or take away his cell phone for a few days. Normal stuff like that."

"Did they ever beat or neglect him?"

"No." I shook my head emphatically. "If anything like that had been going on, Deacon would have told me. I never saw any marks on him either."

"What about the alleged rumor that Louis Cormier was involved in money laundering for the mob? Or the drug trafficking rumors?"

"Who told you that?" I asked, anger bristling the hairs on the nape of my neck.

"Like I said before, it's a small town. The Cormier case was huge news. Of course, I've heard these kinds of rumors for years. I take it you don't believe those rumors."

"Not for a single minute," I snapped. "Why is everyone so quick to judge them? Just because he was a successful attorney? Because he hadn't been born and raised in Enigma? Because that's crap. Something bad happened to them."

"I'm not disputing that something horrible occurred. If Louis Cormier was involved in criminal activity, it's possible that his associates wanted him to disappear. I can't divulge everything I've learned. Suffice to say, we have reason to believe they were murdered. Always have, contrary to the rumor mill around town when they disappeared."

My heart squeezed, and I drew a deep breath. This was good news, right? Not that they were sure the family was murdered—I'd always believed that. But that finally somebody didn't believe the Cormiers had been so devious as to let everyone assume they'd been killed when they were still alive.

Deacon's face flashed before me, the wide-spaced blue eyes and his slow, easy grin. No, there was no happy news in anything this officer had related.

"I-I don't know what to say," I stammered at last.

"Not only that," Blackwell continued, "but I've stumbled on a connection between the past and present murders. Two weeks before Mr. Cormier disappeared, he visited Raymond Strickland at Fountain Correctional Facility."

"Why?"

"We don't know. Inmate-attorney meetings are confidential, so no recordings were ever made. There were also two prison phone calls between Louis Cormier and Raymond Strickland before Cormier's disappearance. All I know for sure at this point is that they did meet."

"Strange," I whispered. I never would have guessed those two had ever met. But maybe it shouldn't have been surprising. Louis had been an attorney, and Ray might have wanted Louis to represent him in some matter like an appeal. It wasn't like Bayou Enigma was a large town.

"Very strange," Blackwell agreed.

Neither of us spoke for several minutes.

"Let me ask you once more," Blackwell said, her tone soft and encouraging. "Can you recall *anything* suspicious happening at the Cormier household? Anyone ever over there that seemed out of the ordinary or anything the Cormiers might have said that, in hindsight, might be significant now?"

I started to again deny it but pulled up short as the image of Cash Johnson rose in my mind.

Blackwell caught on at once. "What is it?"

"This is embarrassing, but yeah, I thought of something. It's probably nothing. Maybe I shouldn't even mention it. I don't want to get an innocent person in trouble."

"Tell me. You'll feel even worse if you discover later that they're guilty or have a clue about the old crime."

I nodded and spoke, hoping she couldn't see the color heating my face. "I used to sneak out at night to visit Deacon in the old smokehouse on his property," I admitted. "More times than not, when I'd leave the smokehouse to return home, I'd run into Cash Johnson. Even if it was before dawn, he'd be carrying a rifle and say he was going hunting. It always made me feel uncomfortable."

"Who is this man? A neighbor of theirs?"

"Yes. He's my Uncle Buddy's business partner at Enigma Expeditions and lives in a cabin near the old Cormier home."

"Buddy Munford? He's a county commissioner, right?"

"Right." Everyone seemed to either know Uncle Buddy or have heard of him.

"I'll check that out. Thank you. If you think of anything else—anything at all—you call me."

Still, Tegan didn't rise to leave. She rocked in the chair, her gaze off in the distance, as though debating something in her mind. Finally, she faced me.

"What I'm telling you needs to be kept between us. Because of the connection between the cases, I wanted you to know we're taking the threat against you very seriously. We'll continue to have sporadic drive-bys of your house. Be careful, Ms. Trahern."

I looked through the front window where Zach and Mimi sat side by side. Zach's head rested against Mimi's shoulder, and she absently patted his hand as they watched their movie.

"I will," I promised. "I can't let anything happen to me or my family."

Tegan followed my gaze. "You have a lot of responsibility for someone so young."

"Nothing I can't handle."

"You must care about them a great deal."

"I do." I continued staring at the intimate tableau—my little brother who depended on me and the woman who helped raise us after the death of our mother. "Mom died of cancer when I was in high school," I explained. "Near the end, when it was obvious she wasn't going to make it . . ." The back of my throat burned, and I swallowed hard before continuing. "Mom asked me to always look out for them."

"A deathbed promise," Tegan said softly. "The teenage years are tough even without the loss of a parent."

I glanced at her curiously. "I take it that high school was no picnic for you either."

"Nothing that a year of counseling didn't help fix."

I started to grin, then realized she wasn't joking. "I-I'm sorry."

She lifted a shoulder and let it drop. "I don't talk about it much. We all have our problems, and you've had more than your fair share. Not only with your mom's death, but your boyfriend up and disappeared into thin air. Must have been tough."

"It was. At least I had Mimi. And in his own way, Zach's a comfort. He has this calm, Zen-like quality most of the time. Unless you change his routine—then all hell breaks loose." I smiled thinly. "They're all I have left. The thought of them being in danger makes me crazy."

She nodded slowly. "I'm a single mother of two children. Twins. If anything happened to them, well . . . they're my whole life."

We smiled at each other in understanding.

Blackwell stood. "Like I told you several days ago, leave the detective work to us. We'll get this figured out. I also want you to know I'm doing my best to discover what happened to the Cormiers. I'm no psychologist, but I believe closure on that case would be helpful for you."

"Thank you, Deputy." I also rose, my legs shaky.

"Call me Tegan," she said softly. "You still got my card?"

"Maybe you should give me another one."

Dutifully, she plucked one from her uniform shirt pocket. "We'll stay in touch. Call me if you have any concerns, Ms. Trahern."

"Jori," I corrected. "And I will."

She extended her hand, and I shook it. Her smile was not unkind. "Anytime at all, you hear?"

I watched her saunter from the porch. "Wait," I called out as she reached the bottom step. "Did you ever get closure for what happened to you in high school?"

Tegan slowly turned to face me, an odd expression flickering across her eyes. "One hundred percent closure. Justice was served quickly. Permanently. The past can never harm me again."

What an odd choice of words. I could do with a little justice myself. To arrest whoever sent those threats and to punish whoever had harmed Deacon and his family.

I waved at Tegan as she drove off. It felt good to have someone in my corner.

Chapter 15

TEGAN

"We finally got clearance to hire an undercover narcotics agent," Oliver told me by way of greeting. "No thanks to Mayor Rembert. Cheap bastard fought me every step of the way. Had to go over his head to the state guys."

I dropped into the chair across from his desk, fatigued from my late-night reading of the Cormier file. "Hank's not going to be happy about that," I observed.

"At this point, I don't really give a damn about Hank Rembert's feelings."

"How did you justify hiring an agent with the state folks?" I asked, surprised at the news. "Don't get me wrong, I'm thrilled we're getting one, but it's not like we have a clear drug connection with the Strickland murder. I mean, sure, we found drugs at the crime scene and Raymond used to be a small-time dealer in his youth, but other than that, there's nothing concrete."

Oliver leaned back in his chair, steepled his fingers, and regarded me in an odd, assessing manner. He nodded, as though reaching a decision. "Shut the door," he ordered.

I hurried to do his bidding and then returned to my seat. "What's up?"

"We're going to be working closely together, and I've grown to trust you. If we're going to crack this murder case, I need you to be aware of what's going on behind the scenes." He leaned forward, drumming his fingers on the battered desk.

"You can trust me," I assured him.

"It's no coincidence I came here to fill a vacancy," he continued. "State and federal agents have been suspicious for some time about the integrity of Bayou Enigma's police force. They wanted someone from outside the area—but not too far—to step in and observe operations."

This was news to me—no tiny feat in a town as small as ours. "You mean, they think our local cops are dirty?" Another shocking realization hit. "Do they think the sheriff's office is dirty too?"

He didn't respond, but his silence was answer enough.

"Damn," I muttered. "So they're suspicious our town has a flourishing drug trade and we're all in on it?" An absurd outrage coursed through me. "Enigma's not like that."

"How can you be so sure?" Oliver asked.

He was right. Rural areas were no stranger to corruption. I thought of my coworkers. They were annoying, but I found it hard to believe they were involved in anything nefarious. But as for Dempsey and Granger—yeah, I could see that. Though, in all fairness, perhaps it was my own dislike of that duo that colored my perception.

"What kind of proof do you have?" I asked.

"Can't reveal everything to you, except on a need-to-know basis. What I can say is that we've got a local informant who's proven fairly reliable. This person has furnished names, and we're hoping to make several major arrests over the next few weeks. With the recent murder, it became imperative to get to the bottom of the matter as quickly as possible."

I sat in silence several moments, absorbing this new information. "Who is this agent and when does he start?" I finally asked.

"Name's Carter Holt, and he's already started."

"But you said—"

He grinned. "I was pretty confident his pay would be approved. Holt started work yesterday and is already starting to make inroads."

"That quick?"

"I was informed he was the best. Has a real knack for infiltrating rings. And with the goods our informant provided, I'm hopeful we'll have answers soon."

"Great. I have some news too," I began hesitantly. "I found a connection between Strickland and Louis Cormier."

Oliver's face drew into a scowl.

"I'm reading the files on my own time at home," I assured him. I quickly filled him in.

"I'll be damned," he muttered. "Makes me wonder about the rumors you told me about, that Louis Cormier trafficked in drugs, same as Strickland."

"Could be he wanted Cormier to represent him in a new trial. There's no telling. But I thought it interesting that the two had a scheduled meeting."

Oliver scratched his head. "Definitely. It was such a long time ago, but I'll call George Blankenship. He was the warden at Fountain for decades and a friend of my father's. I'll ask if he remembers Strickland and any of his known associates in prison. If we're lucky—extremely lucky—someone will remember why Strickland contacted Cormier."

Thank goodness for the good ole boys' network. "Perfect. I'll get back to work on my reports."

He waved me off, already punching out numbers on his cell phone. When I returned to the office, Sinclair grinned when I walked by.

"Looking kinda puny today, Blackwell. Case getting to you?"

"Shut up, jerk wad," I replied good-naturedly, walking to my desk.

Haywood felt the need to chime in. "Need any help yet, rookie?"

I ignored him and raised a brow at Mullins. "You ready to pile on, too, big guy?"

"Nah." He laughed. "When you're ready for my superior expertise, which should be soon, I'll be right here. Waiting."

I snorted, pulling up a screen on my computer. "The day I—"

Oliver rushed into the office, as fast as I'd ever seen him move. His features were lit with excitement.

"Just got a call from Dempsey. A fisherman called the station, reporting a human skull found in Black Bottom Creek. Let's go."

I grabbed my sunglasses and raced to the door.

"Some people get all the luck," Mullins complained under his breath as I went by, clearly disappointed not to be part of the breaking action. I rolled my eyes at him.

Oliver was already starting down the stairs at the end of the hall, and I hurried to catch up. "Is the skull a child or adult?" I asked, flying down the stairs.

"Don't know yet. Forensics has been called. They might be there already."

By the time we got to the cruiser, Oliver was sweating and huffing. "Getting old and out of shape," he complained as he backed out of the parking lot.

As we motored through town and then headed south on a county road, I wondered if the skull belonged to one of the Cormiers.

"By the way, I spoke to the former warden at Fountain before I got the news," Oliver said. "No dice on finding any records that old. He told me that visitor logs weren't kept over a year."

"Bummer." I'd been expecting that news but was still disappointed.

"Still an interesting find," Oliver noted as we rounded a bend.

"You'll have to tell me exactly where this place is," he warned. "Been a long time since I've been fishing this way."

"Another mile and a half, you'll turn right on Turnipseed Road."

We soon came up on it, and Oliver turned onto the dirt road, stirring up dry red dirt that swirled around us.

"Another fifty yards and—"

"I see the cop cars up ahead. County coroner and forensics people already here too."

We pulled up next to a car and scrambled out of our vehicle. I had to fight my way through a ring of several people before I saw it.

A human skull with empty eye socket cavities and a mouthful of teeth.

A stark, ominous artifact dredged from the stygian waters. An older man dressed in camo and khaki stood off to the side with his fishing pole still in hand, looking unsettled. I could imagine his horror as he thought he had a bite, only to pull up his line and discover grisly human remains. Dempsey and another cop were still questioning him, writing notes in their cell phones.

Cameras flashed as everyone stared at the ground. One of the forensics team members knelt on one knee and closely examined the skull. I recognized many of the same faces I'd seen last week at the Strickland home.

The sight of the skull disconcerted me more than the fresh corpse of Raymond Strickland. It was so . . . final. A total absence of tissue and flesh. The home of our brain, the part of us we used to think and feel and act. That defined our very being. The bony cavity was empty now, with hollow eye sockets, no nose, and protruding teeth from a squared jawbone. A flash of something glimmered on the ground.

"Gold cap on the left molar tooth," one of the techs murmured. "Pronounced jawbone," another said. "Most likely male."

More cars arrived at the scene. Four men emerged from a van and began donning black wet suits. Where there was one bone, more might follow.

How many bones? How many people? Had they finally found the remains of the Cormier family?

I glanced at Oliver. "The Cormiers?" I whispered.

"Maybe. If not, we might have a whole new mystery to solve on top of everything else."

"Who has the quickest access to the dental records?"

"Checking it out now," he assured me. "Already sent a text."

The divers entered the shallow water, a small creek banked by reeds on either side. If one had to dive in the swamp, spring would be your best choice. The mosquitoes and other insects were horrid in the summer, and in the winter, though not frozen, the water would be chilly.

"Whatever they're paying those men, they're earning every cent," I said softly for Oliver's ears only.

"Amen," he agreed.

We watched in silence over the next couple of hours as the divers rounded up their grisly collection and handed it over to the forensics experts—a foot with a healed broken big toe, a long femur, a hand, a broad pelvis bone that the techs examined. "Definitely female," they concurred after measuring the distance between the ischium bones—an opening that was large and oval in shape. Other pieces of the laid-out bones were too fragmented for me to recognize where they'd once been located in the body.

Lastly, the divers extracted three large cement blocks and placed them upon the shore.

"Bodies must have been weighted down with them," Oliver stated grimly.

Three.

Louis, Clotille, and Deacon? I knew my boss was wondering the same. His phone pinged, and he opened a text. A moment later he stuffed the phone back in his pocket. "Dental records of Louis Cormier confirm he had a gold cap on his back left molar."

It was the Cormiers all right. That broad pelvis bone must have belonged to Clotille. On a whim, I texted Jori Trahern.

Deacon ever have a foot injury that you know of?

She answered almost immediately. Broken right big toe. Soccer injury. How did you guess???

Later, I answered her, shutting off my phone. I'd call her as soon as I could and give her a heads-up before word of the grisly discovery spread around the bayou.

The spread of nearly a dozen skeletal parts was laid out upon a large black plastic tarp. The forensics people tagged each one with the date, time, and a brief description of the bone. A clinical end to the decades-old mystery of whether or not they'd ever left town. I hoped the remains would soon be given a proper burial and a memorial given for the Cormiers. The town had been so quick to judge and think unkindly of this family.

Had the killer, or killers, hoped a nest of gators would swallow up the bones? Most likely, the large reptiles had feasted on their flesh. Not all the bones had been recovered. Alligators were capable of digesting bone, muscle, and cartilage, but there was no guarantee they'd conveniently swallow up all the remains left for them by the murderer. I thanked heaven that the reptiles had left us a few scraps.

At last, the work was completed, and the forensics crew and dive team packed up to leave.

"How long do you think it will take for official confirmation these bones belonged to the Cormiers?" I asked Oliver.

"I'd guess later this afternoon or first thing tomorrow morning. There'll be a priority placed on identifying them."

The reeds on the creek embankment nearest us had been crushed by divers and techs walking along the shore. But the black murky water appeared the same as always, offering no hint that beneath its surface it had contained a dark secret for over a decade. A grisly mass grave that held the key to what had happened to a missing family thirteen years earlier.

The solemnity of the scene stayed with me long after Oliver and I had left. Even through the rest of the busy day, the tragedy weighed heavy in the back of my mind.

As soon as I was alone, I made the phone call I dreaded. Jori picked up at once, her voice breathless—tense. "What's happened?" she asked. Before I could answer, she rushed on with another question. "You found Deacon's body, didn't you?"

"Yes. The entire family, most likely."

A weighted silence fell between us. I breathed in her pain, her loss. Jori didn't care about the particulars; all that mattered was that whatever small hope she'd carried—perhaps even so small she hadn't even realized it existed—had now been forever extinguished. A tiny match flame in the darkness smothered.

I filled her in and then disconnected the call, hoping it would be a long, long time before I was the deliverer of bad news again.

Chapter 16

April 1991

I watched as the taillights of the red Mustang disappeared into the night. From afar, I'd seen the girl get in his car and less than fifteen minutes later observed Jackson exit the back and climb into the driver's seat. I hadn't expected him to leave the party with the girl. Maybe tonight wouldn't provide the right opportunity.

But I bided my time. The evening was early, and chances were he'd reappear. After all, his connection hadn't arrived yet. Only minutes later Raymond Strickland pulled into the cotton field that doubled as an impromptu parking lot for the dozens of partygoers crowded inside the old barn. Ray sat on the back hood of his desperately ugly Pontiac sedan, which was painted olive and covered with rust patches. The tip of his cigarette glowed in the darkness. I figured he was waiting for Jackson, same as I was. We were both rewarded when Jackson finally returned. Ray and Jackson stood outside by the Pontiac, talking.

From where I stood I was close enough to observe a wad of cash and then a large baggie exchanged between them. Jackson inspected the bag's content before the two of them divided its contents into smaller baggies. Right there, right out in the open. They were that brazen.

Their business took less than five minutes.

Ray flung his cigarette to the ground and then waved goodbye before taking off. Making more deliveries, no doubt.

Jackson returned inside the barn, and I presumed it was to sell the drugs he'd just bought. Losers. All of them.

It was so easy to slink from behind the trees and then slip unnoticed into the back seat of the unlocked Mustang. I crouched low on the floorboard and resumed my wait, slipping on a pair of latex gloves. It didn't take long for him to return.

The front door abruptly swung open, letting in a blast of cold wind. Jackson heavily sank into the driver's seat. With a metallic cling, the key slid into the ignition, and he started the motor before slamming the door shut. Moments later, the radio blared, and he put the car in reverse.

I picked up the gun I'd laid beside me on the floorboard. *Patience,* I chided myself. It was too early. The sports car bumped along the rough field until it reached the smooth pavement of the deserted country road. At least I hoped it was deserted. I'd made the drive earlier today and concluded I should count to thirty before making my move. By then, we would be out of earshot from everyone.

Twenty-eight, twenty-nine . . . thirty. Showtime. Adrenaline slammed through every cell in my body. I rose up swiftly and pointed the barrel of the gun against the back of his head. Jackson stared at my reflection in the dashboard mirror as he slammed on the brakes.

"What the hell are you doing?" he demanded loudly. The brakes squealed as the car zigzagged across the narrow road before jamming to a shuddering halt. I concentrated on keeping the gun trained on his head. Equal measures of panic and shock lit his eyes when he turned around, the gun now pointed inches from his face.

"What are you doing?" he asked again, voice trembling this time.

I supposed he deserved an explanation before he met his maker. "Turn off that radio."

Hurriedly, he obeyed. First time in my life I'd ever seen him do that.

"You've caused a lot of people a lot of grief," I began.

"I-I'll be better."

"The hell you will. You're nothing but trouble."

"Please." His lips were white around the edges with fear. "Forget I asked you for any money. Okay?"

"Asked?" I snorted with disbelief. "You tried to blackmail me."

"It won't ever happen again," he promised, talking quick. "I promise. I made a mistake and—"

"Who else did you tell?"

"Nobody. I swear."

"Not even your dealer, Ray?"

"No, man."

I didn't believe a word coming out of his mouth. But I had another plan for that potential problem.

"Turn around," I ordered Jackson.

"No. Please." Tears streamed down his cheeks.

No trace of the belligerent teenager remained, and my gut clenched with momentary guilt. But it was too late to change my mind. This punk wouldn't ruin what I'd worked so hard to build. Not a chance.

"I said, *turn around.*"

Instead, Jackson suddenly ducked beneath the seat and slammed his foot against the accelerator. The car lurched forward, and then he turned the wheel sharply. We U-turned in the middle of the road, and I slid across the seat. He was heading back in the direction of the party.

"I wasn't gonna hurt you, Jackson," I lied. I repositioned myself behind him. "Just stop the car."

He drove faster. I'd have to take my chances now with the speeding car, or I'd never surprise him like this again.

I pulled the trigger.

My ears rang with a thunderous explosion. Blood and sparks of fire strobed inside the car as it spun in a circle. The Mustang rumbled off the side of the road and hit a tree, at last coming to a halt.

It took several seconds for me to catch my bearings. Wet, hot liquid ran down my face, and I brushed it away with my arm, smearing my jacket with blood. I'd take care of all that mess later. Methodically, I scanned the vehicle, making sure I left nothing behind. Nothing that would incriminate *me*, that is. I withdrew the plastic shopping bag hidden in my coat and pulled out Raymond Strickland's hoodie sweatshirt. I'd pilfered it from his car a couple of weeks ago. You'd think drug dealers would be more careful about locking up their cars to keep out thieves. Carefully, I smeared the front of it with Jackson's blood. Satisfied, I climbed out of the vehicle and headed into the woods, where I'd change clothes and dump the gun in the swamp.

Tonight hadn't gone exactly as planned, but I'd done what was necessary.

Chapter 17

JORI

"This is where I found that . . . that thing. Right there. It was gross." I still shuddered at the memory and found myself looking over my shoulder whenever I entered or exited a room. Maybe I always would.

Dana peered into the closet and shook her head. "You've always been a fraidy-cat, but I'd have totally freaked out too."

I left her standing there and sat on my bed. "Right? Every time I open the closet, I remember it lying there on the floor."

"Did the creep destroy all your journals?"

"What he didn't tear up, I went ahead and burned. At least he didn't get all my keepsakes from high school."

Dana crossed the room and sat down next to me. "What else have you kept?"

"Open the bottom drawer of my nightstand."

She did so and then chuckled, pulling out our old school yearbooks. "I lost all mine in the fire," she said.

A fire had destroyed the house she'd shared with her first husband, Kenny. They'd lost everything, but at least Kenny had managed to escape. He'd been home alone asleep and had almost died from smoke inhalation. Thankfully, Dana had been visiting her cousin in Montgomery at the time.

She opened the book from our senior year, and I marveled at how outdated the clothes and haircuts already appeared in our individual photos. Dana pointed at my picture. "You were so pretty back then."

"Meaning what? I'm nothing but chopped liver now?" I joked.

She nudged me with her elbow. "No! You know what I mean."

It was true. It wasn't like my face had deteriorated to a mass of sagging wrinkles or that I'd gained a ton of weight. But the schoolgirl in the photo had that youthful gleam and innocence in her eyes that could never be recaptured. I wished I were that girl again. To experience that unbridled optimism and happiness I hadn't managed to achieve since then. Not since Deacon's disappearance and the terrible weeks that had followed.

I flipped through the book on her lap and located Dana's old picture. "And there you are. Pretty then, but even more attractive now."

Her mouth twisted. "Don't lie. I looked like shit in high school. My acne was photoshopped for the yearbook, but I haven't forgotten how hideous it was or that I was a good twenty pounds overweight."

"You're way too critical of yourself," I protested loyally. "Besides, look at that long blonde hair. I remember it came all the way down to your waist."

"My only saving grace."

"Kenny adored you." I wanted to bite my tongue after the words slipped out. Their marriage had lasted less than three years, much to everyone's surprise. Dana always maintained they'd grown apart, although I suspected the real reason went deeper, even if she didn't want to talk about it.

"Eh, Kenny." She shrugged dismissively. "He wasn't near as cute or exciting as Deacon. You were so lucky to have him as a boyfriend."

Her words caught me off guard. Was this some backhanded passive-aggressive remark—as in, who was I to have attracted such a great guy as Deacon? I immediately vetoed the thought. More likely, she still harbored bitterness about Kenny as well as the fairly recent divorce from her second husband, Mark. She probably just thought she'd picked the wrong men while I'd lucked out with a better choice. Or it could be that what I'd heard about her drug rehab was true and her drug addiction had wreaked havoc in her marriages.

"Hardly lucky," I reminded her softly. "I lost Deacon."

"Lost." She winced. "You're right. Sorry."

"It was a long time ago." Silence stretched between us, and I asked what had been weighing on my mind. "Listen, you've stayed here in town all these years. Have you ever come up with any new theory on what happened to Deacon and his parents? Have you heard anybody say anything recently?"

"Not even a whisper. As shocking as their disappearances were, it's been a long time. People have moved on."

And so should you. She didn't say it aloud, but I felt the unspoken words. "What's everyone saying about Ray Strickland's murder? Do they think it has anything to do with Jackson's long-ago murder? Like some kind of revenge killing?"

"That idea's been floated. As well as the idea that Ray was either dealing drugs or involved in some other criminal mischief and got in trouble with a bad crowd."

"Are drugs really a major problem in Enigma?" I asked skeptically.

"Yep. Just like anywhere else." Dana hugged her arms to her chest. "We've never talked about it, but I've had my share of addiction problems. Spent several months in rehab after my last divorce and got my life back in order."

"I'm sorry," I said softly. "That must have been rough. But I'm proud that you overcame it."

She flashed a twisted smile and shrugged. "I finally decided it was time to get it together. I started smoking pot in high school and graduated to harder stuff over the years. Eventually, I got hooked on opioids."

Dana searched my face. "I never told you, but I had a serious crush on Deacon back in the day."

For the second time this afternoon, she'd surprised me. "I had no idea."

"Deacon never looked twice at me. Not in the way he looked at you." She laughed, a tad too off key to be a real laugh. The notes of green arrows in her voice appeared sharper and sleeker than normal. "I even came on to him a couple of times. He acted like he didn't notice what I was trying to do. Insisted we were just buddies."

My teeth ground together, and my thoughts raced. I was at once thankful for Deacon's steady, loyal character and irritated at Dana's confession. What kind of friend would come on to your boyfriend? I stared at her, the clear-eyed, freckle-faced woman I'd known all my life. How well did I really understand her, after all? Until seconds ago, I'd have sworn Dana was my best friend and I trusted her completely.

"I shouldn't have told you," she said at last. "Do you hate me for it?"

"Hate? Of course not. Forget it. We were kids." I tried to believe my reassurance to her, but a secret part of me was shaken. I doubted I'd ever feel as close to her as I once had.

Dana exhaled loudly. "Whew. That's a relief. While we're playing true confessions, I might as well admit that I've always been a little jealous of you." She slanted me a curious glance. "Good grades came easily for you; you were pretty and had the best-looking guy in school as your boyfriend."

I said nothing, not sure what to think of this new side to Dana. It wasn't like her to be so open. Sure, we'd been friends for ages, but she'd always had a wall of reserve and often kept silent on private matters. Which was fine by me—I had my own secrets.

Dana tapped a finger against her chin, regarding me quizzically. "What I want to know is—why haven't you ever married? I mean, you're attractive and available. Plus, you're fun and easy to get along with when you make the effort."

I squirmed uncomfortably on the bed. "Just haven't met the right one yet, I suppose."

"Such a shame."

She rustled through the yearbook some more, and several faded color photographs fell from the pages. "What's this?" she asked, picking up the photos from the floor.

"Homecoming photos," I said, staring at the half dozen images of me and Deacon after the football game. In one of them, my favorite, he had an arm tossed over my shoulders. Even sweaty and dirty in his uniform, he was still handsome, his grin looking even cuter and sexier than ever. A rush of pleasure mixed with pain flushed my body.

"I'd totally forgotten all about these," I said slowly.

A thundering crash sounded from the front of the house. "Mimi!" I cried, jumping off the bed and racing through the hallway.

I found her in the kitchen, standing by the counter, the coffeepot shattered all around her on the floor.

"Don't move," I cautioned. Her feet were bare, and I feared the broken glass would shred them. Quickly, I gathered the broom and dustpan and swept up the debris.

"I don't know how it happened," she said with a whimper. Her eyes were clouded with confusion. "All of a sudden . . ." Mimi's voice trailed off as she swept a trembling hand over the mess at her feet.

"It's okay," I reassured her. "I'll have this cleaned up in a jiffy."

After I was sure I'd gathered every tiniest shard, I took her hand. "Why don't you take a nap until Zach gets home?"

Like a child, she let me lead her to bed. I tucked her in, then shut her bedroom door behind me. Dana stood in the hallway.

"She okay?" Dana whispered.

"Just a little shaken and tired. I hope she sleeps for a while—I have to pick up Zach. His driver's out today."

"You want me to stay here with her while you go? Or I could pick him up if you want."

"If you could get him, that'd be great," I said with a rush of gratitude. I felt a little guilty at my earlier irritation. So what if she'd crushed on Deacon in high school and had hit on him a couple of times? Probably half the girls at Enigma High had done the same. What mattered was that she was here now, offering to help when I needed it.

The cell phone vibrated in my back pocket, and I pulled it out.

A text from Tegan Blackwell. Maybe they had a lead on who'd broken into our house.

The blood drained from my face as I read her message asking if Deacon had ever broken his toe. The question could only mean one thing. I quickly texted her back about his old sports injury.

My ears filled with a rush as loud as the ocean, and I leaned my weight against the wall. Dana stepped to the other side of me and put her arm around my waist. The phone slipped through my numb fingers and crashed to the floor.

"What's wrong? What's happened?" Dana cried. "Here. Let's get you seated. Can you walk? I'll steady you."

I leaned against her, and we made slow, stumbling progress toward my room. One step in front of the other. There. And again and again. At last I flopped onto my bed.

"Would you like a glass of water?" Dana asked.

"No," I protested, taking deep breaths. "I'm okay."

"Who was that on the phone?"

"A sheriff's deputy."

Dana's face hovered next to mine, her skin pale beneath her freckles.

"She believes they've finally found Deacon," I explained.

Dana gasped, and her mouth hung open. "He's alive?"

"No, no. I mean . . . I think they've found his bones."

Dana sat beside me and squeezed my hand. "I'll get Zach," she said at last. "Will you be okay?"

"Sure," I answered woodenly. Dana gave my hand one last squeeze before leaving. The front door opened and slammed shut. Cars motored up and down the street; people called out to one another from afar. Normal, everyday sounds. I envied everyone to whom this was just another day, business as usual. I held the phone in my hand, staring at the blank screen. How long would it take before Tegan called back? It seemed to take forever, but at last Tegan's name flashed on my screen. Tegan identified herself and then hesitated. That silent pause told me everything.

"What's happened?" I asked flatly. "You found Deacon's body, didn't you?"

She confirmed it and a weighted silence fell between us before she spoke again.

"I'm sorry. From what you told me of his old sports injury, I feel confident we've at last discovered why he disappeared."

"Murder?"

"Most likely."

I tried to infuse my voice with a calm strength I was far from feeling. "Tell me everything."

"We received a call early this morning. A fisherman retrieved a skull on his line at Black Bottom Creek. A team of divers arrived shortly afterward."

Tegan again paused slightly, and I braced myself for the grisly details.

"They collected over a dozen bone fragments, one of which was a tarsal with a healed fracture in the right toe."

"Did all the bones belong to Deacon?" I asked quietly.

"No. We're awaiting confirmation that the remains also include Louis and Clotille."

Silence charged the phone connection.

"Go ahead. Tell me anything you can," I urged. "It actually helps."

"We expect dental records and other bone fragments will confirm the identity of Louis's and Clotille's remains."

Black Bottom Creek was less than five miles from their old home. All this time, they'd been so close by, lying at the bottom of the stygian waters.

"Wh-why the fragments?" I asked finally, my voice catching. "Do you think their limbs were severed prior to being dumped in the swamp, or do you think it's the work of alligators? Maybe even wild animals?"

"Could be any of those things," she answered. "We'll know more soon."

I was unable to speak past the lump lodged in my throat.

"That's really all I can say for now," Tegan said gently. "It will be on the news tonight, so I wanted to tell you first."

"Thank you," I managed to say past numb lips. I hung up and drifted from my bedroom, stopping along the way to check in on Mimi. She still slept. Her silver-white hair was so thin that the delicate pink skin of her scalp peeked through. Her mouth was parted; her chest slowly rose and fell with each breath. How delicate and fragile life seemed, as though she could easily slip from life to death, her heart worn out and ticking its final beat.

Unlike the violent and early deaths of Deacon and his parents. They'd been cheated out of years and years. Who had killed them? Why had they done it? But the questions came and went, my anger sparked and then was extinguished by a drowning grief. Tonight, at least, I mourned for what could have—should have—been.

Be careful what you wish for. Mimi's words whispered in my mind. All these years, I'd hoped and prayed their bodies would be discovered, their killers sent to prison, and the unfounded, unsavory rumors of their fleeing the country finally put to rest. But I'd been wrong. All of the above would provide me closure, but not comfort.

I returned to my room and picked up the photographs Dana had tucked in the yearbook, stared at Deacon grinning at the camera, an arm possessively slung over my shoulders. Through a film of tears, I couldn't help smiling as I remembered the moment. I set the photo aside and looked through the others. I frowned as I laid each one out on the bedspread. I could have sworn there were several more photos. Shifting back through the memory of our visit, I recalled seeing at least a couple of pictures where a group of us—Deacon, Dana, myself, and others—had sat together on the bleachers after the game, passing around a flask of whiskey.

Those photos were gone.

Chapter 18

TEGAN

The excitement of discovering the Cormier bones was tempered by my sympathy for Jori. But as sad as this day must be for her, I believed that finally finding answers and eventually getting justice for that family would be the best thing for Jori in the long run. When Oliver buzzed me into his office later that day, I'd already forgotten we were scheduled to meet the new narcotics officer. I hurried into his office just in time to be seated before Carter Holt arrived.

Disheveled, sporting a scraggly beard and mustache, an oversize army coat, scuffed boots, and a ratty T-shirt, he indeed appeared as if he'd seamlessly blend into the underbelly drug culture he'd been hired to infiltrate.

"Thanks for meeting with us this afternoon," Oliver said, motioning to the extra chair beside me.

It was 3:45 p.m., but Agent Holt looked like he'd just rolled out of bed, bleary eyed as though he'd been up all night.

"Next time let's make it later in the day, 'kay?" he grunted, dropping his ungainly, tall body into the chair. His legs sprawled in front of him in a manner that suggested irritation without being insubordinate. He frowned at me. "Who are you?" he demanded.

"Deputy Blackwell," I answered, matching his unfriendly t...

Holt had a surly attitude to match the grungy attire. Was th...
a for-real cop or a junkie who'd found a way to get high and get ...
for it?

I bit the inside of my mouth to keep from saying anything I...
regret. This was my first encounter with a narcotics agent. What did I
know of their protocol and methods? Oliver had reviewed Holt's work
record and was pleased with what he'd found.

"Whatcha got?" Oliver asked, getting right down to business. "Any
progress discovering who's distributing in town?"

"Absolutely. I'm the best at this work," Holt boasted. "I've been
meeting with your informant. Shouldn't take too long to bring down
this two-bit ring."

"Two bit or not, I thought Enigma was too small to have an organized operation," I said.

"I told you there'd be one," Oliver said. "If I didn't believe there
was, I wouldn't have bothered hiring an agent."

My face heated with embarrassment. Yeah, he'd told me that, but
I'd been skeptical. "Right," I muttered, averting my head and fiddling
with my cell phone. Damned if I'd say another word.

"Strange thing is, my leads indicate that the drug drop in Enigma
isn't coming from Mobile's port," Holt said.

My head jerked up. "What do you mean?" So much for keeping
my mouth shut. I'd never been one to refrain from asking questions.

Holt ignored me and kept his gaze focused on Oliver. "Enigma's
drug pipeline appears to be sourced from a minor distributor. Now,
when I say *minor*, keep in mind that it's still big money, more money
than any of us will ever earn in our lifetimes, but it's not a major operation with a platoon of boats. My guess is it's one or two people who
have a smaller boat delivering the merchandise directly in the bayou
backwaters."

...nd that way they avoid the larger, riskier Port of Mobile," Oliver
...

"What kinds of drugs?" I asked, tired of being ignored. "Because
.. the past couple of years, pot and meth were the drugs found on
...ost people here who were convicted of possession. Both of which,
unfortunately, can be homegrown."

"Cocaine and heroin use are still common," Holt said, with barely
a glance in my direction.

Oliver leaned back in his chair, stroking his chin. "Good thing
we have a strong informant, because our arrest records don't provide
you many leads. The few trafficking possession cases we've had weren't
because the arrestee had a large volume of drugs. But the fact they were
in possession within a few miles of a school zone automatically triggered
a stiffer trafficking penalty."

Holt shrugged. "Doesn't matter. I'm working my way closer to the
distributor. The last major trafficking bust was seven years ago, when
Dr. Russell Crosby was arrested for prescription fraud. Since then,
someone else has taken over delivery of heroin and synthetic, illegal
pain medications. And I'm going to find him—or her—or them."

I still didn't care for Holt's arrogance, but I had to admit he'd done
his research and wasn't lacking confidence in taking on the seamier side
of the bayou folk.

"What new leads have you got?" Oliver asked.

"I never reveal my sources," he answered smugly. "Last thing I need
is some overzealous cop homing in on one of my informers. Once trust
is blown, any leads will dry up fast." He ambled to his feet and ran a
hand through his unkempt hair. "This meeting's adjourned. Don't be
calling me in for any more either. Too risky. If I have something to
report, I'll get word to you."

Oliver's jaw worked, probably swallowing back an angry retort. But
the fact was, we needed Holt. And the man knew it.

Holt left the office, and neither of us spoke for a minute.

"Guy's quite a character," I said at last.

"That wasn't the word I had in mind."

"More like, *cocky son of a bitch*?" I suggested.

"Nailed it."

"Maybe he can cut through the enigma of Enigma's drug operation."

Oliver winced at my corny attempt to lighten the mood. "Don't ever quit your day job to strike out as a comedian."

"And miss all this fun? Wouldn't dream of it." I turned serious. "Who's the strong informant you mentioned?"

"Like Holt, I don't reveal sources. If it pans out, you'll discover their identity soon enough."

His phone rang, and I took it as my cue to leave. As he reached for it, I rose and headed for the door.

"Oliver speaking. Hey there. Whatcha got for me?" A fist banged on the desk. "Are you fucking kidding me?" he demanded.

I turned and faced him. Oliver waved me over to return to my seat.

"Email me the report. Thanks for the heads-up. I owe you one."

Oliver set his phone down, and I raised a brow expectantly.

"That woman you said Trahern spoke with last week—Grace Lee Fairhope?"

My heart dropped to my stomach. "What about her?"

"She's dead. Died of a heroin overdose last night. Her body was found by a neighbor early this morning."

"Do they think—"

"It's been ruled accidental. No sign of foul play, and nothing to indicate it might have been a suicide." He drummed his fingers against the battered surface of his desk. "Probably only a weird coincidence. She was a known addict."

"Who'd been clean for almost five months," I pointed out. "Jori Trahern said she seemed happy with sobriety and had moved on with her life."

"Could be Trahern stirred up the past and made her feel guilty about giving up her son. The reminder could have been doing a number on her mind, and she turned to drugs, her old friend, to cope."

"Maybe," I answered doubtfully. "Or maybe it wasn't a coincidence at all."

Chapter 19

JORI

I stared at the old photos, willing them to help me make sense of what had gone so horribly wrong. Some clue as to what was soon to befall us. We'd been so young, so carefree. What kind of evil had been lurking in the background of our lives?

The front door banged open and shut. I started, the photos in my hand dropping onto the bed. How long had I been sitting like this, lost in old memories?

Heavy footsteps stomped across the den.

"Eat!" Zach called out by way of greeting. Same thing he always said when he walked in the door from his day program. I smiled ruefully and headed out to meet him. You could always depend on Zach to bring you back to the present with his familiar routine.

Dana waved and gave me a snappy salute as I entered the living room. "Found and delivered," she announced. "Mission accomplished."

"I really appreciate this. Staff didn't give you a hard time, did they? I called and told them you were coming and had permission to pick him up."

"Nah." She waved off my concern. "I know Janelle, remember? She used to date my brother way back when."

"Right. I'd forgotten about that."

Janelle Evans, the day program director, had dated Dana's brother in high school. They'd been a steady item for nearly four years, and we all thought they'd get married and be together forever. Instead, they'd attended different colleges and had drifted apart almost immediately.

Dana gave me a searching look. "You holding up okay?"

"Eat!" Zach insisted, impatient with my chitchat.

I held my palms up in a whatcha-gonna-do gesture and rushed to the kitchen, Dana trailing behind me. "We'll talk in here. The Zach must be fed," I explained. "If not, he'll just keep yelling louder."

"I remember. Just like the old days."

"How was your day, Zach?"

"Mm," he answered noncommittally.

I got out his special green bowl and filled it with mint chocolate chip ice cream. No other flavor would do. Zach settled into his chair and pointed at the fridge. Dutifully, I retrieved the caramel syrup and set it on the table. Zach squirted a large dollop into the bowl and dived into his late-afternoon snack.

"If I ate like that every day, I'd be too huge to walk through the door," Dana said. "Mimi still asleep?"

"Yeah. I'll wake her shortly if she doesn't get up. Otherwise, she'll have a restless night."

"Y'all need anything from the store or whatever?"

I shook my head. "No, go on home."

Dana folded her arms and leaned against the counter. "Did you find out anything else about"—she cast a quick glance at Zach and then back to me—"you know?"

"It was confirmed," I said slowly.

One hand flew to her throat. "They found Deacon's bones!"

I shook my head in warning, not wanting Zach to pick up on the word *bones* and start repeating it. I cocked my head toward the den, and we left Zach in the kitchen.

"Where? Are they sure it's him?" Dana asked as soon as we were out of earshot.

"Black Bottom Creek. And yeah, pretty sure. His parents too. A fisherman got an unexpected surprise when he pulled up a human skull instead of a catfish."

Visualizing that scene made bile burn at the back of my throat.

Dana covered her face with her hands. "I'd hoped it was a mistake," she whimpered. "I wanted Deacon to still be alive. After all these years—stupid, I know."

She was hurting too.

"I wished the same thing," I whispered. Was it really better to know the truth? That his life had been gruesomely cut short? It might give me closure in the long term, but for now the wound was fresh and raw.

"Deacon was such a terrific guy," I continued. "I've never known anyone else like him."

Dana removed her hands from her face, and I was shocked at the wild fury and grief that savagely twisted her angular features. "There you go again," she spat. "Romanticizing Deacon. You never really knew him. Not like I did."

Not this again. "Maybe you should leave," I said stiffly.

"Leave? That's the most Jori thing ever."

I backed away from the venom in her eyes, but she wasn't finished.

"You always run," she continued, the green arrows in her voice buzzing about my ears. "Always turn a blind eye to anything that doesn't fit into the neat, perfect little world you make up in your head."

I'd had enough. "That's bullshit. Where the hell do you get this crap? *Perfect little world?*" I scoffed. "On what planet? I watched my mom suffer from brain cancer and now . . ." I swept my hand to encompass the house where I took care of Mimi and Zach. "And now this."

"Everyone's shocked you came back to the bayou. Your grandmother took care of your mother while you were all wrapped up playing girlfriend to your perfect boyfriend."

That stung. "You know nothing about me. Obviously you never did. I sure as hell didn't know the real you. Get out of our house."

Dana acted as though I hadn't just ordered her off my property.

"Maybe your Deacon wasn't such a swell guy. Ever think of that, Jori? We used to meet up at least once a week to smoke pot and drink."

Dana and Deacon? It couldn't be. He wouldn't.

"Liar," I said through clenched teeth, suppressing the urge to clamp my hands over my ears. None of this was true. Dana was only trying to hurt me.

"You were such a damn goody-goody. No one could possibly live up to your expectations. And look at you now." Her hot gaze swept over me in blazing scorn. "I bet you're single because you've romanticized Deacon as this perfect guy and no other man compares to him. Why would they even try?"

That zing hit home like a punch in the gut. Because maybe there was at least a small kernel of truth in her accusations. Is that why I never formed long-lasting relationships? Was I subconsciously comparing them to what I had with Deacon? It very well could be, and the truth left me breathless. But even if it were true, who needed a frenemy like Dana? I was over her.

I lifted my chin, walked to the front door, and held it open. "Don't ever come back," I said with as much dignity and calmness as I could muster.

She dug in her heels and opened her mouth to say more.

"Get out!" Zach said, rushing into the room. He tugged at Dana's arm. "Get out. Go home."

I laughed shakily and teared up at the unexpected sibling loyalty. "You heard my brother. Get out. Unless you want me to call the cops."

Dana's lips compressed into an angry white line, but she headed to the door. What else could she do?

"Don't expect any more help from me," she said with a hiss, stepping over the threshold.

"We don't need your help." I slammed the door shut and then leaned against it as adrenaline ebbed out of my body.

"What's all this racket?"

Mimi walked down the hallway, smoothing her hair back from her face. "Was that Dana you were arguing with?"

"Yeah. She's gone."

"*Gone*," Zach repeated with a happy grin.

Mimi pulled her robe closer and gave a disdainful sniff. "Never did like that girl."

Chapter 20

JORI

Grace Lee Fairhope was dead.

Tegan's unexpected phone call announcing the news came on top of the already upsetting news about the discovery of Deacon's bones and the argument with Dana. I shut off my phone, and a bone-chilling numbness settled over me. Tegan had insisted the death had been ruled an accidental drug overdose, but I couldn't shake the suspicion that an unknown menace was stalking my every move, destroying anyone I knew.

Had I driven Grace over some kind of mental ledge by reminding her of the baby she'd given up long ago? It was possible I'd stirred her curiosity about Jackson, and she'd discovered his murder.

"Bad news?" Mimi asked as soon as I hung up the phone, her eyes as sharp as ever.

"Deputy Blackwell called to tell me Grace Lee Fairhope died from a drug overdose last night." I watched Mimi closely for a sign of recognition at the name.

Her forehead scrunched. "Never heard of her."

"She's—she *was*—Jackson's biological mother."

"Jackson!" The sharp eyes narrowed on me accusingly. "Why are the cops calling you about that woman? She's no relation to the family."

Zach picked up on the anger in Mimi's voice. He turned away from the television, his gaze sliding back and forth between us, assessing the sudden tension in the air.

"I was curious about Jackson's parentage, so I went to talk with Grace."

Mimi scowled and raked her eyes over me. "So where's your badge? Since when did you become a detective?"

I couldn't explain my obsession to solve Deacon's murder since I didn't understand it myself. I shrugged. "I didn't see how it could do any harm."

"And now she's dead."

Mimi's words echoed my own misgivings and hit like an accusation. "It's not my fault," I protested defensively, trying to convince myself.

Mimi scraped a trembling hand across her face, then regarded me wearily. "When did you talk to her? Was it before you got that threatening note?"

"Yes," I admitted. "I went to Mobile."

"And everyone knows everyone else's business here in the bayou. Let this be a lesson to mind your own business."

Zach piped up his familiar refrain. "Mimi knows."

She smiled and patted his shoulder. "You tell her, Zach. Jori should listen to her old grandmother."

But I couldn't let it go.

The ripples of that fateful night Deacon disappeared had again been stirred, and they were as far reaching and devastating as ever. I'd always believed he'd been murdered. I felt trapped in the middle of a mystery that would forever consume me until I had the truth.

I strolled to my room and tried to think of another avenue to explore. My family was no help. Mimi refused to discuss Jackson. Aunt Tressie was lost in la-la land, remembering only the sweet boy Jackson had been before hitting his teenage years. And Uncle Buddy would only shake his head sadly whenever Jackson's name was mentioned. "Poor kid," he'd say, then immediately change the subject.

I did have another uncle—or at least he used to be when we were related by marriage. Aunt Tressie's ex-husband, Ardy Ensley. I had no memory of him, just old faded photographs of a man in the background of Jackson's numerous birthday pictures and other snapshots. No one ever brought up his name. I only knew it by point-blank asking Mimi the name of Aunt Tressie's ex. Mimi only ever referred to him as "that son of a bitch who skipped town." The only other piece of information I'd gleaned was when she'd once added, "Too bad Ardy isn't another hundred miles away from Enigma. Gulfport is too close."

Was it possible Ardy still lived in Gulfport? The town was only about an hour's drive from the bayou. His name was unusual; surely there couldn't be that many people named Ardy Ensley in Mississippi. On a whim, I entered his name in a search engine and came up with fewer than half a dozen hits, three of which were old obituaries. I read those first, but they were written long before my Ardy was even born. His was an old-fashioned southern name, years out of popular use. On the next-to-last lead, I hit gold. A Mr. Ardy Ensley of Gulfport owned a construction company that had recently completed a strip mall project in Harrison County.

Pretending to be an electrical subcontractor, I called and arranged a meeting with him to discuss a commercial building project. A mere two hours later, I strode into the office of Ensley Construction sporting an attitude of assertive confidence to mask my extreme nervousness.

What is the worst that could happen? I asked myself. If he got angry and tossed me out on my ear, so what? Nothing ventured, nothing gained. Maybe I'd at least garner a scrap of information that could prove useful to Tegan. Something that would make her want to officially interview Ensley for herself.

I sat at the conference table in the empty room while I waited for Ensley to show. He appeared to have done well for himself after leaving Bayou Enigma. The table was polished mahogany, the floor a plush carpet. On one wall, several mounted photographs featured a man I assumed must be Ardy Ensley. In them, he wore a hard hat and business suit, appearing at several groundbreaking sites with politicians, who also held shovels, decked in hard hats and suits. As if those men had ever done a day of manual labor in their lives.

My eyes caught sight of a credenza that held a few personal photographs, and I got up and walked over. There was a handsome silver-haired woman in pearls, Ardy holding a baby in a pink blanket, and a family photograph of Ardy with the same silver-haired woman and three adults who all bore the unmistakable stamp of *family* with the similar slope of their noses and large mouths full of shiny white teeth.

I lifted the group family photo and examined it closely. While my aunt had been left grieving after Jackson's death, slowly losing touch with reality, Ardy had evidently moved on with his life, creating a new family and business. By all appearances, a happier family and a more successful business than the one he'd abandoned in Enigma. Adding a final insult to injury, he'd skipped town with no advance notice, leaving behind three workers unpaid for their last two weeks of labor and a devastated, confused wife.

I reckoned I should be glad for Ardy that the tragedy hadn't wrecked his life like it had his ex-wife's. But all I could picture was Aunt Tressie sitting in her recliner at Magnolia Oaks, a ratty afghan wrapped over her thin legs, gazing forlornly out the room's small window with its view of the wild bayou wetlands.

"J. T. Jenkins?"

I jumped at the voice behind me and spun around, still clutching the photo.

I'd been expecting a big, burly man with eighteen-inch biceps and a tan, weathered face, but Ardy was nothing like that. At five feet eight inches, he was only an inch taller than me. A few wrinkles creased the sides of his eyes and forehead, but he appeared at least a decade younger than Aunt Tressie. His face and arms were lightly tanned, but the shade was uniform and subtle, likely the result of a self-tanning spray rather than hard labor in the sun. The man evidently took pride in his appearance—probably to please his second wife, I imagined, with a small pang of bitterness on my aunt's account.

He regarded me with a raised brow. Clearly, I hadn't been what he was expecting either. When I'd made the appointment, I'd lied about my name and used vague details about my nonexistent company so he couldn't check me out ahead of time.

I raised the photograph in my hand. "Your family?"

He smiled smoothly and slid into the seat at the head of the table, a predictable power move for potential business negotiations. "My wife, Lonnie, and our kids, David, Linda, and Beth. The beautiful baby in the other photo is my granddaughter, Tiffany."

"Good-looking bunch," I said, placing the picture back on the credenza and taking a seat on Ardy's right side.

"My pride and joy," he answered, flashing the familial grin that bared a mouthful of teeth. He folded his hands on the tabletop and waited expectantly. A gold wedding band gleamed on his left hand. So much for preliminary chitchat. The man was ready to get down to business.

Under the table, I dug my fingernails into my palms, the pain a distraction from my nervousness. It was showtime. I'd rehearsed my opening over and over on the drive to Gulfport.

"The initials *J. T.* stand for Jori Trahern," I began. His eyes remained blank and questioning. My name meant nothing to him. "I'm from Bayou Enigma."

That name he did recognize. His body jolted as though he'd been delivered an electric shock. "Jori Trahern," he said slowly. "Of course. You're Oatha Jean's granddaughter."

"And at one time your niece, though I was only two or three when you left."

Ardy's blue eyes grew cold and distant. "Why are you here?"

"Sorry for the deception," I said. "I couldn't get a meeting with you unless it was a business appointment, so . . ."

"What do you want with me?"

"To talk to you about your son. Jackson."

The man went pale beneath his tan. He rose on unsteady feet. "I've got nothing to say. You have no right lying your way in to see me and then dredging up the past." His voice turned hard; each syllable spewed at me like chunks of gravel. "Get out."

I stayed seated.

"Did you hear about the murder of Raymond Strickland?" I asked, hoping the news might pique his interest long enough for me to get in a few questions before he stormed away.

Ardy slowly sank back into his chair. "When?" he asked simply.

"A week ago. Shot in the back of the head, same as your son."

"Damn it." He scrubbed a hand over his face. "I saw the news on TV about the Cormier remains being found—it's made headlines all over—but this is the first I hear about the Strickland murder."

The brash businessman who'd walked in two minutes ago, ready to size up a new business proposal, was replaced by a shaken shell of a man.

"I'm surprised the sheriff's office never contacted you about Strickland."

Ardy grimaced. "No reason for them to—unless I was a suspect in the murder. I cut my ties with Bayou Enigma decades ago. How did Tressie take the news?"

"According to my grandmother, surprisingly well. Mimi told her in person what happened, but I'm not sure Aunt Tressie fully understood the news. She's . . . not doing great."

For the second time today, Ardy surprised me. If I'd been expecting a remorseful man, ashamed of his shabby treatment of his ex-wife during her time of need, I couldn't have been more mistaken.

He snorted. "Don't let the old gal fool you. She's doing better than anyone gives her credit for. Tressie has always been clever. She'll deliberately lead you down a twisted, merry path to suit her own needs."

"I'm not sure what you mean," I said slowly. "She's in her own little world. I don't know what happened when the two of you were married, of course, but these days she hardly even leaves the nursing home except to get her hair done once a month. Most of the time she's in a mental fog."

He threw his head back and laughed. "Mental fog? Tressie?"

I gaped at him, astounded at this reaction.

Ardy pulled himself together and regarded me with a frown. "I see she's really got you hoodwinked."

"I think you've let the acrimonious past cloud your judgment," I said at last. "Ever since I can remember, Aunt Tressie has been, you know, off. That's why she's living in the nursing home."

"She's in that damn place to bleed me dry. It costs me a pretty penny."

"Now I know you're lying," I snapped. "Uncle Buddy pays whatever her Medicare and SSI doesn't pick up."

"Who told you that? Your Uncle Buddy's a tight-fisted bastard who doesn't give a shit about his sister."

"That's not true. He's helped my family out for years."

Ardy shot me a sly look. "If he's helping out Oatha Jean, then it's because she's got something she's holding over that damn tightwad. Your grandmother always was a tough old broad."

I bristled at his characterization of Mimi. "She's strong. She's had to be. Life hasn't dealt her the best hand, you know."

Mimi was closemouthed about her past, but I knew she'd taken care of her husband the last few months of his life after he'd suffered a heart attack. After that, she'd dealt with her daughter's cancer and death, and then she'd shouldered caretaking responsibility for an intellectually challenged grandson. Yes, she was outspoken and rough around the edges. But if I could pin a damn medal of honor on the old gal, I would.

"Believe what you want." Ardy barked out a bitter laugh. "I don't give a damn what you or anyone else in that godforsaken bayou thinks of me. I have a new life."

"So I see. A new wife, new kids. Does that mean you don't ever think of your first son? Of the devastated wife you left behind?"

He banged a fist down hard on the table. "You think I've ever forgotten that miserable period of my life? Not a chance. I pay for it every damn day. Tressie makes sure of that."

"I find that hard to believe."

Ardy pulled a phone out of his back pocket and punched in a number. "Ella, bring me the Magnolia Oaks file." He laid the phone on the table and regarded me with hooded eyes. "You want proof? You'll get it."

This conversation wasn't going at all as anticipated, and I was determined to get it back on track. "Tell me about Jackson," I demanded. "No one ever wants to talk about him."

"Why?"

"Because I want to understand. I feel like if I know what he was really like, what happened to him before the murder, then maybe I can understand who killed Raymond Strickland and why they did it."

"What's it to you? You never knew Jackson or Strickland. You don't have a dog in this fight."

"Because I might be in danger too."

"How's that?"

"I've been warned not to go poking around in the past. So there's something there that someone wants to keep hidden."

"Then maybe you should back off." His voice held a quiet warning that sent chill bumps down my arms. We regarded one another in wary silence. Suspicion created a thick miasma, the room a pressure box of tension.

Was I face to face with the man who'd left me the threatening note pinned to a dead snake? Maybe Ardy was even a killer. He'd been fed up with Jackson's antics and killed him. Then years later, he killed Raymond Strickland.

But I needed a motive for why Ardy would kill Strickland. Ray's words about a business deal echoed in my brain. Had the ex-con been blackmailing Ardy Ensley?

A woman entered the room and silently handed a file to Ardy, casting me a curious glance through her bifocals.

"Thank you, Ella. That will be all. Close the door on your way out." Ardy opened the file and then nudged it toward me. "Take a look for yourself."

I glanced down at the spreadsheet and frowned. Then I went through the thick stack of papers that showed copies of cancelled checks and invoices from Magnolia Oaks. They went back several years.

"Why did you pay for her care if you hate her and think she's lying about her mental illness?"

Ardy took the file from me and pointed at the spreadsheet. "If you'll notice, I went three months in 2014 not paying her bills."

I stared at the figures and nodded. "Okay."

Ardy removed a manila envelope from the file, extracted a thick stack of papers, and placed it in front of me. I stared uncomprehendingly at the phone log record. "What's this?"

"During those three months I didn't pay her bills? She called every day, several times a day, to harass either me or my wife. When that didn't work, she resorted to calling my kids."

Hot damn. Tressie? I couldn't picture her having either the malevolence or presence of mind to mount a methodical campaign of vindictiveness against her ex. Perhaps she'd been pleading with him to return home or . . .

"I have written transcripts of every call," he said, as though reading my mind. He indexed through the papers and rapped his knuckles on the table. "They start here on this page."

Obediently, I began reading.

You bastard. You left me when I needed you most. How can you just forget all about our son? Our life together? You have to pay. I'll never let you forget. I don't care if you live to have a dozen kids. You belong to me and Jackson. Forever.

Every phone transcript was some variation of the same message. Particularly heinous were the calls to Ardy's children telling them that their father could never love them like he had his first child and all they would ever be in his eyes were inferior replacements.

"I-I can't believe it," I said at last. "This doesn't sound like Aunt Tressie at all."

"Oh, it's her all right. Believe me—she's very careful how she portrays herself to the world. You don't know the real woman behind the smiles and the vague, confused facade she likes to present. Inside, she's the devil."

"Did you ever speak to a lawyer about filing a harassment lawsuit against her?"

"Of course. That's why I kept the transcripts. But in the end, it costs less to meet her blackmail demands than get embroiled in court battles. Besides, I don't want to put my family through any more of her bullshit."

"It's unreal. I still can't believe she'd say these terrible things. Could someone else have used her phone without her knowledge?"

"I know her voice."

Of course he'd know the voice of his own ex-wife. I sat back, too stunned to speak. Finally, I gathered myself together. "No wonder you left town in the middle of the night. I don't know how you lived with her as long as you did."

"You become numb. Immune. I didn't even realize how miserable I was until I left and started my life over."

I nodded and cleared my throat. "I'm sorry. I don't mean to bring you more pain. But it would help me a lot if you could talk about Jackson. No one else seems willing. There's been a copycat murder and . . ." I let my voice trail off. "And I'm trying to stay safe."

No need to fill him in on my suspicions that both murders were related to what happened with Deacon. I'd keep that to myself. For all I knew, Ardy might hide a secret, vicious side that was more than a match for Aunt Tressie. Suspicious facts raced through my mind: he'd been known to have rows with his son; he might have killed Strickland in revenge; he might be the one threatening me because I asked too many questions about the past and the private adoption. Aunt Tressie acted vague and confused about the arrangement, but surely Ardy knew what he was getting into.

Ardy stretched and gazed out the office window, his face heavy with sadness. "Jackson was a sweet kid. Or so we thought at first. Tressie and I adored the boy. But he'd started doing bad things by the time he entered elementary school. It got progressively worse. We couldn't have pets because Jackson was cruel to animals. He had fights with other kids. No one wanted to be his friend. Once he started junior high, we lost him for good. He was rebellious, confrontational; his grades plummeted so bad I was afraid he'd flunk out his junior year. We tried to set curfews, but he came and went as he pleased, no matter what kind of discipline we tried to enforce. We pleaded with him and even tried to bribe him to do better, but nothing worked. I finally reached the end of my rope with Jackson and enrolled him in a military school. When I demanded that he pack his bags, we had it out."

He stopped talking and swallowed hard.

"What happened?" I asked softly.

"Jackson said he just wanted to drop out of high school and get a job. I pointed out he couldn't get a decent job without at least a high school diploma. He insisted that he didn't need to graduate, that he had ways of making good money. I told him that was impossible, that he had no work ethic or ambition. My son only laughed at me. 'Think I want to work a nine-to-five job? That's for losers like you,' he'd countered."

Ardy briefly shut his eyes, then opened them again. "It got ugly. Blows were exchanged," Ardy admitted. "I grabbed his arm, determined to drag him to the car and return later for his bags of clothing. Jackson hit me in the stomach." Ardy's face twisted in pain. "At that point, I lost it. We scuffled and began throwing punches, crashing through the house with Tressie screaming at us to stop. I threatened Jackson that I'd have him arrested for assault, and he threatened to have me arrested for child abuse."

"Sounds horrible," I offered. "But you were the adult. You should have kept your temper."

"You think I don't know that? You think a day goes by that I don't remember our fight?"

The anguish in his voice shamed me. What was past was past. I had no right to judge.

He pulled himself together with an effort. "Jackson threatened to run away if I sent him to military school, and he meant it. I realized there was nothing more I could do. He had no respect or love for me. I'd tried showing love, being understanding, talking to him, sending him to counselors, enforcing tough love—not a damn thing worked. It didn't help that Tressie always took his side and made excuses for his behavior. So I threw up my hands and quit trying."

"How old was Jackson when this happened?"

"Sixteen. He died one week later."

Had Jackson's rebellion led Ardy to kill his own son? To finally end the pain and struggle?

Ardy frowned and shook his head. "I know what you're thinking. That I had a motive to want my son dead."

I didn't confirm or deny his statement.

"I didn't do it." Ardy's voice finally broke, and he drew a deep breath before continuing. "I loved Jackson, no matter how bad he treated me. I tried to blame his bad behavior on the drugs, but he'd been trouble since he was a little kid."

"How old was he when y'all adopted him?"

"Less than a month old." His eyes filmed over. "Cute little thing with a mop of dark hair and dark-blue eyes."

"I understand it was a private adoption?"

The unshed tears quickly dried. "Said who?" Ardy asked sharply.

"I heard it mentioned once. And I saw the birth certificate with the birth mother listed. Tressie still has it."

"Tressie was infertile from severe endometriosis. Adoption was our only option for children."

"Why did you go the private route?"

"Because she was adamant that she wanted a baby and wasn't willing to wait for years."

"How much did it cost you?"

"Fifty grand." He stood, collecting his file and laptop. "If that's all?"

"Who made the arrangements?"

"I don't remember. It was a long time ago. Now if you'll excuse me, I need to get back to work."

He was lying. But why? I didn't budge from my chair. "You keep excellent records. I'm sure you must remember who handled the adoption or have paperwork with that information."

"I told you I didn't." Ardy shoved off toward the door, turning his back to me.

"What's your hurry?" I asked. "What are you so afraid of?"

"Nothing. Plenty of people go the private route for adoption."

"Did you know that Jackson's mother recently died of a drug overdose?"

Ardy stilled, then slowly faced me. "You're full of all kinds of shocking updates from Enigma," he said, frowning. "All I want to do is forget that place and everyone in it."

"You can't run away from the past or ignore it," I said. "It always comes back to bite you in the ass." Lord knows I'd tried to do much the same as Ardy. In my case, it was to block out the sinister mystery of Deacon's disappearance.

"It's best to leave some things buried," Ardy grated out. "Digging it up can be dangerous."

I rose from the chair. "Is that a threat?"

"A warning," he countered. "Stay the hell out of it. It's none of your damn business. No good can come from poking your nose around what happened decades ago."

"So I should let dead dogs lie?"

"Exactly." He regarded me evenly, as though those particular words held no special significance to him. Ardy nodded his head once, then left me alone in the room.

I took my leave as well and walked to the parking lot. I'd learned nothing new about the adoption, the whole reason I'd come, but I couldn't count the trip as a total failure either. My eyes had been opened about Aunt Tressie, and I could never again look into her faded, confused eyes without remembering her vile threats to Ardy and his family.

As I got in my car, I glanced at the front office window of Enoley Construction and noticed the blinds twitch to one side. Ardy stood in the sliver of the opening, watching me take my leave. Despite his protestations to the contrary, the man was scared of something. Or somebody.

Or it could be he was afraid of a murderous past catching up to him at last.

Chapter 21

TEGAN

I checked the notes on my cell phone for the name Jori had provided me earlier when I'd questioned her about the Cormier family. *Cash Johnson.* Hunters roaming the woods weren't that unusual in Enigma, but his close proximity to the Cormier's home with a weapon and the fact that he'd made Jori uncomfortable were enough to raise a red flag in my mind. Might as well run him through our database and see if he had any prior arrests or convictions. I entered his name and checked my email while awaiting the results.

I glanced down the email subject lines, skimming past the majority of them, which were administrative matters. But one subject line grabbed my attention—*Sandy Springfield, Family Social Services re: Ensley adoption.*

My heart leaped with excitement that Ms. Springfield had so quickly answered my inquiry on the adoption. I opened the email and read the short message. There were no official, legal adoption papers on Jackson Ensley; at least there were none on record in the state of Alabama. I tapped my index finger against my lip. Perhaps it had been an out-of-state adoption? I'd have to pursue that further.

Sighing, I stretched back in my chair, enjoying the rare quiet of the office. I had it all to myself this early in the morning. I'd awakened early and decided to come on in to work and get a head start on the day. I left my desk to make a cup of coffee and returned a minute later. The information I'd sought on Johnson was up and running on my monitor. Scrolling through, I sipped my drink, only to inhale sharply and swallow burning-hot liquid.

June 12, 2013, Johnson arrested for voyeurism.

That was certainly an unexpected development. All the times Jori had run into Johnson as she'd left her boyfriend, had this man been trying to watch them together? I kept scrolling but found no conviction and no other arrests. This didn't play into my theory of a drug connection between the Cormier and Strickland murders, but I wouldn't be satisfied until I'd ruled out every other possible clue that came my way. After all, the leads were few and far between.

I walked downstairs to the basement, even though I wasn't certain Ginger would be in this early. But sure enough, she sat at her desk munching on a sugar-laden breakfast.

She laid her doughnut on the messy desk and wiped her hands on a greasy napkin when she spotted me.

"Back again?" she asked. "Don't tell me—you've already solved the Cormier murders and are looking for more cold cases."

Ginger cackled at her own wisecrack, and the noise grated against my ears. Instead of responding, I handed her a slip of paper with a case number written on it. "I need the notes from this complaint."

With annoying, deliberate slowness, she donned her eyeglasses and finally read the note. "June 12, 2013." She rolled her eyes. "You got nothing better to do than look at these old files? Isn't Enigma, like, supposed to be in the midst of a crime wave?"

"Yes. So I'm in a bit of a hurry. If you could be so kind?" My tone teetered between sarcasm and sweetness, confusing Ginger.

She narrowed her eyes and lowered her chin. "Are you messing with me?"

"Wouldn't dream of it."

"Humph." Her chubby fingers tapped the keyboard. "There it is." She nodded her head at the clipboard atop a stack of papers. "Sign your name, then write the date and time of your request. I'll email you the scanned notes."

"Thanks, Ginger. You're a peach."

She snatched her glasses off and scowled. "Now I know you're insulting me."

"Yeah. Calling you a *peach* really tipped my hand." I waved at her and smirked. "I'll let you get back to your doughnut."

I strolled back to my office, happy I still had the place all to myself. I opened the notes and began reading, my early-morning calm dissolving as I read the case of a victimized teenage girl. I debated the wisdom of going to Johnson's residence alone. I couldn't see the harm in making a general check. If the interview got weird or confrontational, I'd return to the office and have Oliver accompany me for further questioning. Quickly, I left the office and got in my cruiser for the short ride to Johnson's cabin.

Less than ten minutes later, the impressive Bayou Enigma Outdoor Expeditions headquarters shone like a jewel in the swamp as I slowed my patrol car and admired the place. Plate glass windows stretched floor to ceiling on the front of the structure. Back in the day, the Cormiers' house had sparkled like a palace in this small bayou of fishermen, and the Cormiers were its first and only royalty. I was old enough to remember when it was first being built. My family and others would drive by the site almost daily to glimpse the massive construction and ooh and aah over the size and quality of materials. Mom used to sigh enviously and mutter, "I bet them spoiled rich folk don't even appreciate this place."

I'd recognized the sour grapes note in her voice and others'. Envy had led to mistrust before the family had even moved in. To add fuel to the fire, they'd eschewed the bayou's local building company and hired a Mobile County construction team for all the work. Even more affronting, when the Cormiers finally hired a local landscaper for maintenance work on the grounds and a couple of women as housekeepers, the pay they offered was slightly lower than the standard wages offered in Enigma for the same types of services.

Resentment grew. It didn't help that Louis and Clotille were unlike most of the townsfolk. They were instantly pegged as politically liberal, as well as artsy and pretentious. No matter their wealth, they were considered outsiders. *Not one of us,* people would sniff.

Whether or not the Cormiers cared about the locals' assessment was debatable. Supposedly, they were in love with the view of the gulf the house provided, and Louis enjoyed fishing and hunting in his limited spare time.

The campgrounds in back of the headquarters featured a dozen rustic cabins that were kept fully occupied during hunting season. I continued on, driving another half a mile down the dusty road 'round back, searching for Cash Johnson's residence.

When the road dead-ended into swamp water, I realized I'd driven straight past the place. I turned the car around on the narrow road and then slowly cruised it again. This time I found it, a small nondescript cabin so nestled against a tree line of pine and cypress that it almost blended seamlessly into the woods. There was no driveway or even a mailbox on the side of the road to make it easier to locate.

I called in my location to the dispatcher and approached the cabin with a can of Mace in my palm, my trigger finger on the nozzle, at the ready. Thankfully, I was relieved not to hear the sound of loose dogs barking. I wouldn't admit it to anyone, least of all my fellow officers, but I had a real fear of stray dogs, which was odd since I'd never had a bad encounter with one. But I'd almost rather face an armed assailant than a wild bayou beast.

An old Buick was parked at the side of the house, and I hoped that meant Johnson was home. I'd rather question him here than at his place of employment.

Before I could knock on the door, it was opened by an older man with a short, wiry stature. Physically, there was certainly nothing intimidating about his looks. My grandma could probably beat him in a fight.

"Mr. Cash Johnson?" I asked, pasting on a bright smile. Last thing I wanted was for him to report me to Oliver for harassment.

"Yes?" His voice was so soft it barely registered over the fresh morning breeze.

"I'm Deputy Blackwell with the Erie County Sheriff's Office." I kept my smile firmly in place. Nothing to fear from me, just a casual-chat kind of smile. "I'd like a minute of your time, sir."

He didn't even ask why. Just stood there, hands in the pockets of his plaid shorts, and regarded me impassively with flat eyes, as though he wasn't even curious about my reasons. It was disconcerting.

"We're reinvestigating the Cormier case. As their nearest neighbor, I wondered if you might have any information on regular visitors at the house—that sort of thing."

He spat at the ground, only a foot from my polished black uniform shoes. "Told the cops then that I didn't know nothin' about them fancy-ass folks. Ain't nothin' changed over the years neither."

"Is that so?" I acted puzzled as I withdrew a notepad from my shirt pocket and pretended to scan notes. "Are you saying that you never observed anyone coming and going on the grounds? Maybe even at odd hours during the day or night?"

"Ain't none of my business what people might have come and gone."

"Surely you'd let us know if you saw something unusual around the time of their disappearance, something that might give us a lead to solve the murders."

He deliberately hesitated a moment before answering. "Yeah. Right."

"Excellent. I'm glad to hear it. So perhaps you'd like to reconsider your answer. Did you ever observe anyone sneak onto the Cormier property?"

"Maybe."

I stared him down. Johnson sighed. "Used to sometimes spot a teenager sneaking 'round to the smokehouse to meet up with her boyfriend."

"Her name?"

He gave another exasperated sigh. "Jori Trahern. There—you happy now? I work for her uncle and don't want no grief. It's the best job I ever had."

"What is it that you do around here?"

"I manage the campgrounds, plus I'm over all the tour guides during the busy season."

"How long you been doing this work?"

"Started working for Buddy almost twenty years ago. Got promoted a few years in, seeing as how I'm such a stable employee and live so close. It's been a convenient arrangement for both of us."

"I can see why you don't want to rock the boat. So Jori would meet up with Deacon Cormier in the smokehouse some evenings?"

"Yeah."

"How often?"

He snorted. "Several times a week."

"And how did you happen to observe these meetings?" I gestured to my left. "That old smokehouse is far enough away from your place that you can't see it from here."

His face flushed, and he looked truly uncomfortable for the first time. "I'm a hunter. I'm up early in the mornings roaming the woods."

"Did you ever speak to Jori Trahern or Deacon Cormier when you came upon them?"

"Nope. I reckon if they was sneaking around, they weren't in the mood to chitchat with an adult."

"Did you ever tell either of their parents that these two were rendezvousing in the woods?"

"Weren't my business. They weren't my kids."

"So you didn't think you had any responsibility as an adult to speak to their parents?"

"Hell, no. Nobody likes the messenger of bad news. Besides, they were just being normal kids. Wasn't like I was no saint at their age."

"What exactly did you see in those early mornings?"

"Seen them both leaving the smokehouse and head their separate ways."

"Did you see them kiss?"

He shoved his hands in his pockets and looked over my shoulder, as though unwilling to look me in the eye. "I guess. A time or two," he admitted reluctantly.

I took a deep breath, deciding to take the plunge. "Is that why you were really in the woods most mornings, Mr. Johnson?" I asked softly. "To try and catch them together?"

Johnson's eyes snapped back to me. If he'd been unusually passive earlier, now he was riled, his sense of preservation on the alert. "What's that supposed to mean?"

"It's a simple question."

"Course not," he denied at once.

I didn't believe him for a second. "You sure about that?"

His jaw set in a hard line. "No. I done told you everything. Ain't nothing else to tell."

"So you say."

His gray eyes pierced me with sudden suspicion and a hint of fear. "Why? Did she tell you I did? If so, she's a damn liar."

"Ms. Trahern has told me nothing," I lied.

"You got any more questions?" he asked stiffly. "I got work to do."

I stuffed my phone back in my pocket and gave him a wide grin. "That's all I've got for now, Mr. Johnson. Let's stay in touch, shall we?"

The door slammed shut as I walked back to my vehicle.

———

I made the short drive back to the office, which was now bustling with employees. Straightaway, I strode to Oliver's office, where I found him at his desk, intently reading his computer monitor. "What's up?" he asked, his gaze still on the screen.

"Thought you might be interested in some information I dug up on this guy." I held up a sheet of paper I'd copied from the electronic file Ginger sent. "He works at Enigma Outdoor Expeditions. Their head-quarters is the old Cormier house. Cash Johnson lives within a half mile of it. In fact, he lived there at the time of the Cormier disappearances."

That got Oliver's attention. He pushed the monitor to the side, faced me, and then held out a hand for the paper. "Whatcha got?"

"Guy's a pervert. A Peeping Tom." I handed him the old incident report. "I had a talk with him this morning."

"So? He works there, right?"

"Yes. But Jori Trahern used to run into him late at night or just before dawn when she was sneaking out to meet Deacon Cormier. He always carried a gun, claiming to be out hunting. She thought it odd enough to mention it to me. I checked; he's been reported before. Voyeurism."

A teenage girl had been using the camp shower facilities when she spotted a man watching her. He'd entered the open doorway and had stood there staring. When she screamed, he'd run off—but unfortunately for Johnson, he'd run smack dab into the girl's father.

"One time." Oliver scanned the report. "The charges were eventually dropped."

"I'd be willing to bet they were only dropped because the young girl and her family didn't want the trauma and attention of a trial."

"Unfortunately, that's entirely possible." Oliver handed me back the report. "But I don't see the connection. It's a big leap from voyeurism to murder."

"He's a creep. And one who carries around a gun. Maybe he got caught again being where he shouldn't. He could have been watching Clotille Cormier, and her husband caught the guy red-handed and went ballistic. There was an argument, and in the heat of the moment, Johnson shot the husband and then had to kill the rest of the family for protection."

"Last time we talked, you were sure that the Strickland and Cormier cases were connected. Have you changed your mind?"

"I don't know," I admitted. "But I thought this was worth checking out."

"Maybe. Guess we can't rule out a scenario like that, no matter how far fetched." Despite his dismissive comment, Oliver rose from his seat and grabbed his car keys. "But on a case as dead and cold as this one, it's worth pursuing. Besides, we have time. I've got Mullins and Sinclair doing more legwork on the Strickland murder. They're interviewing the men from the bar again. Figured Tommy Sims and his gang could be leaned on a little harder. Keep the pressure on them."

We'd interviewed them all separately and tried to break them, but each held firm to their story that after leaving the Pavilion the night Strickland was murdered, they'd all gone over to Eddie's place and crashed for most of the rest of the evening.

I tended to believe they were all telling the truth. None of them were smart enough or possessed enough self-discipline to stick to a lie. The men had been buddies a long time, but when push came to shove, any of them would sell out the other for a deal if faced with a murder charge.

Pride had me glowing inside as we headed to the parking lot. It would be amazing to find justice for the Cormiers after all this time, not to mention a real feather in my cap to have helped break a major case. I pictured Ginger's sour, smug face transform to an expression of chagrin when I informed her that I'd been the one to solve the case. That would take the starch out of her sails.

"We'll talk to his boss first. Even I know that Samuel 'Buddy' Munford is a big shot around Enigma. We don't want to unnecessarily rustle feathers."

"Exactly. He's a county commissioner and good friends with Mayor Rembert."

"I'm already on thin ice with the mayor going over his head to hire Carter Holt."

"Have you heard from Holt in the last couple days?"

"He's exploring the possibility of Sims, Yaeger, Booker, and Knight being involved in drug trafficking. So far, all he's discovered is that all four smoke pot. But at least he's worked his way into their group. If they're involved in selling the strong stuff, he'll sniff it out."

"Or if we're lucky they'll all get high together and someone in the group will confess to murder."

"So far they've all hung together tight," he said as we both climbed into the vehicle and buckled our seat belts.

"Do you still feel confident that Strickland's and Ensley's murders were both drug related?" I asked.

"It's the only common thread between them. At least, that's all we know of so far."

I wasn't convinced but realized we had to pursue any path that presented itself.

"Hmm." Oliver's noncommittal tone told me he wasn't nearly as interested in solving the old Cormier case as that of the most recent homicide. We were only interviewing Buddy Munford because we were temporarily at a standstill with the current case.

Oliver switched on the air-conditioning. April in the bayou was sometimes surprisingly chilly, but today the temperatures had hiked. A prelude to the steamy summer season around the corner.

We arrived at Munford's business headquarters in minutes. Before we got out of the car, Oliver cautioned me to let him take the lead in the questioning. "Don't want him complaining to the mayor that we harassed him or insinuated he or one of his employees is in any way a suspect in the Cormier murders."

"Got it." We walked up the path, and I hoped Buddy was there and would let us inside. As much as I'd observed the house from the outside and watched it being built, I'd never seen the interior. Gravel crunched beneath our feet.

"It'll be interesting to hear why he kept Johnson on after that complaint was filed," I said.

"Could be Munford believes his partner wasn't guilty of any wrongdoing. That it was a case of him being in the wrong place at the wrong time."

"Right," I scoffed. "Like there's ever a good time for a man to go inside a woman's public bathroom."

"Keep an open mind," he said mildly as we climbed the porch steps.

I mulled over my boss's gentle warning. Had my past experience with Ensley that horrid night forever tainted my sense of fairness when it came to sex crimes? My track record with men was certainly not good. I'd become a promiscuous teenager, and my marriage to the twins' father hadn't even lasted a month past their second birthdays. None of my romantic relationships had ever lasted. Although I never voiced my suspicion of their love and commitment to me, I could never fully trust a man, and on some deep level they must have picked up on that. Eventually, I simply gave up on relationships, and my life became easier—even if a bit dull. But I never looked back on my decision. Give me peace over drama any day.

Two large hounds lay on the porch, and my right hand automatically reached into my pants pocket for the Mace can. They arose from their comfy pet beds, barking a friendly greeting, and walked to us, heads down and tails wagging. I removed my hand from my pocket and lowered to a knee, one hand extended. They sniffed and then rubbed against me as I petted their heads.

The screen door creaked open, and Buddy Munford filled the open doorway. "I see my guard dogs gave you a warm welcome."

Oliver smiled and extended his hand. "Lieutenant Oliver. Pleasure to meet you."

Munford shook his hand and turned to me, arm extended.

"Deputy Blackwell," I said, shaking his hand.

"Y'all come on in."

So far he'd displayed no surprise or curiosity as to why a couple of sheriff's deputies had arrived at his front door. Johnson must have tipped him off we were asking questions.

The interior was as impressive as the outer facade. Despite the enormous square footage, the living area managed a warm, cozy vibe with its stone fireplace and gleaming oak floors. Leather sofas and chairs were arranged in intimate groupings. An abundance of sheepskin throws and knitted pillows were scattered over much of the seating. Glowing lanterns stationed at every table added to the hospitable atmosphere. Large-antlered deer heads and bass fish were mounted on the walls along with photographs of grinning guests proudly displaying their kill.

Munford led us to a seating arrangement and indicated for us to sit down. I sank into a recliner, my fingers skimming over the rich, smooth leather of its arm. I could envision the adventure-enthusiast guests at night, sipping whiskey from cut crystal tumblers and possibly smoking expensive cigars as they swapped stories about their day's adventures.

"Johnson told me you paid a visit this morning," Munford said, getting right down to business and confirming my earlier suspicion. "I expect you have a couple questions for me on that."

Unlike Johnson and many other people we questioned in crime investigations, his tone was inviting rather than hostile. He sat leaning toward us, elbows resting on his knees and palms open, his expression one of candor. Frankly, it was refreshing.

Since I was the one who'd questioned his employee, I opened the discussion. "I spoke to Johnson. Quite routine, given the proximity of his cabin to this place at the time the Cormiers lived here. I asked him if he'd ever observed any unusual comings and goings back then, especially any that occurred at odd times. He told me he had not. Which I happen to know is . . ." It was on the tip of my tongue to say *a lie*, but I remembered we were supposed to be respectful of his political connections. "Untrue," I concluded, opting for the less stark word.

Munford cocked his head to the side. "Why do you think he was lying?"

"Because I've interviewed a credible witness who's told me the opposite. It made me curious that your employee lied . . . um, wasn't honest, that is . . . so I checked into his background and came across the voyeurism complaint."

"First of all, Cash Johnson is my partner, not an employee. He became an investor years ago. Now, back to the matter at hand. Could be your supposedly credible witness is the liar, or it could be that Johnson doesn't remember the alleged prior encounter the witness referred to."

He seemed hung up on disputing my witness's claim instead of addressing the filed complaint. I guess that was understandable. He wanted to cast doubt on my witness to distract from Johnson's actions.

"What we're trying to establish is whether your partner had, or once had, a compulsion to watch women," Oliver explained, smoothly glossing over the issue of who'd been the one lying to me. "If so, it's possible that he'd been caught spying on Mrs. Cormier, and this might have led to the murders."

Munford straightened until his back brushed against the chair. His hands rested on his thighs, his mouth pursed in a stubborn line. "I've known Cash for years. He's no murderer."

"You understand we have to pursue all possible leads," Oliver said, shrugging one shoulder.

Munford unthawed slightly. "Of course. So how can I help you today?"

"Fill me in on what happened back in 2013. I'd rather hear it from you than call the victim and her family and dredge up the past. But if I have to, I will."

"The girl was showering one evening and claimed she caught Cash in the doorway, watching her."

My fingernails dug into the buttery leather of the recliner arm. His use of the word *claimed* galled me. "What?" I asked sharply. "Are you saying you don't believe her?"

"I didn't say she lied," he protested, thrusting his hands in the air, palms up.

"Good. Because I see no reason why a fourteen-year-old girl would make up a story like that."

An uncomfortable silence settled in the spaces between us, charged with the weight of unspoken thoughts.

"Did you take any action against Johnson in light of the complaint?" Oliver asked at last.

"I spoke to him, and he assured me that he'd gone into the facility for routine cleaning and maintenance."

I couldn't stay silent. "Routine cleaning?" I scoffed.

Oliver shot me a warning glance, but Munford ignored me and continued his story.

"Cash said she screamed when she saw him, and he immediately apologized and ran outside."

"Have there been any other incidents over the years?" Oliver asked.

"Not a one. After this happened, I sat Cash down and had a long talk with him. He convinced me it was all a misunderstanding. I warned him that if I ever received another complaint, he was out of a job."

"So you're telling us that if we call the family who filed the complaint, they'll tell us that they willingly dropped charges because they didn't want to be embroiled in a legal battle without solid proof of the sex crime?"

"That and the fact that I paid them a small amount of money," he conceded.

There. What I'd suspected all along. "Why would you pay them if you didn't believe anything happened?"

"For the misunderstanding. I didn't want them bad-mouthing our company to potential customers."

"How much?" I asked.

"I'm afraid I can't tell you," he said, as though he were truly sorry he couldn't cooperate more fully. "All the details are part of the civil nondisclosure agreement."

Frustration ripped through me along with sharp disappointment. Even if I called the family in question, they could tell me nothing without violating the terms of the settlement.

"I see," Oliver said. "This angle appears to be a dead end. While we're here, though, is there anything you can tell us about the Cormiers that could help us in our investigation? Did you know them personally?"

"Oh, sure, I knew them. Louis more so than his wife and son. He occasionally did legal work for the county commission." Buddy shook his head. "I felt terrible when I heard the news about their remains being uncovered. Damn shame. Especially about the boy dying so young. Had to be the work of professionals to have wiped them all out and then hid the evidence for so long. I hope you find those responsible and make them pay for what they did."

Oliver nodded as he rose to his feet. I followed suit, trying to shake off my frustration.

"Thank you for your time," Oliver said. "We know you're a busy man."

"Anytime I can help, you just let me know," Buddy said, guiding us to the door.

I stepped outside, keeping silent until Oliver and I were ensconced in our vehicle. Oliver started the car and glanced at me.

"Don't take it so hard," he said, swinging the car around the curved driveway and onto the road. "It was worth pursuing. You never know when you might talk to the right person and shake things up. Whoever the killer is might get word we're asking questions and get very nervous."

"And make a stupid mistake? If it's organized crime we're dealing with, I don't think that's likely."

"To me, the mob theory is far fetched," Oliver admitted. "If it had just been Louis Cormier, then yeah, I'd buy it. But the mother and teenage kid? A hit man would have planned a killing so well there would be no need to cover accidental witnesses."

"So it might have been the work of an amateur who screwed up and then had to kill the others to cover up his mistake?"

"If I had to guess, then yes, I'd say so. Look, Tegan. Don't get your hopes up about solving the Cormier case. We'll do our best, but the crime's so old it's likely we'll never discover the identity of the killer or killers."

I said nothing, gazing out the window at the thick tangle of woods on either side of the road. Bayou Enigma was well named—ancient and full of secrets and mysteries. I wondered what stories the old oaks, black-crowned night herons, and stagnant waters teeming with alligators might tell us if they could speak.

Chapter 22

JORI

It was too quiet. *Way* too quiet.

I stopped pulling clothes out of the washing machine and listened, waiting to hear voices or movement, but there was only the low drone of muted plum notes from the television in the den. My ears tingled with unease. I set the damp clothes on top of the washer and checked my cell phone: 4:12 p.m. Where had the time gone? I could have sworn it had only been ten minutes ago that I'd heard a vehicle in the driveway, then the opening and closing of the screen door and a low murmur of voices—Zach returning home from his day program.

But Zach always arrived home between 3:30 and 3:45 p.m. There should be sounds of life from the den or kitchen. Quickly, I stuffed the last load of laundry in the dryer. I'd been pondering the Cormier and Strickland murders as I'd cleaned, absorbed in reviewing everything I knew about the cases. Mimi had promised she'd take care of Zach when he got home, and so I'd allowed myself to focus on the murders instead of caretaking. I should have known better.

Before heading down the hallway, I did a quick check of the bathroom—unoccupied—and then Mimi's and Zach's bedrooms. Both were empty, the perfectly made beds a disturbing omen.

In the den, I found Mimi sound asleep on the sofa, her afternoon show unwatched. Should have known better than to trust her to take care of Zach. A bolt of resentment flashed through my mind that I quickly stifled. Mimi was old and ailing. She and Zach were my responsibility now.

I headed to the kitchen, figuring Zach had fixed his own afternoon snack and would be happily sitting at the table scarfing down his usual treat of peanut butter sandwiches and mint chocolate chip ice cream. But the table was empty and its surface bare and spotless. A quick glance around and I saw no pickle jar, ice cream carton, or breadcrumbs on the counters either.

A knot formed in my stomach, and I returned to the den.

"Mimi! Wake up. Where's Zach?"

Her eyes fluttered open, and she slowly rose on one elbow. "Zach?" she repeated blankly, before lowering her legs to the floor. "He must not be home yet. What time is it?"

"It's after four." I glanced out the front window. No Zach.

Mimi flung off the afghan and stood on wobbly legs. Her eyes were wild with a panic that reflected my own rising concern. "Check the garden," she commanded in a shaky voice.

I ran out the side door, my heart racing. *Surely he's out there,* I thought, trying to tamp down my fear. Zach often enjoyed going outside with Mimi while she tended to the newly sprouted vegetables. But as I rounded the house, only the raw, upturned earth greeted me.

A lone crow swooped in to feast on unsprouted seeds. No doubt the rest of the murder would join in shortly. Mimi would not be happy with that. In the past, she'd tried to scare them away with tin pie plates strung on a line and crude homemade scarecrows, but the crows were too damn smart to be fooled. Thank goodness I'd insisted she get rid of her old BB gun. It wasn't safe with Zach around. He had no sense of danger when it came to moving vehicles or anything lying around the house.

I pressed my hands to my cheeks to ground myself in the present. I was losing it with these random, irrelevant thoughts. I had to focus. Where was my brother?

"Zach!" I screamed and screamed his name until my throat was raw. Even then I didn't stop calling him. "Zach! Where are you? Time to come inside."

My voice died in the gulf breeze, swallowed up in the heavy, humid air. This couldn't be real. Any minute, Zach would stroll out of the woods, puzzled at my frantic cries. I swallowed hard. *Think like Zach. Where would he go?*

"Jori."

I whirled around. Mimi stumbled toward me in her house slippers, her silver hair loose and fluttering in the wind. "Check the tree house," she panted, practically out of breath from running.

Of course. The relief turned my legs to jelly, and I took a deep breath. He'd be there. He had to be. He used to play in it for hours as a kid. My relief was short lived, though, as I remembered it was half-rotten now. It would never hold up the weight of an adult.

Mimi's chest heaved up and down, and I feared the panic and exertion might do her in. I couldn't deal with yet another crisis on my hands. "Go back inside and call his day program," I said, fighting to keep my voice calm. "Maybe there was a problem and he's still there. We'll find him. I promise."

Without waiting to see if she obeyed, I rushed to the opposite side of our property. The tree house Uncle Buddy had built for Zach years ago stood on the edge of the woods. He'd spent every free hour in the tree house as a child, dragging along his LEGOs and toy metal cars with him. I should have insisted the thing be torn down long ago. I raced out to the abandoned structure, my heart sinking at the sight of old pieces of lumber that had fallen to the ground and missing planks on the floorboard that left gaping, dangerous openings.

Frantic, my eyes scanned beneath the tree house, fearing Zach might have fallen and lay unconscious on the ground. I imagined his body crumpled and still from the pain and shock of broken bones.

But Zach wasn't there. Again, the strange mixture of relief and panic rushed through me—until I imagined new horrors of dangerous possibilities.

Let dead dogs lie.

What if . . . what if Zach hadn't wandered off on his own? Had the person who threatened me taken my brother? And if they had . . . what would they do to him?

I felt the blood drain from my face, and I stumbled over to the base of a broad oak tree and leaned my back against it. Prickly bark dug through the thin material of my T-shirt, and the pain grounded my thoughts. I took several deep breaths, lifting my face to the sky. Sunlight warmed my cheeks. I couldn't give in to the dark despair that my brother might be held somewhere against his will, frightened and confused. Not yet. Not until I'd searched everywhere first.

"Call your friend."

I jumped at Mimi's voice and opened my eyes. She stood in front of me, hair disheveled and one thin arm extended, holding my cell phone. "You know. That cop woman. The day program said Zach left at his usual time with his usual driver."

I took the phone and with trembling fingers located Tegan in my contacts and pressed call. She answered immediately.

"It's Zach. My brother. He's missing." I hoped she could understand my words between my gasps for air. No matter how much I breathed, I couldn't seem to suck in enough oxygen.

"How long has he been missing?" Tegan's voice was crisp, calm, matter of fact. It temporarily braced me.

"At least thirty minutes. We've looked everywhere. I think he came home from his day program because I was in my room and heard a car in the driveway, and then our door opened and closed. But when I checked later, Mimi was asleep in the den, and now we can't find him."

"Have you called his day program yet?"

"Yes. They said they dropped him off as usual."

"I'll organize a search immediately. In the meantime, check to see if any of his belongings are missing. Is there anything special he likes to keep with him? Are any of his clothes missing?"

That hadn't occurred to me. "I'll go look and call you right back," I promised.

"Has he ever wandered off before?" Tegan asked.

"Never. Do you think . . ." I couldn't speak the terrible words.

"We don't know that he's been taken. Hang in there and call me back."

I nodded, even though she certainly couldn't see me, and hung up.

"What did she say?" Mimi asked.

"Tegan's organizing a search. While we're waiting, she told me to see if any of Zach's stuff is missing."

Mimi nodded, and we hurried off. "If there was one thing Zach would take, it's his bucket of LEGOs," she said.

At the house, we rushed inside to his bedroom. The nightstand where he kept the toy bucket was completely bare. What little optimism I'd had drained out of me. Just how long had my brother been missing? Was he even still in the bayou? The county? The state?

"It's gone," Mimi whispered, so soft I could barely hear her. "What does that mean? That Zach took them and wandered off on his own?"

My skin crawled with fear. It didn't make sense.

Let dead dogs lie.

The refrain beat a steady drum of fear into my heart. Zach—so innocent and so vulnerable. He had no conception of evil and limited communication skills.

I sank onto his bed and covered my face with my hands. From afar, the wail of sirens blasted in the air.

Chapter 23

I'd set up the room to make Zach as comfortable as possible.

He slouched on the couch, his hands constantly shifting the LEGOs. Grab a scoop of pieces, let them fall back into the bucket. Clickety-clack. Clickety-clack. A mechanical waterfall of plastic bits. Over and over ad nauseum. The constant clatter was getting on my last nerve. I wanted to yank the bucket of toys away from him, but I feared that would result in even worse noise. We were in a remote location, but you never knew when someone might be out walking the backwoods or boating along the bayou creeks.

I'd only done what was necessary to protect myself and my secrets. Nobody would understand that, however.

Zach stood up, LEGO bucket in hand. "Go home," he said, a stubborn, determined set to his face.

I raised my voice. You had to be firm with others, apparently something his grandmother and sister didn't seem to understand. Growing up, my dad never hesitated to use the strap on us kids. Or coddled us in any way. It had been a harsh, hardscrabble kind of existence in the bayou backwoods, but it had made me strong. You had to fight for every scrap of money and power in this world, a lesson I'd learned early as a kid. I'd do whatever was necessary to keep my world from imploding. I'd done it before, and I'd do it again. "Sit down," I ordered. "And shut up."

Zach flung the LEGO bucket across the room. It smashed against the wall; hundreds of plastic pieces clattered around us on the rough-hewn floor, loud as an explosion of gunfire. He started to walk around me, and I grabbed his arm.

"You will mind me," I warned, forcing him back onto the couch. "Now sit down. Or else."

I didn't yell at him or grab him hard enough to leave a bruise. It wasn't necessary. Not yet. And I hoped it wouldn't be. I prided myself on only using the right amount of force called for in any situation.

But if lethal measures were necessary, so be it.

Chapter 24

TEGAN

Jori and her grandmother sat on the edge of the sofa, their bodies poised and tense, as though ready to spring into flight. Jori's eyes were dark and wild and large in her pale face. If Linsey and Luke were missing, I'm sure I'd look the same.

Uniformed cops swarmed their small house and the property.

"We're doing everything possible to find Zach," Oliver said in his most reassuring voice. "It's possible Zach returned home, grabbed his toys, wandered outside on his own, and then got lost in the woods. We've organized a volunteer search crew to comb the woods, and I have officers interviewing everyone employed at the day program. Hopefully, somebody has seen something out of the ordinary."

Jori stood and paced to the window, pulling back the curtains. Already, twilight had begun to gather, casting long shadows and cooling the spring air to a slight chill. "He must be cold. And frightened."

"He doesn't know how to swim," Mimi interjected. "If he fell in the water . . ."

Nobody spoke. Less than fifty feet from their house was one of the many winding creeks that threaded its way through swamps about the bayou. They teemed with water moccasins and the occasional alligator.

With the advent of spring, the reptiles were stirring from their dormant winter, mating and sunning in the warmer weather.

Zach's grandmother looked terrible. She seemed to have aged a decade since the last time I saw her. Her frail limbs trembled, and her face was a sickly shade of white and ash. Her eyes were red and swollen. She was a pale shadow of the saucy woman I'd met earlier.

"It's all my fault," she kept muttering.

Jori left the window and strode to the couch, then took a seat beside her grandmother and put an arm across her shoulders. "They'll find Zach. I want you to take your medicine and go lie down. Okay? There's nothing you can do."

She nodded meekly, and Jori went to the kitchen, returning a minute later with a pill bottle and a glass of water.

Oliver's phone buzzed. "Mullins. What's up?"

I followed him out to the porch as he answered the call, then watched his expression as he nodded and sighed. "Okay. Come on over to the residence. We need every able body in the search. If we don't find him before dark, our chances dramatically decrease."

A quick glance over my shoulder reassured me that Jori and her grandmother were heading down the hallway and couldn't overhear.

"Any news?" I asked as he stuffed the phone back in his pocket.

"No. Mullins and Haywood interviewed every employee who worked at his day program today. No one observed anything unusual. At approximately three twenty, he and two other clients got in the car with their driver. The other clients were safely returned home."

"What about the driver?"

"He said that when he pulled into the driveway, Zach climbed out, and he watched him until he was safely inside the house, then left."

"He didn't find it strange no one was at the door to meet Zach?"

"No. He said sometimes Zach's grandmother came to the door, but not always. He didn't think anything of it."

"What do you think?" I asked. "Surely it's not a coincidence that Jori Trahern receives threatening messages and then this happens. Would her brother really wander off on his own? According to his family, he's never done that before."

The door swung open, and Jori eyed us. "What's happening?"

"We've interviewed all of the day program employees and his afternoon driver," Oliver said. "Nothing out of the ordinary happened today. There've been no reports of suspicious people hanging around the building or any employee who exhibited an inappropriate relationship with your brother."

"How's your grandmother?" I asked.

"Crying herself to sleep. The one time I want her to be confused and unaware of what's happening, she's one hundred percent lucid."

"Sleep's the best thing for her right now," I said gently.

Jori acted as though she hadn't heard me. "This is all my fault," she said, repeating the same words her grandmother had used. "Someone's after me, and they're using Zach to hurt me."

I only had an inkling of how she must feel. Once when the twins were five, my ex was three hours late bringing them home. We were going through the worst of times in our relationship, and I'd feared he'd taken off with the kids. He didn't answer his phone. He wasn't at his house. Every minute with no news ticked by like an hour. Even with my extended family gathered around me, it had been a special kind of hell. Finally, he'd called from a car repair shop and reported that his transmission had died and he'd been stranded. Typical Josh—he was careless about charging his phone, and the battery had died. The twins corroborated his story when they arrived home.

Jori needed more resources, I decided. She toted a lot of responsibility on her young shoulders, and even though she'd grown up in the bayou, she'd been away a long time and needed to forge new connections. I'd make sure to help her with that. But for now, I kept my mouth shut, unwilling to utter false platitudes that Zach had probably just wandered off on his own and would be found shortly.

It could be no coincidence he was missing so soon after Jori received threats. Had Strickland's killer kidnapped Zach? If so, I feared for Zach's life. The person who'd murdered Strickland had proven he had no qualms in permanently silencing his victims.

Chapter 25

JORI

I sat on the back porch steps, rubbing my arms as I watched the woods, willing with all my heart and mind for Zach to materialize out of nowhere. But I knew better than anyone that any amount of wishing and hoping was useless. It hadn't brought Deacon back alive, it hadn't kept my mom from dying of cancer, and it sure as hell wasn't helping Mimi ward off the ravages of dementia. Each minute, the darkness seeped a degree deeper, extinguishing my hope.

The sound of footsteps trampling on twigs and a low murmur of voices drifted on the wind. Even though I couldn't see them at the moment, dozens of civilian volunteers along with uniformed cops were in the nearby woods, combing the ground for Zach or any clue of where he might be.

Warmth pressed across my shoulders and back, but I kept my gaze forward, staring at the empty yard.

"You're shivering," Tegan said. "Thought you could use this afghan from your sofa."

My fingers grasped at the blanket edges, pulling it in closer. It was true— my entire body shook uncontrollably. You'd think I was in Antarctica instead of Alabama.

"Any idea what might have driven someone to take Zach?" she asked.

"You agree this is from whoever threatened me last time?"

"We have to take that option seriously. Can you think what might have angered them?"

"Yes. Like I said, this is all my fault. I went to Gulfport a couple days ago and talked to Jackson's adoptive father."

"His name?" Tegan already had her phone out, ready to make a note.

"Ardy Ensley."

"What happened?"

I quickly filled her in on my conversation with Ardy. "It was so stupid of me. It's like I've become obsessed with what happened in the past and why someone doesn't want me to dig it up."

"I'll contact Ensley at once. Maybe he can help." Tegan jumped off the step, started to walk away, and then turned back. "Just in case . . . do you have a friend you can call to stay with you tonight and keep you company?"

I thought of Dana. That bridge had been burned. "No one," I admitted.

She nodded and strode away from me, already on the phone with another cop to get in touch with Ardy.

Had Jackson's father abducted Zach? I saw no reason for him to do so. All he wanted was to forget everything and everybody in Bayou Enigma and concentrate on his current family. But, presumably, I'd made my enemy very nervous.

That's how I thought of the intruder now. He was an enemy who'd dared harm one of the two people I loved. Guilt slammed into me as I remembered how I'd selfishly worked while Zach had been kidnapped right under my nose. To think I'd been complaining ever since I got home about having to take care of Zach and Mimi. I'd give anything to have my brother back now.

"I'm sorry, Mom," I whispered. "I failed you." The only thing Mom had ever asked of me was to watch out for Zach after her death. I'd done a horrible job of it. I'd run away to Mobile, leaving everything in the hands of my aging grandmother, and had only returned when her health was too precarious to care for Zach anymore.

Where the hell was Zach? I pictured him in a series of disasters, each progressively worse: lost, scared, walking in circles as he tried to find his way home; gulping swamp water as he sank into a pond; being tied and gagged and beaten at the hands of my enemy.

My vision blurred from a film of tears that overflowed and trickled down my face in hot salt tracks that I didn't bother wiping away. Misery and fear had me locked in a death grip that made it hard to breathe. Each second ticked by like an eternity. A chill that had nothing to do with the lateness of the afternoon seeped into the marrow of my bones.

I stared ahead, unseeing and numb, the world a blur. A shout went up somewhere beyond the tree line of the yard. A voice boomed from the woods.

"Zach! Zach! He's here!"

Zach? I stumbled to my feet like a drunk emerging from a weekend binge. Excited voices rang out from somewhere in the darkness.

Was he alive? Or . . . I flung the afghan from my shoulders and ran toward the noise. My breath was loud and labored, hope and fear warring within me. Before I got to the edge of the woods, a group of cops ran forward, waving and pointing.

"Over here!"

Zach walked in the middle of the group, his gaze drifting from one person to another, as though trying to understand what all the excitement was about. He clasped the LEGO bucket firmly in his right hand. One of the cops tapped him on the shoulder and pointed at me.

I ran to him where he stood and then wrapped my arms around him. He was alive. I pressed him tight, and he stiffened uncomfortably before wiggling out of my embrace. I had to laugh through my tears.

Even though my heart was bursting with love for him and relief that he appeared unharmed, Zach still didn't want to be hugged. It was just who he was.

"Are you okay?" I asked, rubbing his hands. It was the one gesture of affection Zach allowed.

"Okay," he repeated, the echolalia automatic and rote. I scanned his body to check for obvious signs of abuse. There were no bruises, blood, or rips in his clothes.

"We'll need to do a full-body scan and question him when he gets inside," a cop said.

I nodded, not hopeful that their questions could ever be answered. Still, I asked what we all wanted to know.

"Where've you been, Zach?"

"All done," he answered, walking toward the house. He grabbed my hand and pulled me along.

"What does that mean?" a cop asked.

"It's his standard answer when he's finished talking," I explained over my shoulder where he scurried behind us. "Or when he doesn't want to be bothered anymore."

"Keep trying," he urged.

I stepped up next to Zach, keeping in stride with his pace. Thank goodness he wasn't limping or crying or indicating that he hurt anywhere. "Zach, where have you been?" I asked again.

"Mimi knows," he mumbled. "All done."

The cop stepped in front of us, blocking our path. "Who's this Mimi?" he asked suspiciously.

"Our grandmother. She's home. But she doesn't know where he's been either," I said quickly. "*Mimi knows* is one of Zach's pet expressions to any question he can't answer. Like *all done* when he wants to be left alone or *get shoes* when he wants to go outside. It's like a code."

His brows furrowed together, as though he wasn't buying my explanation. I sighed. Poor Mimi might be getting the third degree when we got home. I understood that police had to be suspicious and cynical by nature, but for the first time I worried about the consequences of Zach's mysterious disappearance. Would the cops think we had something to do with it? Or that we were negligent, incapable caregivers?

The worry that we were indeed negligent only fueled my paranoia.

A thirtysomething woman in jeans and a *Keep Calm and Do Yoga* T-shirt sidled up to us. I recognized her as a neighbor from a block away. "You think he went outside to play and just wandered off?" she asked.

"No." I directed my answer to the cop, noting his name was Dempsey. I needed to impress upon him that this was no accident. I couldn't dismiss the threatening messages I'd received. It was too much of a coincidence to think he'd wandered away for so long for the first time in his life right at the time I faced an unknown menace. "Officer, I believe he was abducted."

Zach walked around the guy, careful not to accidentally brush against him. "Home," Zach said, tugging my hand impatiently. He led all of us into the house, where Tegan awaited with a broad smile.

"I just checked," Tegan said. "Your grandmother's still asleep. She'll be so relieved when she wakes up. Do you want me to get her?"

"No. Let her sleep."

As though not noticing the entourage of people crowded around him, Zach headed down the hallway.

"We'll need to do that body search before we go," the officer reminded me.

"I want Deputy Blackwell to do it, if she's willing. Zach's met her a few times. She won't be a complete stranger."

Tegan nodded. "Sure. Let's go ahead and get this over with."

Mimi stumbled out of her bedroom, blocking our way to Zach. "What's going on?" she asked, hands on her hips, glaring at the noisy crowd in the den. "What are all these people doing in my house?"

She didn't act surprised Zach had returned; the memory of his disappearance had apparently dissolved during her nap.

The cop raised an eyebrow at me. He must think we were the craziest family ever. But after today's crisis, I didn't care what anyone thought as long as Mimi and Zach were safe.

"Listen up, everyone," the officer called over his shoulder. "Everyone head on home or back to your jobs. Thanks for your help."

"Thank you," I added. "We're so grateful."

"I'll stay until I'm sure Zach doesn't require medical attention," the officer said.

"Medical attention?" Mimi asked. "He's perfectly fine. Who are you?"

"Officer Dempsey, ma'am."

I intervened. "Why don't you go in the kitchen and make a cup of coffee, Mimi? I'll explain everything in a minute."

Mimi shook her finger at the cop. "I want you out of here, young man."

"Sorry," I mumbled as I walked past him.

Tegan snickered as we walked into the bathroom. I had the feeling she didn't particularly care for the cop.

We quickly assessed that Zach had no marks on him. Zach dressed, and a scrap of paper fell out of his jeans pocket and landed on the floor. "What's this?" I asked, picking it up. Zach ignored me and left the bathroom.

Large typed block letters delivered a succinct message.

I warned you. Next time he won't come back.

The words hit me like a sucker punch. I dropped to my knees on the hard tiled floor. My lips numbed, and blood drained so fast from my face that the tiny bathroom walls began to spin and close in on me. The faded wallpaper of poppies swirled like a psychedelic field of blue and pink. A rabbit trap that threatened to suck me into its vortex.

"Jori? Sit down." Tegan's face swam into my vision. She grasped my shoulders and guided my body so that my back leaned against the wall. "Put your head between your knees and take deep breaths."

The shock of the message, piled on top of the intense stress of the last few hours, left me exhausted as adrenaline suddenly bottomed out of my system.

"Will you be all right for a minute?" she asked.

I nodded, and she left me alone, promising she'd return in a minute. "Leave the paper where it is and don't touch it," she warned.

I had no intention of touching it again.

Voices carried from the den for several minutes until Tegan entered the bathroom pulling on rubber gloves and carrying a manila envelope. "We'll see if we can get fingerprints from this note," she said, tucking the evidence into the envelope.

I watched listlessly, my hope as drained as my energy. Whoever had taken Zach was too smart to have left fingerprints behind.

"Your grandmother's made coffee. How about we go in the kitchen. Can you get up?"

Tegan leaned over me and grasped my elbow, helping me to my feet. The room whirled once, twice, and then my vision cleared.

I peeked into Zach's room as we walked down the hallway. Zach briefly glanced up, then went back to his own world. You'd never guess he'd spent the past couple of hours at the mercy of a killer.

"I hope Zach's not traumatized from all this. I know he appears calm, but who knows what he's really thinking?"

Tegan cocked her head to the side. "Maybe you can ask his day program director if she thinks he could benefit from speaking to a counselor?"

"I suppose," I answered, not believing any good would come of pursuing that. But I could at least try.

At the end of the hallway I pulled up short. "I'm worried with everyone gone. What if the kidnapper returns?"

"Don't worry," she assured me. "Your house will be under round-the-clock police protection for at least the next forty-eight hours."

The smell of freshly brewed coffee and the absence of dozens of eyes on me—which I imagined as critical and accusatory—revived my spirits. Stirrings of anger also fortified me. Whoever had taken Zach needed to be arrested. He needed to pay for what he'd put us all through this harrowing afternoon.

Mimi was already seated at the table sipping coffee. Her hands were steady and her eyes clear, fully awake and alert. "I'm sorry, Jori," she said.

"For what?"

"Falling asleep. I can't believe he disappeared right under my nose like that. If only I'd woken up."

Her memory had returned. "And if only I hadn't been so busy. I should have come out and checked on Zach. Thank God you weren't hurt. If you'd woken up and seen someone with him—"

"Then I'd have killed the son of a bitch," Mimi said, slamming her cup on the table so hard I was surprised it didn't shatter to pieces.

"I'll pretend I didn't hear that," Tegan said wryly.

For the first time since Zach disappeared, a smile flirted at the edges of my mouth. That was the Mimi I knew and loved. A no-bullshit, don't-mess-with-me woman.

I'd need to channel that kind of strength if our little family was to survive the invisible menace pressing in on us.

Chapter 26

TEGAN

It was good to see the color return to Jori's face and the suggestion of a smile play across her features. When she'd sunk to the bathroom floor minutes ago, I'd feared she wouldn't have the strength to take care of herself and the family dependent on her.

For now, anger was a healthy emotion, a fuel for action. A first step in moving past a victim mentality and fighting against an unknown enemy.

I took a deep breath. It was time for the hard questions. Oliver left this to me since I'd forged a relationship with one of Zach's caretakers and might have the best success.

"I have to be honest with both of you," I began. "In these situations, it's almost always someone close to the victim. It seems obvious that whoever took Zach knew him well. By your own admission, Zach is agitated around strangers. Yet he returned calm, unharmed, and not hungry or thirsty."

They both regarded me blankly. Either they were good liars, still in shock, or clueless where Zach might have been during the missing hours.

"Think hard," I told them. "Let's start with family and then friends. Who knows Zach well?"

"If you have to interrogate anyone, look at the day program staff," Mimi said, eyes shooting daggers at me.

"Absolutely. We'll continue questioning them. The afternoon driver has agreed to submit to a polygraph test. He's at the station now. I want you both to come to our office at eight o'clock tomorrow morning for a polygraph test as well."

Jori flinched as though she'd been struck.

"I'm sorry. The quicker we can rule you out as suspects, the quicker we can explore other leads. You can bring Zach along with you."

"He'll love that." Jori rolled her eyes. "All those strangers, all that noise . . ."

"Is there someone who can stay with him here at the house?"

"No," Jori said immediately. "I don't trust anyone."

"What about Dana?" Mimi asked.

"No," Jori insisted.

"Who's Dana?" I asked, pulling out my phone to make notes.

"A . . . friend."

I raised my brow at her hesitation at using the *friend* word. "You sure she's a friend?"

"I used to be sure," Jori admitted. "We had a recent falling out."

"Is it possible she took your brother in retaliation? Wanted to hurt you in some way?"

Jori's eyes widened. "I-I don't think so."

"I'll have a talk with her. Her full name?"

"Dana Adair."

Mimi made a small snort of derision. "Always thought that girl was shady."

"Anyone else you two have had trouble with recently? Another friend or family member?"

Jori shook her head no, and Mimi continued to regard me stonily.

"I'll need a list of close family members that live in the area."

"There's Tressie Ensley, my aunt and Mimi's sister; Uncle Buddy—Buddy Munford, that is—Crystal Donley, a cousin on my dad's side of the family . . ."

I dutifully wrote down another half dozen names of various cousins. I'd contact each of them tonight and get their alibis. "Is that everyone you can think of?" I asked again. "Have you had any trouble with neighbors or anyone else?"

"Nope. We don't have any close neighbors, and I can't think of a single person who would want to hurt us or Zach." Jori turned to her grandmother. "Mimi?"

"No. Isn't it possible he just wandered off alone and decided to return?" the grandmother proposed.

"You said he'd never done that before," I reminded her. "Why now? Besides, there's the threatening message he carried back."

She gasped. "What are you talking about?"

I held up the evidence bag I'd placed in the chair beside me.

"We found it in Zach's pants when he came home," Jori admitted.

"What did it say?"

I repeated the message to her, as Jori appeared to want to gloss over the matter. She was understandably protective of her grandmother, and I noticed she tried to cushion her from bad news as much as possible. But they both needed their eyes wide open if they were going to protect Zach.

"One more thing," I added as I rose to leave. "We're obligated to report this matter to Adult Protective Services. They'll probably send a social worker out here tomorrow."

"Terrific," Jori muttered. "Just what we need."

Neither of them made a move to walk me to the front door.

"May I see you a minute, Jori?"

Reluctantly, she walked outside with me to the front porch, and I faced her square on. "I am sorry. I'm doing my job. You and your grandmother have nothing to fear. Take the polygraph, talk with the social worker, and keep a close eye on your brother. We're going to do everything possible to find who's responsible."

"How can you be sure it's not me?" she asked bitterly. "Maybe I'm secretly a crazy narcissist who's done all this for attention."

"I don't believe that. Look, we're on the same side here. We both want to capture who's responsible and for your family to be safe."

Some of her anger melted, but she still held her body stiffly. "Thank you. Anything else?"

"Not unless you have anything else to shed some light on this situation. I get the feeling you don't feel free to talk in front of your grandmother."

"I have nothing to say."

I nodded, not surprised at Jori's reticence. It'd been a long, stressful day for her, and tomorrow promised to be hard as well. I started to suggest she contact Family Services for a list of respite care providers, but now was not the time. Jori would be mistrustful of any stranger until we solved this case.

"Call me if you need me," I reminded her, but I had a feeling my phone wouldn't be ringing. I left the porch and headed down the driveway, my gaze shifting to the woods on either side of the house. Who had been here earlier, lying in wait for Zach? While I was relieved he'd been returned unharmed, frustration knotted my gut. If only someone had seen something—anything—for me to pursue. The various threads of old and new crimes were a tightly woven web, a mystery that so far eluded me. But surely we were close to finding answers, or else Jori wouldn't have been threatened and Zach wouldn't have been kidnapped.

"Whoever you are, I'll find you," I whispered into the gulf wind.

Chapter 27

JORI

What monster lurked behind the smiling faces of everyday friends and family? Tegan had insisted that most likely our stalker was someone I knew and knew well.

Only two people with motive and opportunity came to mind—Dana and Aunt Tressie—I realized as I tried to focus on the last-minute details for the Blessing event. But my mind wouldn't cooperate. Dana's motive might be because of some old, deep harbored jealousy. As ludicrous as that sounded, I couldn't rule it out. And then there was Aunt Tressie. Her ex-husband had opened my eyes to the realization she wasn't who I thought she was.

I continued my pacing, feeling as hemmed in as a chicken in a crowded coop.

"Why don't you come sit down and watch a show with us?" Mimi asked.

"Sit," Zach echoed, pointing to the empty spot on the couch beside him.

"For a minute," I conceded, dropping onto the sofa. Much as I knew Zach hated the physical contact, I ruffled his hair. "You doing okay?"

He frowned and leaned his body away from my touch. "Okay. All done."

I didn't mean to annoy him, but it was impossible not to constantly touch his shoulder or hug him every time I passed him in the den, unharmed and seemingly content as always.

The social worker had briefly stopped by this morning and had reassured us that we were in no danger of being declared incompetent to care for Zach.

"Accidents happen," she said. "No one can be one hundred percent vigilant one hundred percent of the time."

The polygraph test had proved more stressful. Being shoved into the room and hooked up to the wires intimidated me, even though I had nothing to hide. Tegan had watched Zach while I was being tested. Later, she told me it had taken half a dozen trips to the vending machine to keep Zach pacified. The bags of chips and soda kept him occupied and distracted. Mimi was another story. It had not been a good morning for her. Her mind was hazy, and even asking her simple questions such as her name and today's date proved too much. Mercifully, the polygraph examiner had concluded testing my grandmother would be a waste of time.

Within five minutes, I was bored to tears with the game show that had Mimi and Zach engrossed. I jumped up from the couch and for the dozenth time since yesterday worked my way clockwise around the house, checking to make sure that all windows and doors were locked, that the curtains were drawn, and that there were no signs of disturbance.

"Why don't you get out of the house for a bit?" Mimi finally suggested. "It'll do you good."

"No, no, I can't leave y'all alone."

Mimi set down her knitting. "If you won't do it for yourself, do it for me. You're making me nervous. We can't become prisoners in our own home."

I hesitated, toying with the idea. It would be nice to get some fresh air.

"If it'll make you feel any better, I can have Rose stop by to keep Zach and me company."

"If she's free . . ."

While Mimi called Rose, I went out on the porch and called Tegan.

"Are you positive a cop car will be watching us all day and night this evening?" I asked.

"Positive. If you need to leave the house for groceries or any other reason, that's perfectly fine."

I waved at the cop watching me, and he waved back. The guy was evidently paying attention and not sleeping on the job. A good sign.

"How did the social worker interview go?" Tegan asked.

"Better than I could have hoped for. Actually, she was very nice."

A brief silence settled between us.

"Anything else?" Tegan said at last.

It wasn't until that moment I realized the real reason I'd called her. "About the messages," I began hesitantly. "If you were me, would you stop questioning people about Jackson Ensley's murder?"

"Aren't you at a dead end with that?" she countered. "You told me about your conversation with his adoptive father. At this point, there's nothing more you can do."

Ah, but I hadn't told her what Ardy had said about Aunt Tressie. All my life, Mimi had so ingrained into me the importance of family loyalty. Speaking to outsiders about "private matters" was taboo, and my upbringing left me reluctant to speak ill of any blood relation.

"Yeah, I'm at a dead end," I lied. "But hypothetically, would an outside threat prevent you from asking more questions?"

"If you have more questions for anybody, we can get the answers for you," she said. "That's our job, not yours."

"Well, there is one person," I began reluctantly. "Ardy was pretty bitter about his ex-wife, my aunt Tressie. And he has reason. He showed

215

me phone transcripts where she's been coercing him for years to pay for her cushy residence at Magnolia Oaks." I filled Tegan in on my conversation with Ardy.

"Your aunt sounds like an extremely unpleasant person, but what reason would she have for kidnapping Zach or threatening you?"

"Because I've been asking questions about her son's adoption. Have you found out anything about it?"

"Still looking into it," she replied cryptically. Which told me much of nothing.

"Do you have any clues about who took Zach?" I asked, turning the conversation in another direction.

"Not yet. The day program driver passed a polygraph. We interviewed staff again but haven't learned anything new."

My heart sank, even though her news was hardly surprising.

"But in searching the woods," she continued, "we found a trail of LEGOs that led to the edge of a water pathway. It appears that whoever had Zach might have kidnapped him in a boat."

"Any footprints?"

"No. We found a muddy track going into the water. It looked like someone erased all their footprints with a branch. Do you think Zach might have deliberately dropped the LEGOs to leave a trail of bread crumbs?"

"Doubtful." I couldn't imagine Zach doing that. "Must have been an accident. He leaves LEGOs all over the house. You have to watch your step around here."

"Has he said anything that gives you a clue where he might have been?"

"Nothing," I reported with a sigh. "If he does, I'll call right away."

I hung up the phone and marched back into the house. "Is Rose coming over?" I asked Mimi.

"She'll be here in five minutes."

"I've decided to go out for an hour or so," I said, grabbing my car keys from the fireplace mantel. "Sure you don't mind?"

"Go," Mimi said, shooing me off.

"Go," Zach repeated. "Bye-bye."

"Call me if you need me."

I made my escape. Once in town, I tapped my car brakes and slowed down as I neared Winn-Dixie. At the last possible moment, I shut off my blinker and hit the accelerator, my decision made.

A hint of twilight clouded the skies by the time I pulled into Magnolia Oaks. The magnificent antebellum mansion with its white columns, wraparound porch, and well-manicured lawn was striking. I'd never been out quite so late in the day. Every window glowed with warmth, and it looked as inviting and welcoming as a Norman Rockwell painting.

Poor Ardy had been stuck funding most of Tressie's living costs, and I suspected Uncle Buddy also regularly slipped his sister extra money. There were less expensive assisted living facilities in nearby Mobile that would have been perfectly decent for Aunt Tressie, but according to her ex-husband, she'd chosen grander accommodations as a way to punish him for deserting her.

Inside, there was plenty of activity as a local church choir performed in the ballroom. At the reception desk, I signed my name as usual and headed down the south wing.

An LPN I recognized waved. "Oh, honey, you should have called before coming out. Your aunt isn't here."

"Not here?" I repeated stupidly. "Tressie Ensley?" A series of possible explanations shifted through my mind: Had she fallen? Had a heart attack? My hand fluttered to my throat. Maybe whoever had taken Zach had now targeted my aunt. "What's happened to her?" I asked.

"Nothing! Sorry, I didn't mean to scare you, sweetie. She just decided to run get a bite to eat. Pot roast was on the menu tonight, and she had a hankering for barbeque."

Debbie Herbert

"Since when did she start driving?" I asked, confused. Up until this moment, I'd thought the only time Tressie left the facility was when she had an aide drive her to the beauty shop once a month. Ardy was right. Her deceptions went deep, and I'd best remember that from here on out.

The LPN cocked her head to the side, brows creased with confusion. "She's always driven. Ever since I've been here anyway, which is almost a year. She goes out regularly. The only restriction we have is that all residents return by nine in the evening."

"I-I see. Do you happen to know if she was here yesterday afternoon?"

"We can check the log. Everyone's supposed to log in and out when they leave. It's a safety measure."

The LPN cast me curious glances as she walked with me to the nurses' station.

"Any particular reason you want to know?" she finally asked.

I shrugged, unwilling to go into the kidnapping with a stranger. The woman asked another employee for the logbook, and a thick blue binder was handed over.

"Yesterday . . . ," the LPN muttered, her index finger scanning a page. "Let's see. No, I don't see where she left the premises. Hope that helps you?"

She slammed the book closed, but not before I was able to briefly scan the open pages. Aunt Tressie had checked out regularly. Ardy was right: Tressie's mental fragility appeared to be an act.

But why? What purpose did it serve? Was it merely to play on others' sympathy and extort money from her family? Or was there something more sinister at play?

"If you'd like to wait for your aunt, you can listen to the church choir in the ballroom. They're really good. They come twice a month, and our residents love them."

218

"Th-that's okay," I managed. "Thanks for all your help."

I made my way outside and stumbled to my car in a daze. All these years, Aunt Tressie had been putting on this poor-pitiful-me act, and I'd fallen for it like a complete chump. As far as I knew, Mimi had fallen for it too.

Darkness settled by degrees. There was no point in remaining, but I couldn't find the energy or the will to leave.

Car headlights snaked up the driveway, and my heart hammered as I recognized the dark-blue Town Car. Tressie was at the wheel, her features calm as she turned into the parking lot.

I sprang out of the car and headed to her, my footsteps loud and reverberating on the asphalt. A crow cawed a warning that Aunt Tressie didn't heed. She was so smug, so confident, so . . . normal as she exited her Town Car clutching a bag of take-out food and a cup of coffee.

"Enjoy your evening out?" I asked once I was merely two feet away.

Tressie jumped, and hot liquid sloshed out of her drink and onto her hand. "Damn it," she whimpered, staring at the burnt flesh already inflamed and bright red.

"Let me get that for you." I moved in, removed the drink from her hand, and stared into the face of a stranger. This Aunt Tressie was focused. Aware. A hint of calculation in her gray eyes that were the same distinctive pewter color as my own and Mimi's and Mom's. An inherited family gene through the generations.

"Jori!" she screeched.

In less than two seconds, this version of my aunt morphed into a more familiar one. Confusion clouded her eyes; her shoulders slumped forward an inch, and her lips trembled.

"Um, thank you, dear." Her voice warbled as though weak and infirm. "What a surprise to find you here."

If I hadn't been holding a cup of hot liquid in my hands, I'd have given her a slow clap of satiric admiration.

"Bet you're not as surprised as me," I commented. "You led me to believe the only time you ever left this place was to get your hair done. And even then, you'd pay one of the nurse's aides to drive you there."

"I've been feeling much better lately." She offered a wobbly, apologetic smile. The gray eyes promised a nothing-to-see-here-move-along flash that downplayed her deception. "The doctors put me on a new round of medication that's working miracles."

"Really? I don't believe in miracles myself."

Tressie aimed her keys at the Town Car and locked it with a decisive click. "What brings you here? Is something wrong with Oatha? Or Zach?"

She could shove the fake concern. "You didn't hear the news? Zach was kidnapped yesterday."

Alarm flared across her features. But not surprise. "Yes, I-I did hear that. The TV news reported he was returned unharmed. Is he okay?"

"If you knew, why didn't you pick up the phone and call us?"

"I didn't want to intrude. I mean, I figured it must have been a madhouse. I was going to wait and call tonight."

"Where were you yesterday afternoon?" I asked flatly, ignoring Tressie's attempt to downplay her lack of concern.

"Why—right here, of course. In my room like always."

"The whole afternoon? Can the nurses and other residents verify that?"

Her shoulders straightened. "What are you implying?"

"That you could have been the one who took Zach."

"That's . . . that's absurd!"

"No, it's not. According to the checkout log, you come and go from here all the time."

"They showed you the log? I'll have a word with them. That should be confidential information. At any rate, if you looked at it, then you saw that I didn't leave the grounds."

"Maybe. Officially. But you could have snuck out without reporting it."

"What possible reason would I have for taking him? That's ridiculous." She walked around me, moving at a surprising clip for a person supposedly old and feeble.

"It's not ridiculous at all," I insisted, catching up to her. "You've pulled some pretty shady stuff over the years."

That brought her up short, and she abruptly halted. "What are you talking about?" she snapped, all pretense of Poor Little Old Aunt Tressie obliterated.

"Don't play games with me. I talked to Ardy."

Her lips pursed together, trembling with rage. "Why would you go see him?"

"Because I think there's something fishy about Jackson's adoption."

Fury blazed from her eyes. "How dare you? It's none of your business."

"Somebody—maybe you?—made it my business."

"What do you mean?"

"The threatening notes. Zach's kidnapping."

"I have no idea what you're talking about."

She resumed her march to the building. Her own private sanctuary where she lived in ease and manipulated others out of spite.

"Why should I believe you?" I asked, easily keeping pace with her.

"I don't give a good damn whether or not you believe me. Go home."

I gave a bitter laugh. "Watch it. Your true colors are showing. If Ardy hadn't had proof of you threatening him, I'd never have believed you had a role in anything illegal. Now, well, I wouldn't put anything past you."

"That bastard owes me," she seethed. "He ran out on me when the going got tough like the coward he is."

"He only left after Jackson died. But he stayed with you when Jackson was a troubled teenager in trouble with the law. He told me he tried to instill discipline but—"

"Ardy was too harsh on my boy," she interrupted. "Jackson was just going through an unruly adolescent phase, that's all. If he hadn't been murdered . . ."

Her wrinkled face crumpled like wadded tissue, and I suspected this was the first real emotion I'd ever seen from Aunt Tressie. She drew a deep breath.

"If my boy had lived, he'd have turned out fine. Jackson had a good heart."

I couldn't argue might-have-beens, although I highly doubted Jackson would have "outgrown" his criminal "phase."

The more I puzzled out all that had happened, the more I believed Aunt Tressie was the one behind it all. Where had she taken Zach? Her old house had never been sold because she'd insisted she couldn't sell the place where she'd raised her only child. It would be a perfect hideout for keeping Zach out of sight.

"I had nothing to do with Zach disappearing or the threats you say you're getting," she insisted. "Now go away and never come back." Her step quickened, and we were almost at the Magnolia Oaks back door, where three employees were gathered on the patio smoking cigarettes. Once we reached the employees, I knew the conversation would be over. Tressie would play a poor victim hounded by a thoughtless niece.

"Does Mimi know you bought a baby?"

Aunt Tressie whipped around. "We didn't *buy* Jackson. We paid for a private adoption."

"Which the police are looking into."

Her face paled, and her knuckles whitened on the take-out bag.

"Does Mimi know about this?" I asked again. "Who else knows?"

"There's nothing to know because nothing happened." Her eyes dropped to my hands. "Now give me back my coffee."

My aunt had no shame. Her callous selfishness infuriated me. I held my arm out straight to the side and let go of the cup. Milky mocha liquid splashed on the pavement and formed a puddle.

Tressie raised her voice, high pitched and full of angst, amber notes glowing like molten lava. "What are you doing, Jori?"

She turned to the employees, widening her eyes as though frightened. One of them started to make their way over to where we stood.

Tressie faced me again, a smug smile on her thick lips. "Don't ever come back here. I'm going to put you on my restricted visitors list."

"I'm heartbroken. By the way, I let a deputy know you've got an extortion scheme running with your ex. Are you extorting money from Uncle Buddy too?"

"I'm not extorting anyone. And if my brother wants to slip his poor little sister a bit of cash from time to time, that's no one else's business but our own. Because family is family. We help each other."

"Old lady, you better stay away from us. You got that? If you ever take Zach again, I'll—"

"Is there a problem, ladies?" A tall, burly man who looked to be in his midthirties came to stand by Tressie.

"My niece was just leaving," Tressie simpered. "Weren't you, dear?"

"You betcha." I conjured a fake smile. "We've both said everything we have to say to each other."

Chapter 28

TEGAN

"About to break the Strickland murder?" Sinclair asked the moment I stepped in the office. "It's been several days, and no one's been arrested yet." He made a tsking sound.

"Just the Strickland case?" Mullins snickered. "Hell, our superstar's about to break every unsolved murder that's ever happened here in Enigma. News report at ten tonight."

"Jealousy isn't a good look on y'all," I chided as I slid into my seat. "We really should get partitions put up in this place. I need a private cubicle so I don't have to see you clowns."

"You'd still hear us," Haywood said.

"But I could pretend not to."

I entered my computer password and, while I waited for the monitor to light up, checked a stack of papers in my inbox. Who knew being in law enforcement meant dealing with so much paperwork? It certainly wasn't how I envisioned my career while at the police academy learning how to shoot weapons and struggling through physical agility tests.

My three coworkers began speculating on the cost of converting our office to individual cubicles. Haywood suggested putting in a request to

Oliver. I knew they wouldn't follow through with the idea; they loved jawing back and forth with each other too much.

From outside the open window came the sounds of sawing and hammering. The city maintenance staff was hard at work finishing the final construction for the Blessing of the Fleet events that would start tomorrow. Even getting to our parking lot this morning had been a trial as I weaved around vendor setups and volunteers setting up water stations for the runners in the annual 5K race.

"How are we supposed to get any work done around here?" Haywood mumbled.

Sinclair rolled his eyes. "Close the damn window and turn on the AC for starters. Duh."

I tuned them out and scribbled a list of my daily to-dos. One, reinterview Eddie Yeager; two, email the courthouse for a list of—

Oliver burst into the room, looking more intense than usual. "Carter Holt's been shot," he announced without preamble. "He's in critical condition." He pointed at me. "Let's go."

"Goddammit," Sinclair swore, banging a fist on his desk. I jumped out of my chair without bothering to shut down the computer and followed Oliver out to the cruiser.

"Any more details?" I asked, buckling into my seat.

"Report just came in from Enigma PD. He was found in his car at five thirty-six a.m. on Gilmore Road, slumped over the wheel, bleeding and unconscious. He'd been shot once in the chest."

"Who found him?"

"A local driving to work at a bakery. She called it in. Officers and EMTs responded less than five minutes later."

Shot in the chest. That sounded dire. Much as Holt and I had taken an immediate dislike to one another, his shooting hit me hard. It was a brutal reminder of what could happen to me on the job at any time. Even though my ex-husband and I couldn't stand to be in each other's company, I had to admit he was a good father. Our twins would always have a loving home with him if need be. I never would have accepted this job without that assurance. Still . . . I wanted to be around a long, long time. Time enough to at least see Luke and Linsey grown, employed in a solid job, and happily married with their own families.

At the emergency entrance, we ditched the cruiser and hurried to the ICU unit. There was no need to inquire which room was Holt's. Four uniformed cops milled outside a door at the end of the hallway.

"Is he conscious?" Oliver asked by way of greeting.

"He's in and out," Officer Granger reported.

"Anyone asked him yet who shot him?"

"Yeah. He's tried to answer, but we haven't been able to make out what he's saying," Granger answered. "They've got him pretty drugged up."

"What's his prognosis?" I asked one of the newer cops I hadn't met before. I avoided speaking with Granger and Dempsey whenever possible. I read the new officer's name tag: *J. B. Lyles.*

"Doctors told us it's seventy to thirty that he'll make it," Lyles said. "Luckily, Holt was found shortly after the shooting, and the bullet missed hitting his heart."

Better odds than I'd feared. The tight knot in my stomach loosened a fraction.

Oliver pushed past the crowd and walked into the ICU unit.

"Hey," Dempsey said. "No one's allowed in. Doctor's orders."

Oliver didn't slow his stride or give any indication he'd heard Dempsey's warning. Without hesitation, I also entered the ICU room.

Holt lay in a raised hospital cot with a myriad of tubes protruding from both arms. A thin line of blood trickled out of a thicker drainage tube inserted into his chest. His skin bore a grayish cast that was obvious even in the slightly darkened room. Buzzes and bleeps from several monitors formed a continuous background cadence.

Holt's eyes slitted open as we approached his bedside. "About time y'all showed up," he grumbled.

"Feel like a Mack truck just ran you over, buddy?" Oliver asked, giving his hand a quick squeeze. "Did you see who shot you?"

"Yeah. Listen." Holt struggled to sit up, then winced and flopped back down on the mattress, casting an uneasy glance at the open doorway. "Shut the door," he whispered. Despite his lowered voice, the urgency in his request was undeniable, and I was amazed at his ability to converse with us, given his condition.

Holt tightly gripped the blanket's edge that was pulled up past his waist. "Don't let them in here. They came in twice already, and I pretended to be out of it. Oliver, promise to get me a cop from Mobile PD to guard my room. Make sure the locals stay away."

Lines of worry creased Oliver's forehead. "Is there some reason not to trust the Enigma cops?"

"Damn straight. They're dirty. The drug ring's headed by your mayor, and some of the cops are on his payroll. I don't know how many, but Dempsey and Granger are definitely dirty."

"Hank Rembert?" I asked doubtfully. "Are you sure?"

"One hundred percent."

Oliver and I glanced at each other, brows raised at the bombshell. Although Oliver didn't appear as surprised as me.

"Could it be you aren't thinking clearly?" Oliver asked. "They must have you pumped with a ton of painkillers."

"How can you be so surprised?" Holt asked. "I only corroborated what Dana Adair already told you."

The name jolted me with recognition. Dana Adair, Jori's estranged friend. "Is this woman your informant?" I asked Oliver and Holt, glancing back and forth between the two men.

"Yeah. And turns out she's a damn good one. Unless . . ." Holt wiped a hand over his face, and for the first time I noticed a slight tremor in his body. His heart-rate monitor sputtered and then resumed.

"Unless you think she's behind the shooting?" Oliver asked. "Maybe she had second thoughts and turned on us. Could be the mayor got wind of her passing information and threatened her to set you up."

"You can never be sure in this business," Holt conceded, his lungs rattling as he drew a breath.

"Hey, you want the doctor?" I asked.

"No, man. I'm just . . . I'm exhausted. They gave me a shot of morphine thirty minutes ago. I'm tired but can't sleep with those jokers hanging around my door. For all I know, they might finish the job if they think I'm on to them."

"I'll stay here with you until a Mobile cop arrives," Oliver promised. "Tell me what you remember about the shooting."

"I was waiting on a delivery. Two guys I didn't recognize pulled up alongside my car. Before I could react, the guy on the passenger side unrolled his window and shot. My chest exploded. That's the last thing I remember."

"What kind of car?" I asked. "Can you describe the men?"

Holt shook his head. "It was dark. All I can tell you is that it was a black truck. The shooter wore a mask."

Oliver and I exchanged a look. Holt hadn't given us much to work with.

"We'll question Dempsey, Granger, and the mayor," Oliver said.

"No!" Holt's eyes snapped open. "You do that now, it'll ruin everything. I have no proof yet, only Dana's info. We need to set up a sting. They have a shipment coming by boat Sunday."

"Then there's no time," I said, shaking my head. "It's already Thursday."

"I'll be out of here by tonight or in the morning," Holt assured us. "You move now, we can't prove shit. We have to catch them in the act."

"But this Sunday?" I asked, full of skepticism. "That can't be right. The main activities for our Blessing will be in full swing. Cops and tourists will be everywhere along the waterway."

"What better time?" Holt argued. "They'll deliver right there under everyone's noses, and no one will think to question what's happening. It's damn perfect."

Oliver nodded, his face grim. "We'll do it. In the meantime, I'll contact Mobile PD. Get your rest—we'll make sure you're safe."

"Thanks, man." Holt needed no further encouragement. He closed his eyes, and within seconds his taut face relaxed and his chest slowly rose and fell in slumber.

"I was hoping Dana was wrong and that the operation didn't go so high up." Oliver sank into a chair and set to work.

Wearily, he withdrew his cell phone and started making security arrangements with the Mobile chief of police, explaining the need for utter confidentiality in the case. He kept his voice low so the men outside the door couldn't understand what he was saying. I strolled to the window and peered into the vista. From this view on the top floor, you could make out the horizontal line of the Gulf of Mexico in the distance. No matter what human tragedies played out, the sea was a familiar constant, its rhythm a steady comfort in my life.

Hank Rembert. Gilbert Dempsey. Leroy Granger. All dirty. I'd never liked any of them, but the thought they were involved in drug smuggling had never entered my mind. The room grew silent as Oliver wrapped up his phone call. That done, he walked over to stand next to me.

"Mind blowing, isn't it?" he murmured. "What kind of town do you have here anyway? Bayou Enigma's always had a somewhat shady reputation for cops turning a blind eye on crime, but this . . ."

"Unbelievable," I agreed. "Guess you were right all along. The Strickland and Ensley murders might be drug related too. It seems to be a common motive here."

"Your other leads were worth checking out," Oliver said. "But it's looking like the Trahern kidnapping and threats against their family appear to be unrelated to our murder case."

"Yeah. Maybe that's good news. Could just be a disgruntled relative causing trouble for Jori. They left threatening notes and then took Zach to their house for a couple hours, never intending to harm him."

"It's still a serious crime, but for now we need to focus on the drug sting."

"You're right, of course. I was just so sure that the Cormier case might have been linked to the other murders."

"It's still possible Louis Cormier was involved in drug trafficking. Once we arrest Rembert and the others, we'll ask them who else was involved in the ring over the years."

He shot me a warning glance. "Don't say a word to anyone or act any different than normal around the mayor and cops. We can't tip them off or give them any reason to change their scheduled delivery."

"Of course," I agreed. "Are you going to ask the Mobile chief to help us catch them?"

"Yes, along with the ALEA top brass."

"If you want to get back to the office, I can stay here with Holt until the Mobile cop arrives."

"Good idea," Oliver said, glancing at his watch. "Someone should be here shortly. I'll text you the name of the officer they're sending as soon as I'm notified. Don't let Dempsey and the other Enigma cops set foot in this room. Make up any excuse you have to."

Grim satisfaction pooled in my belly as I thought of thwarting Dempsey and Granger. It would be great to see those jerks get their comeuppance. "No worries," I told Oliver. "It will be my pleasure to deny them entrance."

Chapter 29

JORI

I systematically walked from checkpoint to checkpoint, crossing items off my list as I confirmed that every facet of the Blessing event was progressing smoothly and on time. But amid the flurry of activity and cluster of tourists, I kept worrying about Zach and Mimi. Thank goodness Rose had agreed to stay at our house for the entire weekend; otherwise I couldn't concentrate on my job.

My worry had increased after last night's call from Tegan informing me that the police watch of our house would be reduced from full time to an occasional drive-by. Effective immediately. Anger still roiled my gut at the news. Tegan had seemed preoccupied and distant during the call, in a rush to move on to other matters, even after I'd explained that Aunt Tressie was most likely the one behind the threatening notes and Zach's abduction. Her response? Come to the office first thing Monday morning for us to discuss the matter.

Did that mean she didn't believe my theory? Or were Zach and our family considered unimportant? If it'd been the mayor's son who'd been kidnapped, I'd bet every law enforcement officer in the county would be working around the clock to discover the culprit.

The injustice of it simmered inside me behind my professional calm and polite smiles at the Blessing volunteers. Without their support, the event would never have grown the way it had.

At the waterfront pier, the smell of seafood gumbo mingled with the scent of Vietnamese cuisine. Judging the cook-off was one of my favorite Blessing moments every year. I settled at a picnic table with the other judges and dug into the food, marking my rating of the individual fares.

With a full, happy stomach, I left the pier to check the progress of the 5K Blessing Race, but my attention was caught by a group of sheriff's deputies clustered by the marina. Tegan was part of the crowd, her expression intense and serious. It struck me that the entire group's mood was different. Usually, the deputies and cops on security detail casually strolled about, seemingly enjoying themselves as much as the tourists. Despite my grudge with Tegan, curiosity propelled me to walk toward them.

"Hello, Officers," I said cheerily, edging into the group. "Everything going all right?"

They all abruptly turned to stare at me. Lieutenant Oliver spoke first. "Everything's under control, Ms. Trahern. How's your brother doing?"

"As far as I know, he's fine. Presumably right at home where he should be. Of course, I'd feel more certain if there was a cop car still parked in front of our house, so . . ."

Oliver didn't appear the least bit fazed by my dig. "Good to hear he's doing well. Deputy Blackwell's told me that you two have an appointment on Monday to talk about a possible lead on the case."

I had to bite my tongue to keep from asking if they believed their mere presence at the Blessing meant more than solving an actual crime. Bottom line—they worked for the mayor, and this event was a huge financial boon to Bayou Enigma.

"Yes. It wouldn't take that much of her time to hear me out before then. But, whatever. Good day, everyone."

I hoofed it back to the pier, eager to exit before my bitterness caused me to say more that I'd probably later regret. Cheers and clapping erupted by the picnic area. I'd missed the cook-off winner announcement.

"Jori, wait."

Tegan popped up beside me. "I can spare a few minutes to talk if you'd like."

"Gee, thanks." I kept walking. "Wouldn't want to impose."

"I'm trying to help you the best I can, given the circumstances. If you'd rather wait until Monday, then okay. I realize you're busy too."

I came to a halt. "I don't mean to be ungrateful. It's been super stressful for me ever since I came home. The transition would have been difficult enough without all the added drama."

She nodded and folded her arms. "Of course. I'm a single mom, so I understand a little about stress. Not that I'm comparing my situation to yours. Tell me more about your aunt and why you think she's behind everything."

I filled her in as succinctly as possible, conscious of her valuable time ticking away. "So you see, my aunt's a great actress. For years, I never dreamed she had this dark side—until I talked to her ex-husband."

"Your theory is that she threatened you and kidnapped Zach to keep you from exposing her crime of buying a baby."

"It sounds far fetched when you repeat it back to me like that, but yeah, that's exactly what I believe."

Tegan nodded thoughtfully. "Maybe. But you can't believe your aunt killed her own son that she loved or had anything to do with the Cormier murders. You used to think the threats were all tied into everything else."

"True," I admitted. "I was way off there. I wanted so much to help discover what happened to Deacon that I lumped everything together in my mind."

"Do you think your aunt's really capable of murdering Strickland?"

I didn't hesitate with my answer. "Yes."

"Very well. Lieutenant Oliver and I will interview her as soon as possible. If she confesses or we uncover evidence to arrest her for suspicion of murder, I'll let you know. In the meantime, don't speak with your aunt or tip her off in any way that we're investigating her."

"Absolutely."

Tegan turned to the group of officers by the waterfront and waved. "I should get back."

"Wait. Before you go. Have y'all made any progress in the Cormier case?"

"I can't answer that."

"You told me there's evidence that law enforcement was always aware they'd been murdered. Can you give me anything more specific?" I'd been eaten up with curiosity ever since she'd slipped me that tiny bit of information.

"Why are you so obsessed with that old case? I know you used to date Deacon in high school, but still."

Dating in high school. Put like that, it sounded as though Deacon and I merely had a passing crush for one another as kids. But as corny as it might seem to outsiders, Deacon had meant so much more to me than a teenage crush. He always would.

During a difficult time in my life when my mother was dying and Zach was in his own bubbled world, he'd been the one person I could talk to. Really talk to. Mimi was great, a solid presence in my life, but hardly one who invited emotional conversations or wanted to listen to my vulnerabilities. She was old-school tough and would merely tell me to accept what was and move on, just as she had done.

I struggled to explain this to Tegan. "Call it closure. I may have only been a teenager when he disappeared, but I've never felt closer to anyone than I did Deacon. Not even now."

Her face softened, but she shook her head. "I'm sorry, but I really can't jeopardize the investigation by discussing it."

Even though I'd expected that response, I sighed, and my shoulders hunched forward. "I get it."

"Blackwell!" One of the men called her name from the waterfront. She nodded at him and began walking away. "Later, Jori."

I watched as she marched toward her peers. Halfway there, she held out an arm to them, an index finger waving. *One moment,* she signaled. To my surprise, she turned around and headed back to me.

"We discovered a recording," she said. "On it, Deacon was being filmed by his mother. He wore a tux and held a corsage in one hand. Moments later, someone entered the house, and gunshots were fired. There's a long pause on the recording, but before the battery died, there's the sound of the killer and one or more of his accomplices returning. Presumably to clean up and dispose of the bodies."

My heart pounded painfully against my ribs, so hard I wouldn't have been surprised if it crushed those bones. In the last moments of his life, I had to have been on Deacon's mind, as he was dressed in the rented tux and holding the corsage meant for me.

A recording. The significance of it slammed into my brain. "You couldn't see the killer?"

"Wrong camera angle."

"What about the voices?"

"Too garbled to identify, and forensics couldn't match them to any known suspects. None of the Cormiers' nearest living relatives could identify them either."

"Send it to me."

"No. And don't repeat what I've just told you."

"But I can help you. I'm great at identifying voices. I have synes—"

"Blackwell!" Lieutenant Oliver's voice had a hard edge.

Tegan turned and hurried back to her job.

My heart pounded in my chest. If I could just hear that recording, I might be able to solve the case. That is, if the killer was anyone I knew.

Chapter 30

TEGAN

Sunday. The final day of the Blessing of the Fleet activities and the much-anticipated blessing by the archbishop. Ships were lined up by the drawbridge, awaiting their individual blessing before heading into the gulf to begin the fishing season.

The small ship that Holt claimed held packages of heroin, cocaine, and fentanyl was midway in the line, awaiting its turn for the priest's blessing. Of all the hypocrisy. Its name, *Zephyr*, was painted on the side of the hull.

Dressed in an ankle-length black cassock with red piping and white miter headwear, the archbishop stood on the wooden dock and spoke into the microphone, his voice loud and clear.

"Dear Merciful God," he began. "The sea surprises, delights, and sometimes terrifies us. It is the source of your wondrous bounty—fish, shrimp, oysters, and mullets—and its beauty and mystery delights us while we respect its power and the secrets which lie beneath its surface."

Mayor Rembert and several other politicians were seated at a place of honor where the priest spoke on the wooden pier. Nothing about the mayor's demeanor suggested he was nervous about the nearby ship with its illegal cargo. I scanned the silently respectful crowd, watching for any unusual activity.

"Lord be with those who sail your waters and brave its precarious moods . . ."

Jori stood near the shore, head bowed, still clutching her ever-present clipboard she'd used all weekend to check off the agenda time-line with vendors and volunteers. Even from this distance, I detected subtle signs she was tired. Her weight shifted from foot to foot, and her shoulders slumped. Compassion washed over me. I knew that despite the long hours at work, she'd returned home to take care of her family.

"Protect our brave men and women from the perils of wind, rain, and the deep. Grace them with an abundant harvest as they . . ."

What if Jori really could help with the Cormier case? What would be the harm in allowing her to listen to the recording? I played with the idea. Lieutenant Oliver would be angry if he knew I'd shared the recording, but the potential reward of Jori actually identifying the killer outweighed any possible censure by my boss.

"And may they return home safe to be reunited with loved ones who have waited . . ."

On my cell phone, I located Jori's name in my contacts, hit the attachment icon, and scrolled to find the MP3 recording Ginger had provided. My index finger hovered. Was this a fireable offense? Recklessly, I hit send.

Moments later I observed Jori pull out her phone. Her mouth dropped open an inch as she read, and then her head snapped up, eyes scanning the crowd. Our gazes met. I nodded with a slight smile, and she waved before returning her attention to the phone. Hastily, I sent another text.

Don't listen in public.

As low key as Oliver was trying to keep this drug sting, several undercover officers roamed about.

Jori faced me and gave the *okay* sign before wandering off on her own.

The booming, mournful peal of a bell suddenly tolled, once, then twice, for the two sailors who'd perished at sea over the past year. My attention returned to the job at hand. The archbishop lit a bronze censer and blessed the lead boat in line. Even from here, the sweet scent of copal, myrrh, and frankincense was notable as the smoky incense drifted on the bayou breeze.

Slowly, the boats inched forward for their blessing. At last the *Zephyr* received its blessing. I carefully watched the mayor, but his expression of bland geniality did not falter. It was as though this particular boat was of no particular significance to him. Was it possible Carter Holt had been wrong about a drug shipment?

I strolled to my unmarked vehicle and entered, trying to appear casual. Cruising along below the speed limit, I turned off the main road in minutes and onto a deserted, dusty road.

The two-way radio crackled. "Proceed to location."

"Ten-four."

A mile farther, I pulled over to the side of the road to await further instructions. No one appeared anywhere near, but I picked my cell phone up from the passenger seat and scrolled through it. Should any car come by, the passengers would hopefully believe I'd stopped to read an important message. Only seconds after I shut off the engine, humidity blanketed my skin. *Screw that.* No telling how long I'd be sitting here. I turned the key in the ignition, and air-conditioning pumped out cool air. Much better.

The absolute quiet was eerie. Oliver had elected to include as few law enforcement personnel in the sting as possible, handpicking several officers from the Mobile PD who he knew personally. He'd requested, and been granted, assistance from Homeland Security. A US Coast

Guard cutter had been arranged. The beauty of involving the Coast Guard was that it had sweeping authority to board any vessel at any time or any place without need of a warrant or even probable cause. For over two hundred years, US courts consistently had upheld their right to do so.

So where were all these people awaiting delivery? If the drug smugglers already had their workers and a vehicle in place for the shipment, I wouldn't be notified. Oliver had wisely ordered that radio silence be maintained as long as possible.

Churning water sounded, and I quickly rolled down my windows again to hear better. Was it the *Zephyr* after all? Had it broken rank from the steady procession of shrimper boats headed out for deeper waters?

The still of the bayou suddenly shattered as shouts emerged from across the woods. My radio crackled again with the same message as before.

"Proceed to location."

Adrenaline flooded my body in waves. I stomped on the accelerator and emerged onto the dirt road, dust flying and tires squealing. No need for stealth anymore.

Another right turn, and I was upon the mayhem. The *Zephyr* swarmed with US Coast Guardsmen in their navy-blue uniforms. Alongside the *Zephyr*, their white cutter was moored with its red-and-blue bands, their official emblem, and the letters *USCG*. The Coast Guard standard flag whipped in the breeze, white with yellow fringe and a dark-blue US coat of arms.

Mobile cops escorted two handcuffed men from the boat. Another cop had a third man handcuffed against a nearby rusty truck and was reading him his rights. Everywhere, men and women barked orders.

Guardsmen began carrying out crates to waiting personnel. Oliver motioned to me, and we hurried over. One of the men cracked open a crate, revealing tightly wrapped bundles.

"What do we have here?" He smiled grimly. With a box cutter he carefully ripped off the paper on one of them. A solid brick of white powder appeared.

"Heroin?" one of the guardsmen asked.

"Definitely."

A total of four crates were unloaded. In the last one, instead of white bricks, there was a large clear bag of bluish-gray pills.

"Pretty sure the lab will find this is fentanyl," the guardsmen said. "Perfect for cutting with heroin."

Oliver and I smiled at one another with grim satisfaction. Carter Holt had not been mistaken. Mayor Rembert's political career was dead in the water. The men apprehended today would no doubt soon be spilling the names of everyone involved in their operation. It was a shame Holt couldn't be here in person to witness the takedown. His bosses had insisted that he remain undercover and far from the action. That way, they could still use him to bust other drug operations.

I continued to watch the guardsmen unload the drugs, mesmerized at the large number of packages, each a bundle of misery and heartache for addicts and their families. It was much later before I finally noticed that I'd received a text from Jori.

Chapter 31

JORI

I rushed toward the shade provided by a copse of live oaks as I hurried to open the recording Tegan had sent. At long last, would I be able to recognize the voice and discover who'd killed Deacon? I paused at the edge of the woods and glanced around.

I was alone.

My fingers trembled as I turned up the phone volume all the way and hit play.

The past rushed up to greet me in an explosion of sound and color as the recording began.

Clotille spoke— pale lavender spiked on flowering lily pads.

A second ticked by, and then Deacon spoke.

Deacon. Dark violet waves, crested with foaming whitecaps, flooded over me. I swayed, gasping as though doused, and my arm reached out automatically, finding solid grounding against rough tree bark.

A distant sound of gunshot was followed by Clotille's scream. Lavender gushed and spiked with Clotille's high-pitched cry. I'd never heard such a desperate edge to a sound. The closest I could compare it to was when I'd heard the pain and panicked screams of a feral cat in the death throes of a coyote attack. There was a rawness to it that could never be faked in a movie.

The camera fell to the floor with an abrupt crash.

A door squeaked open. My breath caught in my throat. Who had done this? Did Deacon and Clotille recognize whoever had appeared on the threshold? Or was this a hired gun paid to carry out brutal executions?

Clotille's voice sounded again before a new voice murmured, garbled and indistinct. Umber swirled like a tornado spiraling toward a random target. It was a remembered musical note, but my brain couldn't quite put the correct shape and shade to what the tornado tried to form.

A gunshot exploded, this time from close range.

"Mom!" Violet-and-white foam swirled with Deacon's anguished voice.

Again, the new male voice muttered something.

Bam. Another shot rang out. The noise reached across time, squeezing my heart in a vise with the burst. My knees gave way beneath me, and I sank onto the ground, my back scraping against the oak for support. Footsteps thudded on the recording, their vibrations treading on my chest. A door opened and shut.

And then there was only the whirring of the recording, more menacing than the screams and the footsteps and the gunshots. It was the sound of death. Had Deacon and his mother bled out on the living room floor as the tape continued? I never, ever wanted to see the actual video footage; the audio alone was traumatic enough.

I closed my eyes and continued to sit as the mechanical noise tunelessly droned on. Ordinary sounds of life carried on all around me—the gentle backdrop of ocean swells breaking on the gulf, talk and laughter by the dock as the ships left for open sea, birds singing and squirrels scurrying in their busy business of survival.

I imagined Deacon's heart still beating, growing slower and more erratic, his breath more shallow. Or had he died instantly? I hoped to hell he had, that other than the few seconds when the killer entered his house, aimed, and fired the shots, the end had been quick and merciful. Much as I didn't want to, I had to rewind and listen to this tape again and again, as many times as necessary, until the colors and shape of the unidentified voice revealed itself.

"Jori?" Green arrows—Dana's voice. "Are you okay? Someone thought they heard a scream this way."

I jumped to my feet with a startled gasp. My phone dropped to the ground. "I-I'm fine."

"You look like you've seen a ghost." She cocked her head to one side. "What's that noise?"

I scooped up my phone, but not before the endless whirring of the recorder gave way to the sound of garbled voices again and the squeak of a door opening.

"What are you listening to?"

"An audiobook." I switched off my phone and wiped at the tears gathering in my eyes. "Go away, Dana. I told you I'm fine. We have nothing more to say to each other."

Dana shook her head sadly. "I'm sorry, okay? Can't you let it go? We've been friends since grade school."

"No. I just thought we were friends." I leaned over, this time to pick up the clipboard with my event agenda.

"We were friends. Still can be if you'll let bygones be bygones."

"Leave me alone, Dana."

"But I—"

"Here." I held the clipboard out in front of me. "You want to help me, give this to Ashley Rogers. You know her, don't you?"

"Yeah. She works with the mayor's office."

"Give it to her and say I had to leave unexpectedly. All that's left to do is make sure the city maintenance crew starts cleanup and answer any questions that might pop up from vendors or guests."

I turned my back on Dana and stepped into the woods. Obviously, I needed to find a better place if I wanted to be left alone. The path was narrow but well traveled. Kids still rode their bikes through here to get to Choctaw Beach, a small strip of sand in a secluded area. The place was only a fifteen-minute hike by foot. While there I could sit on a patch of sandy soil. With any luck, I'd catch sight of several kayakers as they rowed their way to the final lap of the event course.

Minutes later twigs snapped behind me, and I whirled around to face Dana. "Why are you following me?"

"I can tell something's wrong. Come back with me, and we'll get a drink at the Pavilion."

"Go. Away."

Without waiting for a response, I spun around and marched forward. Minutes later, after hearing no sounds of being followed, I glanced back over my shoulder. Dana was gone.

I'd worked up a sweat by the time I arrived at Choctaw Beach. I plopped down on the warm sand and scooped a handful of hair up from the back of my neck. The forested banks offered seclusion from open ocean views. Tall willows, sycamores, and other tree species reflected green in the slow-moving stream. Here in the primitive, mysterious heart of the bayou, the humidity was tempered by shade and cooling breezes over water. Here my heartbeat slowed under the spell of ancient tree roots that veined on the bank sides and reached deep into the earth. Here I sunk into the peaceful rhythms of nature, the unceasing wail of cicadas, the splash of turtles sunning on rocks and then returning to their murky underwater domain, and the eternal backdrop of breaking ocean waves in the distance. A gentle breeze passed over my bare nape, and I drew several full breaths, growing calm for the task ahead.

At last I was ready. I turned on my phone and started the recording over from the beginning. The gunshots still shook me to the core, but not with the intensity of the first listen. I still couldn't make out the tornado of sound that refused to settle into a specific color and shape.

Again, the file reached the long whirring period. According to my phone, there was a little over twenty minutes remaining. I waited it out as though it were a lifeline spanning across the past thirteen years and I was lying in blood on the floor with Deacon, together for one last time. I stared at the phone screen. Only another eighteen seconds left. Seconds before I expected the whirring to end, a large thud sounded, as though the camcorder had been dropped again.

Someone—Deacon? The killer?—was still in the room. Perhaps they'd tossed the camcorder to hide it, or the killer had thrown it, thinking to break the machine.

Distant voices sounded. Footsteps grew closer. The door opened.

"Let's get this over with," uttered a deep voice—or words to that effect. The recording was so muffled it was hard to tell exactly what was said. It sounded as though the camcorder might have been stuffed under a pillow or blanket.

Yet—I knew that voice. The umber whirlwind settled and transformed into burnt-orange cubes. My lungs seized with shock. More faint words came, undecipherable, yet my colored hearing picked up on the tone, and I recognized the patterns as clearly as a thumbprint.

Burnt-orange cubes flared again as the voice issued some command that I didn't quite catch. So this was the killer.

"Jori? What are you doing here? Everything all right?"

I turned. And stared into the face of the devil himself.

Uncle Buddy.

The man I'd always believed to be our family's benefactor, the reliable uncle who could be counted on in a financial pinch, the respectable businessman and community leader in the bayou. He was a fraud. A murderous fraud. All this time. I'd never really known the man at all.

Chapter 32

BUDDY MUNFORD

One look into Jori's eyes told me all I needed to know. Panic and shock radiated from every tense muscle in her body. She was a gazelle, set to run at the least provocation.

I walked toward her slowly, as though I didn't recognize her fear. As though I were still her dear old kindly uncle—the one who'd lent them money for so many years. Actually, I had been a damn good uncle. I'd helped out my sister and her ill daughter for years, paying their bills, making sure Zach received excellent care for his special needs, and making sure Jori's mom had the best medical care when she was struck with cancer. Wasn't my fault that it had to end. I'd done my best to scare Jori off from sniffing around that damn adoption.

How was it possible that she'd discovered the truth? And after all these years too. It wasn't fair.

"Dana told me you were acting strange. That something was wrong."

"I-I'm fine," she lied.

Deception had never been her strong suit.

"Well, now, that's debatable," I said, smile in place, easing forward. "When Dana told me what direction you'd headed, I figured this was where you'd end up."

Jori glanced left and right, then over a shoulder at the blue expanse behind her. "Kayakers should be here soon," she said quickly. "They have to pass by here to get to the finish line at the dock."

I stopped walking. She was right. I'd forgotten all about that damn kayak race. Jori hurriedly punched something into her phone, and I frowned. Was she texting for help? My fingers curled into my palms, my hands tightening into fists. I had to get the phone from her.

I marched to Jori and grabbed her arm. "I'll take that."

She cried out as I pried the phone from her hand.

"Give me my phone back," Jori demanded with false bravado.

Keeping a firm grasp on her arm, I scrolled up the screen with my opposite hand and read the message Jori had just sent.

It's Buddy. Help.

Above that line was a link to an MP3 recording. The recipient of Jori's text was Deputy Tegan Blackwell. I clicked on the link.

It wasn't until I heard the gunshot and the screams that I realized what it was. Shock gave way to panic, then anger. Someone had recorded the shooting? How had we missed finding it when we cleaned up the house?

A sharp kick on my shin sent pain radiating up my right leg. My grip loosened at the surprise attack, and Jori took off running into the woods. Twenty feet inside the confines of the wooded area, I caught up to Jori and tackled her to the ground from behind.

She didn't even have time to let out a scream before her body hit the dirt with a loud thud. I fell on top of Jori and grabbed a handful of her hair.

She yelled, and I pulled her hair tighter. "Shut up and I'll let go. We need to talk. Understand?"

"Yes," she said, moaning and whimpering.

I flipped Jori onto her back and wrapped my hands around her throat. "Now you're going to answer a few questions. What did you mean when you told the cop *it's Buddy*?"

"N-nothing," she stammered, eyes glazed with panic.

I pressed my thumbs into the soft hollow of her neck. "Liar. I don't have much time. Why do you think it was me on that tape?"

She didn't answer right away, and I realized I was squeezing her throat too tight for her to speak. I eased up on the pressure. "Well?"

"Your voice," she whispered hoarsely. "I recognized it."

I frowned. "How could you possibly . . ." Then I remembered. Oatha had mentioned several times in the past that Jori had something called *colored hearing.*

"What bullshit," I said fiercely. How could something so abnormal . . . so freaky . . . defeat me? I refused to let it.

I thought fast, realizing I had very little time before either a cop or maybe even Dana came looking for my niece. I'd have to kill her. And quickly. The cops couldn't prove anything, especially if her body were never found. Momentary guilt stabbed my heart, but I tamped it down. Killing Oatha's beloved grandchild, the great-niece I'd watched mature into a kind, intelligent young lady . . . well, it was such a shame.

Keeping one hand wrapped around her neck, I retrieved her cell phone from my pants. "Password?"

"Noscam8871." Despite her fear, loathing filled her eyes. "You sick bastard."

I winced inwardly at the insult. Jori didn't understand that you could care about someone but recognize that all that really mattered in this world was your own survival. My needs came first, always. Quickly, I dialed Cash. "We've got a problem. Bring the car around to mile marker five on Conch Road. I've got a hostage and need a quick get-away. How soon can you get here?"

"Five minutes," he promised, then hung up. That's what I liked about Cash. He never asked questions, never acted surprised. Just did what he was told. If only everyone were so malleable, there'd be no need to silence them.

"Here's what we're going to do," I said to Jori. "We're going to walk toward the road and then go for a ride."

Her eyes shot daggers at me, but she wasn't stupid. Reluctantly, she nodded. "Okay."

"Up you go." I twisted one of her arms behind her back and jerked her to her feet.

I guided her off the beaten path and shoved her in front of me, still twisting her arm behind her back. She stumbled forward at a slow clip in what I suspected was a deliberately passive-aggressive move. Didn't matter. Even at this slow rate, we'd reach our destination before Cash arrived with the car.

I didn't like this situation one bit. But I'd do what was necessary, even if she was family.

Chapter 33

JORI

"You little witch," Uncle Buddy muttered, strengthening his hold and twisting my arm another degree tighter until tears ran down my face. "Why can't you just mind me? It will be easier on both of us that way."

A car motor sounded from the distance and roared closer before coming to a complete stop. From the trees, I made out a black truck. Cash Johnson opened the door and stepped out.

"Buddy?" he called.

"Over here."

Fear paralyzed my muscles, and I sagged against Uncle Buddy. If those two forced me into the car, my fate would be sealed. Buddy's voice wasn't the only one I'd heard on that tape. Cash had been there as well. "Please don't do this," I begged. "I won't tell anyone."

"Cat's out of the bag already," he said. "I'm truly sorry."

"I'll make up some kind of story for Tegan," I promised. I'd promise him anything at this point.

Cash walked to the edge of the woods, then entered, stomping through the dense underbrush.

"What kind of story?" Uncle Buddy asked.

"Like I was mistaken. That I can't identify your voice."

"Don't believe anything she says." Cash burst through, scanning me from head to toe with open contempt.

I swallowed hard. The man had always creeped me out, but until this moment his disdain had been shadowed, hidden beneath a thin veneer of politeness. The mask was stripped away now.

"Jori Trahern's been nothing but a slut since she was in high school," Cash continued. "Always sneaking around at night meeting her boyfriend. Screwing him in that old smokehouse."

The memory of Deacon and what these two had done to him fueled me with rage. He shouldn't have died so young. He'd been denied so much, his life stolen.

"Why did you kill him? Why?"

They ignored my anguished question. Cash grabbed my free arm and twisted it behind my back. I was trapped between them as they dragged me forward. We reached the street, and I desperately searched in both directions. Not a car or person was in sight. Cash opened the passenger door to the back seat. I stared at the gray interior with mounting terror. My inner voice screamed a warning.

Do not get in that truck.

If I did, there'd be no escape. I'd be totally at the mercy of these two psychopaths. They would kill me.

My feet dug into the ground like leaden weights, and I leaned backward, struggling to free my arms from their grasps. Their fingers dug grooves into my already abused biceps. Still, I screamed and flailed from side to side, hoping against hope to break free of their grip for just one second. If I could, I might be able to outrun them, considering they were so much older than me.

"You bring some rope?" Uncle Buddy asked Cash. His voice was strained, and he panted from exertion.

Rope? I redoubled my efforts to get free.

"It's in the back floorboard," Cash said. "You get it while I hold her."

The moment Uncle Buddy dropped my arm, I kicked Cash in the shin with all my strength, desperate to get away.

Sharp pain exploded from my left shoulder with a loud pop. The dislocation burned like a hot poker and stole my breath.

In a haze of pain, I screamed uselessly as Uncle Buddy returned to my side and bound my wrists behind my back. Next, he bound my ankles with rope as Cash kept the pressure on my dislocated shoulder. I was shoved into the back seat, Uncle Buddy beside me. The truck door slammed shut, sounding like a death knell.

I was entirely at their mercy—a quality I knew they both distinctly lacked.

Cash entered the front of the truck and threw a torn piece of cloth at Buddy. "Want to gag her?"

Without answering or any hesitation, Uncle Buddy grabbed my jaw. I twisted my head from side to side. He slapped me hard in the face. The stinging flesh on my right cheek temporarily stunned me. He placed the cloth between my teeth and roughly tied the gag. It was suffocating. I felt like I couldn't breathe properly. I forced myself to calm down, slowly inhaling and exhaling.

Uncle Buddy shoved me to the floorboard, and the truck began to roll. The vibrations rumbled through my body as I attempted to collect my wits. I had to think. I had to develop a plan. The first step was to be aware of my location. If I made it out of the vehicle alive, I needed to know which direction to run.

"Where to?" Cash asked Buddy.

"Number eighteen."

The answer made no sense to me.

The truck made a sharp right, and the pitch of the tires changed. We were on the main road, heading past the dock. The sounds of other vehicles passed by—so close, and yet I could do nothing to signal my distress. A boat horn sounded from the gulf. Probably the last of the shrimp boats headed to open water for the first day of the season. Tourists as well as the locals would be heading home about now.

I struggled to rise up and pound on a window for help, but Uncle Buddy yanked on my hair, pulling out a handful.

"Don't you dare," he threatened.

I moaned around the gag. "Please, stop." My words were garbled, but I'm sure he understood what I was trying to convey. He let go of my hair and leaned back in his seat, smiling and waving at a passerby.

My heart pinched as I thought of my grandmother and Zach waiting for me at home. How many hours would pass before Mimi called the police? Too many to do any good, I was sure. And that was even if she was thinking clearly today. Poor Zach. With Mimi's descent into dementia and me gone, what would happen to him? He'd be dependent on the kindness of strangers. Or—my heart dropped as it occurred to me—Uncle Buddy might become his guardian.

That horror redoubled my determination to escape. If that meant lying to these two bastards, then I would. I'd never been much of an actress, but I'd do my best.

Cash turned the truck left. We were heading downtown.

"Here." Cash tossed a blanket over the seat to Uncle Buddy. "Better cover her up to be safe."

Thick wool was thrown over me, scratchy and hot against my skin. It smelled of musk and wet dog. With each breath I drew, the wool formed a suction over my mouth. Suffocating. The dark was as complete as though I were buried in a coffin.

From outside came the muffled sounds of people talking and laughing, other vehicles humming along the road, an occasional blast of a horn. I longed to be free. To feel the fresh gulf air with its tang of salt, to see the decorated ships with their colorful triangular flags and Old Glory flapping in the breeze.

Another left turn, and the sounds grew more distant.

"Anyone on our tail?" Uncle Buddy asked.

"Nope. We're good."

I swallowed my despair and tried to refocus on where we were. We must be on the Shell Beltway, which led to 1-10 toward Mobile. Only a minute later, Cash took another left. But which road? It could be any of a dozen dirt roads that lined the highway. The truck veered left, and the ride became bumpier. The tires dug into less-compacted sand. My body bounced painfully as we ran over a deep pothole. The road must have narrowed, as tree limbs scraped along the truck sides, resulting in a metallic screech that sent indigo flames zapping my brain. It was one of the few sounds that actually sparked an unpleasant physical jolt through me.

We were driving farther and farther from a chance encounter with anyone.

Abruptly, the truck stopped. My heart beat wildly. Now what?

A door opened. The blanket was lifted. I squinted up at Uncle Buddy. Cash's rough hands grabbed me under my arms, and he pulled me out of the truck. Unceremoniously, he dropped me to the ground, and I fell on one side, the pain in my dislocated shoulder flaring on impact. Despite the agony, I rolled my bound body from his booted feet, afraid he'd kick me.

Uncle Buddy stooped down and grabbed my legs. "Don't want to carry her inside. She's too heavy."

Cash loomed over me, a silver buck knife glinting in the bright sun. He swooped down closer, and I let out a strangled scream. I braced myself for more pain, and Cash chuckled. But instead of plunging the knife into my chest, he angled it toward my feet. With a deft, experienced twist of his wrist, the ropes fell from my ankles.

"You're going to be a good girl, right, Jori?" Uncle Buddy asked. As though I were a child and he was taking me out for a walk in the park. There was even the tiniest suggestion of sadness, as though he were a reluctant disciplinarian who had my own good at heart. "No kicking," he admonished.

I nodded my agreement.

"And no screaming," he continued. "I don't think anyone would hear you, but . . ."

I vigorously nodded, eager to have the gag removed. Instead of untying the knot at the back of my head, he took Cash's knife. The cool blade against my face sent shivers down my spine. The lethal edge of the blade ripped through the fabric, and it fell off.

I took long gulps of air, thankful for the small mercy. Cash reached for my arm, and I scrambled backward.

"I can stand on my own," I said, not wanting his rough handling to make my injury more painful. It was an awkward struggle with my bound hands, but I rose to my feet.

Across from me was a small hunting cabin with Uncle Buddy's signature placard hanging on the front door: ENIGMA OUTDOOR EXPEDITIONS, CABIN #18.

"We'll head inside for a talk," Uncle Buddy said.

I walked as slowly as possible without giving them a reason to clamp their hands over me and drag me inside. A quick glance in all directions revealed no one else was around. This might be my only chance. I darted forward, but Cash grabbed my wrists from behind and jerked me against him.

"You ain't goin' nowhere," he grumbled in my ear.

The only hope I had left was that Tegan would somehow find me. But that hope was small—last I'd seen her, she'd been busy with event security.

I felt disassociated from my body, like this was all happening to someone else, not me. Perhaps that was partly the result of physical shock. The sun shone brightly like any ordinary day, yet I wondered if by nightfall I'd be joining Deacon in some vast, mysterious beyond.

I could delay it no longer. With the two men pressed close against my sides, I stepped over the threshold. Musky darkness enveloped me, and it took several moments for my eyes to adjust.

The one-room log cabin was sparsely furnished with only a couch and two chairs. One of the men pushed me from behind.

"Get in the chair," Uncle Buddy commanded.

I dropped into it and faced them, biting the inside of my mouth to keep my lips from trembling. *It's showtime. Act stupid. Act compliant. Buy as much time as you can.*

Uncle Buddy pulled out my cell phone. "Password again?"

I recited the code, and he pulled up a screen, then handed Cash my cell phone. "Jori's been texting a cop. Can you believe this shit? They have a recording from the Cormier incident, and Jori identified my voice for the cop."

"I'll say I was mistaken," I promised. "I won't ever tell."

Cash turned on the recording. Deacon's and Clotille's voices came alive in the tiny cabin, their familiar colors and shapes playing in my mind. The gunshots fired, and the whirring began.

Cash frowned. "I didn't hear us on there. She's lying."

Uncle Buddy raised a brow at me.

I considered lying, telling them that they weren't on the tape, that I'd been mistaken. But Uncle Buddy wasn't stupid. At some point, he'd replay the recording in its entirety and hear it for himself.

"Fast forward to near the end," I said.

The voices returned, speaking only a few seconds, and then the recording stopped.

"You can't tell nothing from that," Cash said. "If you could, the cops would have done taken us in years ago."

"Ah, but now they have my niece."

Cash glared at me. "So what?"

"She has a . . . special talent for identifying voices."

"Bullshit. She can't prove nothing. It's her word against ours."

Uncle Buddy regarded me thoughtfully.

"He's right. I can't prove anything," I said quickly. "Who are they going to believe? A respected county commissioner and prominent businessman—or me? My ID using synesthesia would never hold up in court."

"Syna-*what*?" Cash asked, his forehead drawn in lines of confusion.

"I'll handle this, Cash. You go wait outside and keep an eye out."

"No. I'm in this too. Ain't no way—"

"I said, get out!" Uncle Buddy drew up his fists, then dropped them to his sides, regaining his composure with effort. "I'll take care of everything," he insisted.

With a final glare, Cash stomped out of the cabin, slamming the door behind him.

"Thank you," I gushed. With Cash gone, I figured my odds for getting out of this alive had just improved.

Uncle Buddy paced the room, not even glancing my way. His silence began to unnerve me.

"Like I said, I'll keep quiet." I scrambled for more reasons to sound believable. "I-I know how much Mimi and Zach depend on you. And they need me too. We're family. For their sakes, let's forget this whole thing happened."

"I never wanted to kill Deacon and his mother," Uncle Buddy began.

His tone was casual. We could have been discussing accounting, for all the emotion he showed in that brutal admission of guilt.

"I went there that day to talk some sense into Louis. Make him agree to stop investigating Ray Strickland's claims against me."

"You mean Raymond guessed about the illegal adoption?" I asked, my mind racing. The scattered murders, occurring over nearly thirty years, were finally forming a terrifying pattern, one with Uncle Buddy right at the rotten center. Had Jackson discovered Uncle Buddy's secret depravity in stealing him from his biological mother? Had he at least guessed at the truth? If so, it would have been natural for him to confide in his friend Ray. I kept my eye on Cash as he leaned against his truck, glowering and puffing a cigarette.

"Ray started blackmailing me in prison." Uncle Buddy's face darkened to a murderous purple. "At first, it was chicken shit amounts. I mean, how much money do you really need in prison? You can only buy so many cigarettes and candy bars in the prison canteen."

The pieces of the puzzle still did not perfectly fit the puzzle. "But he must have realized if you killed Jackson over the adoption, then you were the one that also framed him for his friend's murder. That should have been worth lots of money."

Uncle Buddy shook his head. "That's not what he had on me."

"What else did you do?" My mind went to a dark place. Was Uncle Buddy a serial killer with dozens of victims strewn across South Alabama and beyond?

He shrugged as though what he was about to admit was of little consequence. "It was all about drugs, of course. Ray was a dealer, right? He and Jackson got a whiff of what was really going on in town." Uncle Buddy waved a hand over the room. "I have over a dozen remote cabins here in the bayou. What better place to smuggle in drugs and divide up the merchandise?"

I blinked at him in surprise. Drug smuggling? I'd had no suspicion my uncle was involved in that. "What about Louis Cormier?" I asked. "Was he in on this too?"

"Mr. Nice and Clean? Hell, no."

I glanced out the window where Cash paced by his truck. How much longer did I have before they permanently silenced me? The longer I kept the conversation going, the more time it bought me to try to figure out an angle to save myself. "I'm confused," I said quickly. "Why did you kill the Cormiers?"

"Ray started demanding more money. He upped his game, hinted that he had more dirt on me besides the drugs. I called his bluff and cut him off. Ray was furious. He called me from prison to say he'd hired Louis to look into Jackson's adoption and he'd soon have proof that I'd stolen a baby for money." Uncle Buddy snorted in derision. "Stupid bastard never guessed that I'm the one who killed Jackson and set him up for the crime."

My pain and fear momentarily subsided as I absorbed his calm confession. I'd guessed he'd done it, but to hear him say it aloud still shocked me. "You killed your own nephew," I whispered.

Chapter 34

TEGAN

I opened the text from Jori, heart drumming with excitement and full of optimism after the successful drug bust. Really, it was greedy of me to want more. How incredible if Jori could identify the voice on the recorder and solve an old mystery.

It's Buddy. Help.

Buddy Munford? Her uncle? I stared at the screen in stunned disbelief. Was she in danger? Surely she hadn't been so foolish as to confront her uncle with the truth. The text had been sent at 11:27 a.m., nearly forty minutes ago. I started to hit the dial button, then stopped. What if her uncle had the phone? Calling might place Jori in even more danger. Best to track her location. Oliver stood nearby talking to a few cops from Mobile. I caught his eye and signaled him over.

Quickly, I identified Jori's phone carrier and called the company, identifying myself as a law enforcement officer and that I needed the current location of that phone ASAP for an emergency. In training, I'd learned that the phone company could immediately identify a phone location based on tower triangulation, but until today I'd never had occasion to test that fact. I was relieved when seconds later they informed me where the phone, and hopefully Jori, was at this very moment. By the time I disconnected the call, Oliver was at my side.

"What's up?" he asked.

"We have to get to Jori Trahern right now. I'll fill you in on the way."

I raced to my unmarked car, and he ran alongside me. Inside the vehicle I hit the accelerator, and we sped out. I estimated it would only take five minutes to get to the location. If only I'd opened the text sooner . . . no, I could self-recriminate later. Right now, I had to focus on what might lie ahead. If I hadn't provided Jori that recording, she wouldn't be in danger. I should have waited to let her hear it in my presence and then gone after her uncle once she'd identified his voice. I filled Oliver in as I drove. I expected an explosion of anger when I told him I let Jori listen to the old recording, but he took it in stride. I might catch hell later, but that would have to wait too. Nothing Oliver could say to me would make me feel worse than the guilt now eating at me.

I gripped the steering wheel tightly, the road almost seeming to rush up to meet me, as Oliver radioed for backup and asked who owned the property located at 8859 Shadow Wood Road.

Seconds later, we had our answer. Buddy Munford. Jori was with a killer, and she'd texted me for help. Chills slithered up and down my back.

Chapter 35

JORI

I gaped at Uncle Buddy, astonished at his callous nonchalance. He was determined to put his own spin on the murder of his nephew.

"Had to. Jackson was hitting me up for money. He'd intimidated Tressie into admitting that I'd illegally taken a baby from a drug addict. I mean, come on! Jackson should have thanked me for delivering him into a family that loved him. Ardy had the money to spare—his business was going well. Tressie just told Ardy that the fifty-thousand payment went for legal fees and court costs. To be honest, her husband didn't look too close at what was happening. It was a win-win all around."

I'd been right. Everything had stemmed from there. The drug smuggling he'd mentioned wasn't the real issue. The baby stealing was at the core of the matter.

"Tressie paid you for a baby. There was no adoption and no official papers. And you were the middleman between her and Grace. Does Tressie know you killed Jackson?"

"Hell, no," he chuckled. "Tressie was always a little tiger, even as a kid. If she thought I'd killed her precious son, she'd have either killed me or told the cops."

That fit into what I now knew about my aunt. She was an outrageous liar and manipulator, but it didn't go further than that.

"Like I said, it served us all well," Uncle Buddy continued. "I got the seed money to start my business, Tressie got the baby she desperately wanted, and Grace got the means to fund her drug habit. You should have stayed out of it. I tried to warn you," he said, shaking his head sadly, as though I'd disappointed him. "But you had to keep going and talking to everyone."

I scanned the cabin, searching for another subject to distract him and get him talking longer. "Is this where you kept Zach when you took him?"

He shrugged. "No. It was a different cabin."

I began to tremble. Thank God he hadn't hurt my brother. He'd killed one nephew, so he certainly would have no compunction killing another.

"You still couldn't keep from snooping, could you? Had to go and talk to Ardy. That stupid sucker. Tressie always could bend him to her will."

My mind raced ahead. "You must have killed Strickland too. Was that really necessary?"

"Of course. He put the screws on me when he was paroled, threatening to hire another investigator or attorney over Jackson's illegal adoption. I'd already had to kill one lawyer over the matter."

"I still don't get it. Why kill Louis Cormier?"

"Guy was a jerk. So smug and self-righteous when I confronted him in his backyard." Uncle Buddy smiled with grim satisfaction. "He wasn't so smug when I pulled my gun. He told me right quick where he kept his investigation notes on Jackson's adoption."

"And Deacon and his mom?" I asked softly, my throat constricting with pain. "Why did you kill them?"

"That's Cash's fault. Not mine. Cash told me Louis was working in his backyard and that his family had gone shopping in Mobile. So I paid him a visit."

Uncle Buddy's face grew red with anger. "Louis refused to drop Strickland's case at first. Not only that, but he had that knowing look in his eyes. He was running against me for a county commissioner opening. The bastard would have ruined me and taken my power."

His anger suddenly spent, Uncle Buddy sank onto the sofa opposite me. "I couldn't have that," he said, his voice again casual. "So I shot him. Then, unbelievably, I heard a scream from inside the house. So I had to take care of them too."

Take care of them too. His words were like bullets ricocheting in my mind. If only Deacon and his mom hadn't been home. If only they'd spent another hour out shopping.

"You bastard," I said with a hiss, too angry to hold it in. "You damn bastard."

"And now you're a problem," he said calmly.

"If you kill me, they'll know it's you."

He smiled. A chilling, eerie smile that frightened me more than anything else had this day. He picked up my phone. "Noscam8871," he mumbled, then swiped the screen and began tapping the keyboard.

My heart jackhammered, and my breath grew shallow. "What are you doing?"

Uncle Buddy tapped a few more seconds, then read from the screen.

Hey Tegan. Sorry for the earlier message. It was Cash's voice on the recording. I'm off to confront him. Later!

He shut off the phone. "I'll toss this thing in the swamp on my way home. I'll give Cash his orders to dig a hole out here for your body. By the time the cops arrive, I'll be long gone, and Cash will be caught red-handed. Of course, I'll deny any involvement. Who are they going to believe—me, or a guy with a bit of a shady past?"

Uncle Buddy pulled a gun from the back waistband of his pants and aimed it dead at me.

My time had run out.

"Please don't shoot." I closed my eyes, thought of my family. What would become of them? "Think of Mimi and Zach." I opened my eyes and pleaded in a last-ditch effort to appeal to his mercy. "There's no one left to take care of them if I die."

The deadly determination in his eyes didn't flicker. His mind was made up.

I screamed, even knowing it was useless. There was no one to hear me but Cash.

This was it, then. No escape.

Chapter 36

TEGAN

"Here we go." Oliver held up his phone screen showing a Google Earth map of Buddy Munford's property. A small cabin sat only twelve feet from the road. I pictured Jori in there, held hostage. Or was she still alive? I steeled myself, preparing for the worst.

"What's the plan?" I asked. "We have to assume this is a kidnapping, right?"

"Correct. When we get within two hundred yards of the place, we'll pull over to the side of the road and approach by foot. I've warned backup not to arrive with sirens blaring."

He faced me. "Be prepared to take whatever force needed. I'll take the lead, and you follow my instructions. Don't rush in and risk someone being shot. Got it?"

"Got it."

He scanned the road and checked our coordinates. "Slow down. We're close."

I let my foot off the gas.

"Here. Pull over."

I stopped the car on the side of the road, and we exited the vehicles, shutting the doors quietly. Oliver withdrew his gun from his holster and nodded at me to do the same.

Silently, I pulled out my gun and gripped it securely, its weight comforting. We walked quickly toward the cabin, keeping close to the trees. Suddenly, Oliver held out an arm, then put a finger to his mouth. Peering around him, I spotted Cash Johnson outside, pacing near his truck and smoking a cigarette. His movements were jerky, and he kept running a hand through his hair as though agitated. By his side, a gun dangled in his right hand. We were close enough to be in range of bullets. Oliver motioned for me to stay in place while he crept closer.

For his size and weight, Oliver moved with amazing stealth. But with every small twig that snapped beneath his shoes, I feared for his life. Despite Oliver's prowess, Cash swept his gaze along the tree line, squinting and tense as a frightened deer. As an experienced hunter, he was no doubt alert to every tiny noise emerging from the woods.

Oliver took a few more cautious steps forward when the unexpected broke loose. A flock of swamp sparrows screeched in a treetop above Oliver, their wings flapping madly, rustling leaves and limbs in their haste to flee from human intruders. Cash raised his right arm, his gun gleaming silver in the sunlight. He stared straight at Oliver.

"Drop your weapon!" Oliver commanded.

Cash raised his left hand to support and steady the gun in his right hand and squinted, adjusting the weapon's sights. I could hardly breathe. Blood pounded through my ears, loud as the gulf's current. I raised my own gun, ready to shoot.

The crack of gunfire exploded in the remote bayou air. Time slowed to the pace of molasses. My breath was deep and heavy as I struggled to gulp oxygen. I caught the splay of sunshine on the sandy soil, the roar of the Atlantic from nearby, an unnatural metallic scent intruding in the salty air. Oliver still stood. Cash did not. He crumpled to the ground, bleeding.

A single scream erupted from the cabin, breaking my momentary stupor.

"Let's go!" Oliver commanded.

I raced past him, determined to get to Jori. At the small front window I faced the worst-case scenario I'd envisioned on the drive over. Jori was seated in a chair, her hands bound behind her back. Buddy Munford turned toward me, his eyes widening. In his hands, he held a gun.

Chapter 37

JORI

An explosion of gunfire filled the cabin.

"The hell?" Uncle Buddy half turned toward the front window.

A crimson stain mushroomed from Cash's shoulder, and he fell onto the dirt. What was happening? Was there a third person involved in this dirty business? Deputy Blackwell stepped into view, her gun raised as she faced the window.

Tegan had found me. She or her partner must have shot Cash. I spared no pity for the man who seemed to delight in partnering with my uncle's depraved killings. Would Uncle Buddy still shoot me now that she'd arrived? I was still far from being out of danger. My body responded faster than my brain as it grappled with everything going down around me. I instinctually dropped to the floor, providing Tegan a clear shot.

Another gunshot exploded, and I screamed. Shards of glass rained down on me. Who had fired first and was still alive—Uncle Buddy or Tegan? *Please God, let it be Tegan.* Images paraded through my mind in quick succession—Deacon, Clotille, Louis, Raymond. I even pictured Jackson as a young child, which I remembered from an old photograph particularly beloved by Aunt Tressie. Was I going to be the next to die?

Heavy thuds pounded on the front door, and then it burst open, banging against the wall. Tegan and Lieutenant Oliver entered, guns drawn. They were alive. I was alive. Then that meant my uncle had either been shot or had run away.

"Jori? Are you okay?"

I struggled to a seated position and tried to find my uncle. What had been Uncle Buddy's head was mostly splattered across the opposite wall. Bile rose in my throat. I opened my mouth to answer Tegan but couldn't speak. She was by my side in an instant, flinging an arm across my shoulders. "Thank God. You're alive. How bad are you hurt?"

"H-how did you find me?"

A two-way radio crackled in the air, and deep, disembodied voices filled the tiny room as Lieutenant Oliver barked out orders.

"We tracked you from your first text," she explained. "Then followed you from a distance. Let me untie your hands."

Sirens sounded, growing closer by the second. I nodded, barely registering the chaos around me, still stunned that I wasn't the one shot. I kept my face averted from what was left of my uncle.

"Let's get out of here. Can you walk?" Tegan helped me stand and stumble toward the open doorway.

"Don't look back," she warned. She needn't have worried. I had no intention of doing so. Lieutenant Oliver came to my other side and put his strong arm around me as well. Together, all three of us walked out of the cabin with its blood-smeared walls and into the sunlight and fresh air that smelled of ocean.

Alive.

Tegan guided me toward their vehicle. Now that the danger had passed, the remote cabin—which had seemed an impenetrable death trap minutes ago—was a buzz of activity. Radios crackled, and sirens blared, announcing the swift arrival of more cops. My entire body trembled as though ice coursed through my veins.

"Thank you." My voice was choked and broken, but I needed to talk. "They were going to kill me. Just like they killed my cousin, the Cormiers, and Raymond Strickland."

Lieutenant Oliver gave a low whistle. "Munford and Johnson were responsible for all those murders? Are you sure?"

"Positive. My uncle confessed to everything."

Lieutenant Oliver nodded. "We'll get all the details at the office. Unless you need to go home first?"

I shook my head, wanting nothing more than to give my statement before heading home. "Let's get it over with. While everything's still fresh in my memory."

As though I would ever forget a word that had been spoken. Still, I wanted to talk it out with them.

Tegan draped an arm over my shoulders. Its weight was solid, comforting. "It's you we should be thanking. You're the one who solved these crimes."

So many deaths. So many ruined lives. At least now Zach, Mimi, and I were safe.

Or . . . were we? I hadn't told the cops everything yet. Maybe I never would.

Chapter 38

DEACON CORMIER

May 19, 2006

Having Mom record me with the prom corsage was so lame. Actually, the whole prom scene was lame, but if Jori wanted to go, then I'd make her happy. Last week, she and Mom had spent an afternoon shopping in Mobile for her prom dress. Mom had tried to pay for the dress, but Jori had insisted on using part of her savings from working at Winn-Dixie to buy it herself.

"Smile, Deacon," Mom urged as she pointed the camcorder at me. "Hold up the corsage too."

Dutifully, I held up the posy of coral and white roses mixed with clusters of baby's breath. The sooner she finished filming, the sooner I could get out of this uncomfortable rented tux. Me? I'd much rather dance at the Pavilion in jeans and a T-shirt than get gussied up in stiff clothes to dance in a high school cafeteria. No amount of ribbons, balloons, and other fanfare decorating the room could disguise its true function. But no one had asked my opinion. So the prom it was.

"Louis?" Mom shouted over her shoulder. "Come down here and see your son all decked out."

Dad was here somewhere, because his car was in the driveway. But the house remained deadly quiet.

"Must be in the shower," I offered.

She paused, cocking her head to the side. "I don't hear the water running. Stay here while I go up and—"

A shot rang out from the backyard.

Mom and I stared at one another. Her eyes held shock, quickly followed by confusion, then rapidly shifted to fear, mirroring my own progression of emotions.

She screamed Dad's name, and the recorder dropped from her hands.

The back door by the kitchen was yanked open, and a man—not my Dad—walked into the room, a gun by his side. Mom's back was to him, and I stared into familiar eyes that held none of their usual frankness. A chill raked through me from head to toe. Something was very, very wrong. Where was Dad?

Mom whirled around. I opened my mouth to warn her, to yell at her to run, but no sooner had the thought formed when the opportunity to escape shut down.

It was too late.

The next minute of my life slowed down to a crawl. Every sensation of every moment crashed into me. My mind raced to catch up and filter out what was important. The view from the backyard, Mom's roses and tomatoes and cucumbers all ripening at once. The black tilled soil, the sunny blue sky, a group of starlings flying from one tree to another. Moss hanging from live oaks and a car parked around back that I didn't recognize. It didn't belong there, just as this man didn't belong in our house.

I knew him, of course, but something in his flat, emotionless eyes chilled me. It was as though he were a stranger. There was no flicker of recognition or human warmth in them. My gaze traveled down to the revolver he carelessly dangled in his right hand.

An initial wall of fear, then dread, slammed into me. My mouth opened to scream, but no sound emerged. I lurched forward to reach Mom. I had to protect her, to save her.

"Who are you?" she asked, face furrowed in confusion. The eminent danger had not yet sunk into her brain. "What are you doing in my—"

"Such a pity," he mumbled with a tsk. He raised the gun.

My world exploded, roared in my ears as sudden and loud as though a freight train had crashed through the walls of our home. Burnt metallic sulfur assaulted my nose. Mom crumpled to the floor, a red bloom spreading across the front of her white shirt.

"Mom!"

I knelt down beside her. Her eyes rolled back in her head. I looked up, and the man raised his gun again to shoot, aiming at me. I read the intent in the hard set of his face. His finger pulled the trigger. Pain exploded in my chest, and I fell to the floor. My ears pulsed with a loud ringing. A death knell.

Blood gushed from my chest. So much blood.

The point of his dirty, scuffed boot poked my ribs and rolled me over, my face pressed to the floor, and my body went limp.

I don't know how much time passed. I came to slowly. Swimming up from a quicksand trying to suck me back under, pulling at me mercilessly, relentlessly. It was eerily quiet now. Hadn't it just been deafening? What had happened?

Panic electrified me to action, and I scanned the room. Was he still here? The man with the gun? No, I was alone. So alone. The madman had left me for dead. I laid my head back down on the hard floor. It was so quiet I could feel the blood thundering in my ears.

Mom was dead. I was dying. I must be in shock, because the facts registered, but I had no emotional connection to what was taking place.

In a single afternoon, my family had been wiped out. The enormity of that fact was crushing.

Why? Why us?

It made no sense. I wanted to curl into myself, deny what had happened. Go back in time to Mom filming me holding that corsage, thinking of Jori and making her happy. Turned out, I wanted prom after all. I wanted so many things I'd never have now.

I turned my head to the side and caught a glimpse of bits of baby's breath that had fallen from the corsage and landed under the sofa. I touched a petal. Velvet smoothness. Jori would never see it.

A car motor sounded from the driveway. The man was coming back. I could feel an inner knowing of that fact deep in my bones. Probably to make sure we were dead and to clean up the crime scene. He'd get away with this. No witnesses, nothing to implicate him. No explanation for why he'd flipped his lid and turned into a killer.

Was Jori safe from her uncle? I had to protect her, let her know she might be in danger. That there was a madman in her family.

The recording. Mom hadn't filmed Buddy, but Buddy had spoken. And if his voice was on that tape, Jori would immediately know it was her uncle. Like everyone else, he'd have a distinctive color pattern associated with his voice. I could only hope Buddy hadn't noticed the recorder.

Panicked, I scanned around the floor for the recorder and couldn't find it. It had to be nearby. There was only one place I hadn't yet checked. I rolled Mom's bloody body to the side. Her arms and neck flopped like a rag doll, and horror paralyzed me. *Pretend it's a bad dream. A terrible, terrible dream.* She had fallen on top of the camcorder. The red "on" light was still on, the battery light flickering.

Steps came up the walkway, ponderous and deliberate. I pictured him as he'd stood before us earlier, the way he deliberately raised the gun in his hand and shot us point-blank. I listened harder. There was another person with him. They didn't speak. They didn't have to—I knew why they were here. Best for him not to leave dead bodies and evidence around. They were coming to dispose of me and Mom. I refused to let them get away with it.

Hide the recorder. The floor was slick with blood, but I grasped the device. Picking it up from the floor felt like deadlifting a ton of barbells. I opened the bottom drawer of the bookcase and thrust it inside, hoping to hell that he'd never find it. Mom had dropped it before he entered our home. Surely if he'd seen it, he'd already have taken it with him.

The steps grew closer.

I slammed the drawer shut with my last reservoir of strength and waited. My lungs and chest burned like a devil's bonfire, and I coughed up blood.

The latch lifted from the front door, and it began to creak open.

Chapter 39

TEGAN

I dabbed more concealer under my eyes and stared at my reflection in the small rippled silver pane that passed for a mirror. The women's bathroom in the Erie County Sheriff's Office was cramped, ugly, and dark. But even in the poor light, the added makeup piled under the dark circles only emphasized them.

So much for that wasted effort. Sighing, I smoothed down my hair and walked down to my office.

"Deputy Blackwell. You're looking . . ." Mullins took in my haggard appearance. "Um, presentable."

Not good, just presentable. Weak praise indeed. Not that it mattered. Despite the sleepless night as I lay in bed, replaying the shooting of Buddy Munford, I had zero regrets over killing the bastard. If I hadn't, Jori would be dead. And who knows how many other lives Buddy Munford would have taken in the future. Jori had filled us in on everything her uncle had confessed to during her kidnapping. Any potential threat of exposure led him to commit more crimes, thus compounding the tragedy. The web of lies rippled outward with each additional murder Munford committed, expanding his chances of getting caught and creating a riptide that innocent bystanders were fatally pulled into.

"Nice job over the weekend, Deputy," Sinclair added.

I waited for a punch line that never came. Confused, I faced Haywood, sure they had set him up to deliver a wisecrack.

"Not only did you help solve the Strickland case, you also helped take down a major drug ring headed by our mayor, no less," he said. "Kudos, Deputy."

"All the credit to Carter Holt on that one," I protested. "I was just along for the ride."

"Don't forget solving the Ensley and Cormier cold cases too," Mullins said, grinning. "You trying to make us look bad?"

I blinked at all three in confusion. Not only did they appear sincere, they'd each referred to me as *deputy* instead of the usual *rookie*.

"Doesn't take much work to make you jokers look bad." Oliver entered our office, tempering his words with a wide smile across his weathered face. If he suffered any compunction over shooting Cash Johnson, it didn't show in his eyes. But then again, Johnson had survived the gunshot; Munford had not. Just as the criminals caught in the drug operation had cooperated in detailing everyone involved in exchange for a plea bargain arrangement, Johnson had confessed to his crimes and how he'd worked for Buddy Munford over the years. We also had Jori Trahern's account of her kidnapping and Johnson's role in it.

"We've got a small matter to take care of this morning before y'all get to work," Oliver continued.

Mullins, Sinclair, and Haywood all rose from their chairs and stood at attention.

"What's going on?" I blurted.

Oliver held up a manila envelope. "Deputy Tegan Blackwell, it's my pleasure to inform you that you've been promoted to sergeant, effective immediately."

My ears rang with the startling announcement. I'd taken the promotional test last month but hadn't expected to get promoted—not for months or years, anyway. I searched my coworkers' faces for any trace of resentment but found none.

Oliver opened the envelope and removed a single sheet of paper. "Hot from personnel, here's the official notice along with the pay increase amount you'll see in your next paycheck."

I accepted the paper and read the numbers, my breath hitching with excitement. Silently, I vowed to put every cent of the extra money into the twins' college fund.

"And here's your sergeant's bars," Oliver said, holding out the patch—three gold chevrons.

Applause broke out, and I swallowed hard as I accepted the patch. "Well deserved," Oliver said gruffly.

I wanted to thank him for his trust in me, but that would have to come after I got myself together. My coworkers would never let me live it down if I did something so disgraceful as cry. Oliver nodded, as though sensing my temporary inability to form coherent words. "Later, Blackwell."

"This calls for a celebration," Mullins announced. "Dinner at Broussard's tonight. My treat."

"Anything I want?" Sinclair asked. "Because if that's the case, I'll order lobster and—"

"Not you, idiot. I'm only paying for rook . . . I mean, Dep . . . I mean, *Sergeant* Blackwell. You two clowns are on your own. What do you say, Sergeant?"

I cleared my throat to dislodge the giant lump threatening to strangle my windpipe. "That would be great. Just great. Could we invite Carter Holt?" I had to admit the agent still wasn't my favorite person in the world, but he'd done an exemplary job of discovering a drug-smuggling operation that had been running for years under everyone's nose—with the help of Dana Adair, of course. He deserved some well-earned applause, which I felt certain he didn't experience much of in his undercover work.

I debated inviting Dana. She'd proven to be an honest, valuable informant whose only motivation was to stop the infiltration of drugs into the bayou. She'd been through her own personal hell of addiction and didn't want anyone else to go through it. But as far as a victory celebration with cops, I wasn't so sure that would be the right call. I resolved to treat her to dinner in private. It was the least I could do.

"Too bad Dempsey and Granger won't be around to witness your promotion," Haywood remarked with a snicker. "The bastards have been sent to a federal penitentiary and placed in protective custody until trial. Serving time in an Alabama prison is going to be *quite* rough."

My lips twisted grimly. Those two were worse than I'd ever imagined. A search of their homes turned up the gun used in the attempt on Holt's life and other evidence. Both of them, along with the men arrested from the boat, had fingered Hank Rembert as the kingpin of the operation. Our mayor had been arrested, and the trafficking charge against him was solid. I supposed it was wrong of me to find satisfaction in the Dempsey and Granger arrests, but after years of having to put up with their snide remarks, I allowed myself to enjoy their plight. "You know what they say about karma," I said.

"It'll be a bitch for the likes of them," Mullins grumbled. "Dirty cops deserve everything they get in the end."

There had been so much corruption, so much bloodshed. Jackson's face flashed before me—youthful, handsome, and utterly debased at only age sixteen. He'd paid dearly for trying to blackmail his uncle. Justice, as well as karma, could also be a bitch.

Chapter 40

JORI

Mimi appeared to be having a good day. You'd never know from her outward calm that turmoil had rocked our family only two weeks earlier. She'd been shaken at the news of Buddy's death, but not as much as I would have thought, especially because of her stalwart commitment to family over the years. Perhaps the fog of dementia buffered the grief. For half a second, I envied her that fog. When I lay in bed at night, I continuously heard the boom of the shotgun from the recording. Over and over. *Boom, boom, boom.* Red and black shards piercing a black canvas in my mind.

And then my mind would replay Uncle Buddy calmly preparing to kill me. The man I'd regarded as a father figure in my life. He'd reach for the gun, cool as a bite of watermelon, aim it at me, and I was helpless to fight back. Me. His niece.

Mimi stood in front of the stove, stirring a pot of pinto beans. "Needs a little more honey," she announced after scooping up a mouthful and tasting.

I sat at the kitchen table and watched as she removed the cornbread from the oven, marveling at her oblivion. She baked it in an iron skillet so that the bread crisped at the bottom, just the way Zach and I liked it. Mom, too, when she was with us. How many dinners had Mimi prepared for us over the years? Thousands, I reckoned. Had I never really understood my own blood and flesh?

The TV provided a cozy background noise from the den, where Zach sat on the couch with his LEGOs, watching a home renovation program on HGTV. I didn't need to be seated in the same room to know that his blue fleece blanket would be wrapped over his legs, his torso swaying side to side in a rhythm provided by an inner music only he could hear. Since my escape from Uncle Buddy, I'd spent more time with Zach, recapturing our former closeness. Growing up, I'd been the one to care for him while Mom and Mimi worked extra jobs on nights and weekends to make ends meet. We used to play in the old tree house during the day and watch rented movies at night.

In some ways, my colored hearing, unique and idiosyncratic, formed my own private world no one else could envision, much as Zach's world was unexplainable and unknowable to anyone but himself. It wouldn't surprise me in the least if researchers one day discovered a neural connection between synesthesia and autism. Reality might be fluid and flexible, influenced greatly by individual perception instead of set in stone.

"Going to pop the bread in for another minute," Mimi mumbled. The oven door banged shut. Leave it to my grandmother to bring me out of my head and back down to the present moment.

"You don't seem too shaken about Uncle Buddy's death," I noted, probing—hoping to rattle her mask of calm.

She shrugged. "Not particularly. Although I do worry what might happen one day if we get in a financial bind."

"We don't need his money. You know I'll always take care of us, don't you?" The words were thick and heavy on my tongue.

"You're out of a better-paying job now. Remember?"

"I managed fine without him before now," I answered sharply. "Nothing's changed on that score. I still have my own business. What

I'm trying to understand is why you aren't upset that your brother killed Jackson. Your own nephew. I thought family was everything to you."

"If Buddy hadn't killed Jackson, the kid would have ended up in prison or the morgue before he was thirty. He was a bad seed."

"That's cold."

"That's being realistic. Now, Tressie blackmailing Ardy all these years—that surprised me."

Not for the first time, I couldn't read Mimi's emotions. She had a way of announcing facts in a neutral, brusque manner, as though she were merely an observer on the outskirts of events.

"I thought at first Tressie was the one sending me those threats and had kidnapped Zach." I gazed out the window momentarily, collecting my thoughts. "But all along it was Uncle Buddy."

"Cornbread's done," Mimi announced, pulling it again from the oven. "You about ready for dinner?"

It seemed she was through with this conversation about her siblings.

"We need to talk first."

"Fine." Mimi wiped her hands on her apron. "Zach—go on and wash up for dinner," she called out.

The moment had arrived. Dread weighted me down like a stone to the chair. Mimi sat across from me, arms folded on the table. Her eyes stared directly into mine. Calm and expectant.

I thought I'd already made my decision, but now, facing my grandmother, my heart raced, and my palms began to sweat. This was going to be as hard as I'd imagined.

"Uncle Buddy and Cash Johnson weren't the only voices I heard on that tape recording," I blurted.

She didn't so much as blink.

"You were there," I said softly. "The day the Cormiers were murdered."

"No. You're mistaken." Her gaze remained unflinching. Only the tightening of her clasped fingers on the table betrayed nervousness.

"You were there," I insisted. "You showed up after the murders with Uncle Buddy and Cash."

"That's ridiculous. Why would I be there?"

"Must have been a lot of blood to clean," I said. "Uncle Buddy figured there'd be nobody better than you to take care of the mess. You were their housekeeper, after all."

"Is that what you think you heard on that tape?" she scoffed. "I'm telling you: it wasn't me."

"I couldn't make out the words," I admitted. "But I do know your voice—tiger-orange cubes rattling against a black landscape."

Silence filled the space between us—a dark abyss. The gurgle of running water drifted to us from the bathroom.

"Is that what you told your cop friend?" Mimi asked at last. She pressed her thin lips together as though to keep them from trembling.

"Why did you do it?" I whispered. "*How* could you do it?" The question had been eating at me, toxic as cancer, an acid drip on my heart that refused to stop.

"I had nothing to do with the killing. That was all Buddy. Not like I could change what he'd already done to them people."

I leaned back in my chair, dumbfounded. Secretly, foolishly, I'd hoped I'd been wrong. All these years—she'd known. Had even mopped Deacon's blood from the floor and covered up the murders for her brother.

"Why?" I asked, my voice breaking. "Why?"

"I did what I had to do." Her gray eyes darkened and glowed with fierce determination. "No regrets."

"You knew I loved Deacon." I hurled the accusation at her. "You knew how much it hurt me when people said he and his family went into hiding to save themselves from the Mafia. You knew how much I grieved for him."

Zach entered the room. "Mimi knows." His singsong words danced around us. "Mimi knows. Mimi knows."

The familiar echolalic phrase shook me to the core. "Go back in the den and watch TV, Zach."

"Eat!" he demanded.

I rose on shaky legs. "I'll fix you a plate—then you go eat it on the couch."

My hands shook as I buttered him a piece of cornbread, scooped pintos into a bowl, and then carried it out to the living room. I set it all down on the coffee table.

"Tea," Zach said. For my brother, today was just another day, same as any other.

I returned to the kitchen, poured a glass, and took it to him. Mimi remained stoically seated in her chair, back stiff and unyielding. I sat across from her.

"You say you did what you had to," I began, resuming the confrontation. "What's that supposed to mean?"

"I had a ton of medical bills from the doctors treating your mom. I could never hope to pay them on a house cleaner's salary."

"You could have declared bankruptcy."

"And then I had to raise you and Zach," she continued, as though she hadn't heard me. "If Buddy hadn't paid our bills for a time, I couldn't have done it. The state would have taken custody of you both and put you in foster care."

"You'd have found a way to make it work," I insisted. If there was only one thing left I knew for sure about my grandmother, it was that she was a survivor. A woman who did what she believed necessary for herself and her family. "You can't justify covering up all these murders. When I remember all the times you welcomed Buddy into our house, knowing what he did." I stopped and swallowed hard, blinking back tears. "All the times he ate dinner with us. When he came to my high school graduation and gave me a set of diamond earrings." I shuddered. "The man was a monster, and you helped him. That makes you a monster too."

A single tear rolled unchecked down Mimi's paper-thin cheek.

I reached across the table and laid my hands over her frail, thin ones. The same hands that had cooked and cleaned for me and my brother when we had no one else. How could I not still love her? No, she wasn't a monster with no feelings or conscience. Mimi hadn't asked for forgiveness, but she needed to hear the words anyway. "I forgive you because of all you did for Mom. For Zach." I drew a shaky breath. "And for me."

Mimi nodded, her lips trembling. "Are you going to tell the cops?"

I'd wrestled with that very question nonstop. Where, exactly, did the bounds of family loyalty lie? What was the right thing to do for Zach, for my grandmother, and for Deacon and his parents? My death-bed promise to Mom haunted me. I'd told her I'd take care of Mimi and Zach. How could I have known the twisty, dark depths that rash promise would lead to? In the end, I'd made my decision. Good or bad, it was done.

From the window, I spotted a familiar car rounding the bend near our home. She was right on time.

"I've already packed your bags, Mimi," I said wearily, my energy spent. The anger was gone, and only sadness remained. "All the arrangements have been made."

Her faced whitened. "Wh-what? Are you sending me to jail, then?"

"No. Not that. I can't afford Magnolia Oaks, but there's a bed available at a home in Mobile. It's not posh, but it's clean and comfortable. The staff seems nice."

She didn't speak for a full minute, and I held her gaze, steady and resolute. Finally, she nodded, accepting my decision.

"I wouldn't want to live in the same building as Tressie anyway." She attempted a weak smile, slowly rising from the table. "I had enough of Tressie and Buddy growing up."

It was the first time I could remember her voluntarily even mentioning her childhood.

I also rose. An apology formed on my tongue, but I didn't speak the words. Yes, this was hard, but it was a necessary thing. The right thing. And it hurt like hell to send her away. But what was love without trust? Without respect? She'd refused to discuss her past, but over the years I'd gathered bits and pieces that wove together a tale of brutality. They'd had an alcoholic, violent father and a mother who cowered in fear of him rather than trying to protect their children. All three siblings—Buddy, Tressie, and Mimi—had grown twisted, their emotional maturity forever stunted. An unholy trio of damaged minds and hearts.

No doubt Buddy was the worst of the bunch. Tressie had grown selfish and coldhearted. She'd focused all her love on a child who didn't love her in return. According to Ardy, she'd never been an easy person to live with because of her hair-trigger temper, but Jackson's death had completely broken her.

And then there was my Mimi.

She had so much goodness in her. Nothing would ever shake my faith in that. It was hard to reconcile an image of her at the Cormier home, mopping up Deacon's and Clotille's blood while their lifeless bodies lay on the floor.

And yet, she was guilty. Her culpability in the crime was undeniable. A warped sense of family obligation must have driven her to help Uncle Buddy. If she'd turned in her brother, Uncle Buddy would be in prison, and Raymond Strickland would be enjoying a long-overdue freedom.

A rap sounded at the front door, and Mimi shot me a questioning look.

"Door," Zach announced unnecessarily. "Get door."

"It's Rose. I thought it'd be easier this way."

"Seems you've thought of everything."

I pulled Mimi's packed suitcase from the broom closet and followed her into the den. Mimi sat beside Zach on the couch and pulled him to her for a hug. He leaned out of her grasp, avoiding physical contact.

I wished for just this once he'd surrender to a giant bear hug, but that was not his way.

"Bye, Zachary. I'll miss you. Be a good boy, you hear?" Her voice warbled, and she swallowed hard. "Jori will take good care of you."

"Bye-bye," he said, scooting away. Of course, he had no idea the goodbye was permanent. My heart ached for the pain I knew Zach would feel in the days and weeks ahead.

"I'll bring him to visit on Sundays," I promised Mimi.

"Only if he wants to come and it comforts him instead of confusing him."

Rose tapped on the door again and then opened it, taking in our sad little tableau. "You ready, Oatha?" she asked softly.

Mimi stood, one hand on the sofa arm, supporting her weight as she straightened. She looked older, frailer. I silently handed Rose the suitcase, unable to speak. Rose patted my arm. "I'll be right outside the door."

I tried to harden my heart at this goodbye, but the damn thing was already broken and bleeding. I stood there shaking, feeling as vulnerable as a motherless child.

Mimi slowly walked to me. When she was within a foot, she raised both hands. I half thought she was going to shake me, but instead she cupped her weathered palms against my cheeks.

"We're both going to be all right, Jori. You'll see."

And then she was gone. What was left of my family was reduced to only one.

Chapter 41

JORI

The shade provided no relief from the scorching sun. Its rays penetrated every tiny crevice of the trees' canopy, contributing to humidity so thick it clogged my lungs with every breath. My sojourn would have been more pleasant even later in the day, but I wanted to return home before dark completely blanketed the bayou. I wouldn't risk Zach stumbling on a tree root and twisting an ankle.

He lagged several paces behind me, frowning, his attention on the ground's narrow path. Clearly, he was unhappy with this excursion. Ever since Mimi left last month, I'd taken him on daily late-afternoon walks, convinced that the exercise and fresh air were good for him. He'd spent too many years cooped up with Mimi in the house playing with LEGOs and watching TV. I'd also begun taking him to Saturday social events in Mobile, which he disliked even more than these walks. So far, my efforts had been an epic failure, but I still persisted, convinced that in the long run he'd benefit from being out in the world more.

Tegan Blackwell had been a real friend in this trying time. She'd provided me with names of counselors for Zach and me, respite care resources, and best of all, she'd suggested her twins as babysitters so I could have more free time. Zach surprisingly accepted and liked Luke and Linsey.

Dana and I still got together occasionally, but I'd never feel the same warmth toward her as before. Too much baggage in that relationship. And yet, I did respect Dana for playing a major role in bringing down the drug ring and corruption at the highest level in our bayou. At first, I was leery of her claim, but I'd checked it out with Tegan, and it was indeed true.

Zach and I had visited Mimi a couple of times at the nursing home. I'd sat in the lobby while Zach spent time with her in her room. Mimi and I had exchanged glances but not spoken. Maybe someday we would. Maybe not.

"Just a little farther, Zach," I encouraged. "We're almost there."

His head rose. "Home?" he asked hopefully.

I couldn't help laughing. "Not yet. Soon."

I returned my attention to the sprawl of saw palmettos, pine, and cypress. It was all starting to blend together, indistinctive and unfamiliar. Never, ever would I have believed it possible to forget the way to my special spot. I'd seriously underestimated the power of time and distance to change the landscape and my memories.

Had I unknowingly passed by the smidgen of land I'd once claimed as special? Were my treasures forever lost?

I was ready to turn around, conceding defeat, when a particular cypress, several feet taller than the other trees, caught my eye. Could it be? I hurried forward, my heart zinging at the sight of the crooked creek winding near the cypress. Once a foot wide, the creek had dried almost to nothing. All that remained were a mere two inches of stagnant water that stained the ground and saturated clumps of pine needles, leaves, and twigs.

I wiggled the backpack straps from my shoulders.

"Want some water, Zach? Let's sit down and rest." I dropped to the ground and patted a spot beside me. Zach regarded it dubiously, tired but unwilling to get dirty. Anything gritty on his skin inflamed his texture issues. I handed him the canteen, and he leaned against a tree, drinking quickly. He'd be ready to return home, pronto. With or without me.

I'd better finish my business quick.

I pulled the trowel from the backpack and stood. Aligning heel to toe, I counted. One foot, two foot . . . seven foot. I was close to the creek. Hopefully, close enough that the dirt would be damp and uncompacted. The circle of heavy rocks I'd placed there remained, half-buried in the dirt.

Thirteen years ago I'd chosen this spot because it was far enough from the cypress that there was space among the intricacies of its root system to bury my small mementos—sprigs of baby's breath from the prom corsage, the promise ring Deacon had given me only a week before he died, and melted candle wax from the memorial service I'd held right here, witnessed only by the silent trees and the scampering wildlife solely concerned with their relentless hunt for food.

My unborn baby.

Now as then, I whispered my truth. "I wish you had lived. I wish a part of Deacon had lived on."

I placed a hand on my abdomen, remembering the terrible cramping and loss of blood that had accompanied the miscarriage less than a month after Deacon's disappearance. I'd endured it alone, afraid to tell Mimi or anyone what was happening. With only two missed periods under my belt, no one besides Deacon knew of the pregnancy. I hadn't even been sure about it myself until the last couple of weeks before the end.

Behind me, Zach coughed and announced, "All done."

I began to dig in earnest, upturning small clumps of clay mixed with sand. I only had a couple of minutes left until his patience ran out.

A tiny circle of silver glinted in the dark earth. Tears streaked my face as I held it up. The diamond was smaller than I remembered but was more beautiful, more precious than ever. I motioned for Zach to hand over the canteen and poured water over the ring, washing it clean.

"What do you think, Zach—should I wear it?"

"Ring," he said, tapping my fingers.

I slipped it on. It felt right. Like this was where it belonged—attached to living flesh instead of buried underground. The time for mourning had long passed. I filled up the hole in the ground with the upturned soil and patted it down as smooth as I could. From the backpack I removed the LED tea light candle I'd brought, flipped the switch on, and set it atop the pile. I figured the battery would die sometime during the night. Maybe one day I'd return alone and light a real candle and stay until it burned out. For now, I had my brother, and that was family enough.

I took one last, lingering look at the turquoise sky visible through the canopy of ancient trees. "Forgive me, Mom?" I whispered. "I did what I thought was right. Zach's in good hands. I promise."

A gulf breeze rustled through the woods like a gentle affirmation. Mom had been a tender soul, unspoiled by Mimi's inner darkness. Sometimes, as a child, I'd thought Mimi the stronger of the two, but today I knew different. With each generation that passed after Mimi's tyrannical father, his influence had been diluted. I'd gather the best qualities from both of the women who'd raised me and move on. I stood, dusting dirt from the seat of my jeans, and smiled at my younger brother.

"Let's go home, Zach."

ACKNOWLEDGMENTS

To my editors Megha Parekh and Charlotte Herscher for their assistance in developing my stories to their fullest potential. Their insight, vision, and editorial expertise are always spot on and delivered with large doses of clarity and kindness. I cannot thank you both enough for all you do for me.

And to my literary agent, Ann Leslie Tuttle of Dystel, Goderich & Bourret LLC, who was the editor of my very first published novel, a quirky mermaid paranormal romance/mystery that she spotted in the midst of thousands of manuscripts by unpublished authors. She remained my editor for numerous other books until, in a serendipitous turn of fate for me, she became my agent. Her unwavering advocacy means the world to me both professionally and personally. My deepest appreciation.